Prologue

Ophelia was flying north with the pir　　　　　　　　　　star speckled sky, the full moon lighting her way. Holding up her skirts to catch the wind, she felt the air warm in her face. The light slowly rotating through the dark was guiding her forward. Diving down the breeze rushed through her hair and the ground opened up to welcome her. She watched as her bare feet sank into the soft golden sand. She was floating along the sand, her toes enjoying its touch. Giggling with pleasure she slowed and lay down, sinking into the softness. Slowly, the beach ate her up covering her arms, legs and body. She relaxed into sleep.

Awake with a start, the sea was washing over her, the waves carrying her up and down. She started to swim taking broad powerful strokes. She dived down under the waves. Down she sank, deeper and deeper into the dark of the ocean. She felt herself letting go, relaxing in the blackness. She looked back up but there was only a small spot of light on the distant surface. She turned to swim towards it. She pushed up but the weight of the sea was pulling her down. She tried again but the light was no closer. She was struggling to breath. Unseen hands were pulling her down. She thrashed at the water. She was suffocating. But still the sea pulled her down, deeper and deeper.

And then they were around here, watching her with their big black eyes, calming her. They were guiding her up towards the light. Up and up they climbed. And suddenly they were bursting out of the water and surfing across the waves. The euphoria carried her forward and she found herself crying out with joy. She looked down and saw her legs turned into a long sleek tail. Her arms were subsumed into her body. She was one of them. They had taken her. She relaxed into their hold and sleep took her again.

Voices calling her name pierced her consciousness through the cold. She was a child and they were playing hide and seek in her garden at home. She ran on but there was no place to hide. Falling down, she crawled up into a ball and pressed herself against the grass, screwing up her eyes. She took comfort in the darkness. Perhaps they would not see her. But her heart was drumming out a loud beat drawing them towards her and suddenly strong hands were upon her.

'There you are Offie. You know you shouldn't be out here at his hour. Come on, it's time to come back in.'

Helped to her feet she took his hand.

'Do you want to come inside?'

'Please' she whispered.

Hoisted up into his strong arms, her father carried her back towards the light and she felt her heart beat relaxing as he took her home.

***

The boys were playing out the back green. There was the four of them from his close, himself, Ian and his brother Davie and wee Michael from downstairs. They were playing the Brits and were armed to the teeth with sticks and Ian's cowboy gun up against the Billy Brewer and his pals from the neighbouring close as the Gerries.

The Arki gang were defending the den and had blocked the doorway with his dad's barrow and some ginger crates tied together with string.

Footsteps on the grass roof announced the arrival of the Brewer Boys. They could hear sniggering and then a something was thrown in. 'Dog poo, dog poo, dog poo!' they started chanting louder and louder. They were gagging with the smell. Wee Michael said he wanted to go home.

Out they ran brandishing their weapons but the Brewer Boys held the high ground and were already on top of them. He fell with a thud, his glasses tumbling off. Davie and the others were off across the green, but big Billy Brewer held him down.

'Make him eat it' shouted one of the others. 'Yeah, make him eat in' they all chipped in.

He could smell the poo and Billy prizing his mouth open. He squirmed his head to and fro, but Billy had him by the hair. 'Taste dog poo Arki bampot' he shouted, smearing the dog shit on his face. Then Ian was there and thumping Billy off him. 'Leave him be' he shouted, pulling him up and away. He ran away a few yards. Turning back the Brewer gang were already all over Ian, laying kicks and thumps into as he lay on the ground. He hesitated and then ran on, not stopping until he got home.

Part 1 – Before the Island

Friday 14 April

It was five to six on Good Friday morning. The BBC weather forecast for the United Kingdom had promised a warm spell with occasional showers, but way up here an unexpected Artic front had come in overnight. It had brought rain turning to sleet which was currently washing against the split windscreen as the classic VW campervan rumbled slowly along the cobbled dockside. He looked for the ferry that would take him up to the island but the terminal was completely empty other than for a couple of small fishing boats lying in darkness tied up against the quay side. Giving the windscreen wipers a turn to get rid of the accumulating mush, he spied through the darkness a metal post with an old wooden sign sitting atop it at an angle. Slowing to a crawl he was relieved to see that it read '*West Hunday*' and showed presumably where car traffic was supposed to queue, although there was none except for his own to be seen. He stopped the VW and felt it gently rocking in the wind. He kept the engine running to fend off the cold. He cleared the windscreen again. Flicking on the headlights he peered out but could not see anyone. He lent across to the passenger seat and from his backpack pulled the Orkney Ferries 'North Isles' timetable which the girl at the library had kindly printed for him off the internet. He flicked his finger down the table headed somewhat ironically '*Summer Sailing Times*'. Sure enough the weekly ferry from Kirkwall to West Hunday was shown as leaving at six thirty each Friday morning. His eye was however drawn now for the first time to a footnote in smaller type. '*Tides Permitting*' it read. He cursed at his stupidity. He prided himself on his attention to detail. This was not like him at all. Then again, the whole trip was completely out of the character and, not for the first time, he asked himself what on the earth he was doing on such a fool's errand at his age.

As the old van was buffeted back and forth in the wind, he considered his options. He could drive back into Kirkwall town centre to this bed and breakfast but that dragon of a spinster Miss. Kelly had been quite firm last night in emphasising that breakfast was only served between seven thirty and eight thirty and that was no possibility whatsoever of anything hot before then; even, she had taken pleasure in pointing out, if he was willing to pay a supplement. He could try to find somewhere else in the town but when he had earlier driven down to the harbour it been as quiet as a ghost town and he doubted anywhere would be open until much later. He would simply have to wait until the booking office at the pier head opened and ask when the ferry was due to leave. He turned off the engine, pulled up his old coat around his chin and tried to settle back in his seat.

A rap on the driver side window woke him with a start. A menacing looking figure in oilskins loomed in. He fumbled about as he struggled to find the handle for the window. The man outside knocked more firmly. Finding the handle he rolled it down to be met by a gust of cold salt air and rain. A bearded face, dripping water onto his's lap, poked in. 'Youse far West Hun?' he asked. ' Err.. yes, West Hunday' he replied, reaching over and rummaging for his ticket to give to the man. The dock worker ignored it and pointed instead ahead of them. 'They'll call you forward when it's time to board. Keep an eye out'. With that he slammed the door and departed into the storm.

He clicked on the ignition and cleared the rain from the front screen. Ahead of him lay tied up the dock what looked to be as a surprisingly small ship with lights ablaze fore and aft. A sign on its side identified it as the *MV Earl Erland*. A couple of dockers were buzzing in and out of the bow door loading various crates and other pieces of freight with small forklifts. Meanwhile another man in uniform, presumably the boat's captain, leant out of a window on the bridge, called something out and then promptly pulled the window shut.

He looked at his watch. Six forty five. He had dozed for only an hour but the harbour was now alive with activity. Both of the fishing boats had departed their berths and another, much larger, rusty white trawler filled their space, with men throwing up fishing boxes onto the dock-side. The loading of the ferry took proceeded apace and soon the forklifts stopped and everything seemed to be on board. There was then a pregnant pause before a crew member eventually appeared at the ship's bow doors and waved over to him crossing both arms above his head. Carefully, he pulled the van forward and down onto the boat wincing as he heard it scrap over the bottom of the ramp. Not for the first time he regretted not flying. On board, he was directed to pull up by a float holding two bellowing black cattle. He did as instructed, pulling on his handbrake as tight as possible. He stepped out onto the open deck, locking up the van.

'Leave your keys in the ignition and the window down' called a crew member.

Doing as ordered, he took in the mixed smell of sea air and cow shit. He pulled out his backpack and his favourite ivory topped walking cane. He hurried over out of the sleet to an entrance improbably marked '*Passenger Lounge*' and slowly climbed up two flights of steep stairs, balancing his cane under his arm. There he found a simple but clean cabin with several rows of benches and small portholes to each side and to the stern. He was the only person there. Perhaps other foot passengers would join shortly. Sitting down on a bench at the rear overlooking the car deck, he took off his coat, an old army surplus he'd retained from his time with the TA. It was already soaked. He hung it over the back of the bench in front and put his backpack and cane beside him. He kept his wool hat on given the apparent lack of any heating on the boat. Looking out of the stern porthole, he saw that the boat was crammed full of all manner of stuff, including large bags full of gravel, an old tractor and various items of farm machinery including a shiny new plough and of course the cattle float next to his van, and from which he was annoyed to see that one of the beasts was now busy pissing down the passenger side of his van.

The ferry sat shifting up and down at the dock side rolling gently on the water. This went on for some time and he wondered whether the weather was too poor for them to leave the safety of the harbour. He hated flying, which had been the other option for getting to the island, but, if truth be told, he was also not overly keen on sailing either. This was not a journey he was looking forward to and he was already regretting not packing some sea-sickness tablets. Eventually he heard foot steps up the stairs to the cabin and a crew member in a white boilersuit appeared. He ignored him and instead hurried on through a door at the front, presumably to the bridge. He wandered over to the side porthole facing towards the dock but all he could see were distant lights now on along the Kirkwall harbour front. There was no sign of life on the harbour itself, other than from the fisherman workin on the rusted trawler in front of them. He sat down again, and feeling peckish and for want of something better to do, opened up his rucksack and rummaged through it to see if there was anything to eat; but all he could find was some shortbread in a plastic wrapper acquired from his bedroom at Miss. Kelly's. There was however a flask of tea he'd made up this morning and he poured himself a cup. It tasted rather of plastic and metal and was already lukewarm at best. It was though for all that still welcomed being his first cup of the day and for a tea addict like him it overdue. Although it was cold in the passenger lounge he began to doze again, and was only stopped from falling off to sleep completely by the bridge door opening and closing with a clunk. The same crew member as before appeared, again ignored him, and left down the stairs to the freight deck. It promised to be a long journey.

The ferry sat at its mooring for perhaps another half an hour or so but suddenly he heard shouts coming from down below and looking out of the rear porthole he made out through the rain a large SUV pulling onto the boat with WHBO printed on its side. The SUV's driver together with a passenger, both men, stepped out, exchanged unheard words with a crew member and made for the door up to the lounge. When they reached the passenger lounge they looked surprised to see him and look seats on the opposite side of the cabin. They were clearly not expecting company.

They made for an interesting twosome, one being tall with a shaved head. He had the look of someone who worked out. The other was shorter and fatter and with messy hair stretching down below his shoulders. He sported an over-sized moustache. He did not have the look of someone who frequented gyms.

'Good morning' said Fin. 'Are you for West Hunday?'. As the words came out of this mouth he realised what a stupid question it was, given that was the only place to which the ferry went.

The bigger of the two looked at him as if he was a simpleton. 'Humm..'

'Some weather, isn't it?'

Another 'Humm.'

Clearly, they were not conversationalists.

He looked at the large canvas bag they'd lugged up to the lounge with them. Why would you do that, he thought. It wasn't as if anyone was going to steal it if left in their car. As he sat wondering what might be in it, the ship's tannoy clicked into action and a pre-recorded voice announced that they were about to depart and what to do in an emergency. He gave up a little prayer that the instructions would not need to be followed. All the same he checked under his seat for the promised life-belt.

Peering out the side porthole, he saw the ship's ropes being loosened and he felt the bow doors clang shut with a dull thud. Almost immediately the ship started to reverse away from the dock side. With grinding sounds that made him feel decidedly uncomfortable it slowly turned around and then, quickly picking up speed, began to pull out beyond the safety of the harbour walls.

***

He knew from the timetable that the journey to West Hunday should take about four hours which would provide some further dozing time but first things first he had spotted a sign marked 'Galley' pointing back downstairs.

'I'm going to check out the galley' he said to his two travelling companions, but they just stared back at him. 'Would you like me to bring you anything?' he asked. The big one replied 'No, we're OK.' The smaller one just stared.

Carefully, and holding firmly onto the hand rail, he made his way back down the steps. He reached the main deck and then followed a sign pointing down a further set of steps right into the bowels of the ship. There was a pervading smell of engine oil. There, he found an open hatch into a sizable galley where he was surprised to find a group of about half a dozen crew members sitting around a long table eating what from the smell emanating appeared to be sausages, bacon and eggs. He realised with embarrassment that he was interrupting their breakfast. The aroma of the food mixed with the smells of engine oil and salt water, coupled with the rolling of the ship, was already making him feel queasy, but he hadn't eaten since yesterday evening and he wondered if getting something into his stomach might help to settle it down for the voyage ahead. He asked the group as a whole if he could get anything to eat. They all looked up at him in unison. There was a pregnant pause but then one of them, presumably the cook, nodded to him and said. 'I can make you up a roll with a tatty scone and sausage if you'd like'. For the first time this morning, he felt things were starting to look up. The cook quickly rustled up a couple of filled rolls and, suitably provisioned, he took his spoils carefully back up to the passenger lounge. To his surprise neither of his two travelling companions were there. The ship was in open water and was starting to roll to and fro with some gusto. His tea slopped gently around his mug and spilt down onto his boots. He thought of going back down to the galley for a new brew but doubted that there would be much left by the time he'd carried it back up. He settled on the now cool tea from his flask.

The small ship chugged on steadily at what appeared to be unnecessarily close distance to the shoreline of the various islands that make up the Orkney archipelago. For a while he watched out of the windows for hopeful sight of dolphins and seals as indicated on charts on the cabin wall but except for rhythmic white elephants, he was unable to identify anything against the grey water. Eventually he felt the ship turning to port as it reached the far end of a hilly island, which he took from a map in the cabin to be Westray, and they entered more open water. Almost immediately, the roll on the ship increased substantially as the swell from the Atlantic took hold and he was forced to sit back down on his bench. He was starting to seriously regret his breakfast rolls He tried focusing straight ahead and then on the horizon but neither helped. The ship was now rocking and rolling quite violently, and it was then that the crew member he'd first seen again appeared. 'Good morning to you' he smiled. 'You'll be Mr. Tulloch?' He nodded and the crew member ticked him off a passenger list.

'I have a ticket' he said. He rummaged in his pocket and pulled out a rather dog-eared ticket which he handed to the crewman. The man looked at it for some time as if he'd never seen one before and then passed it back.

'Will you be a birder then?' the man asked.

'Sorry… a what'. 'A birder' the man said more slowly. 'Are you coming up for the bird watching?'. He annunciated his words slowly as if talking to a child.

'No' he said. The man waited for him to elaborate and his failure to add anything, said, smiling. 'Come down to the car deck when we arrive and we will see if we can land. If it's too rough, I'm afraid we'll need to turn around and go back to Kirkwall to try tomorrow. You do know you can fly?'

'Aye'. The thought of another four hours on the boat was enough to bring a little sick up into his throat. He swallowed it down and felt himself turning a shade of puce.

As the crewman turned back towards the bridge he asked. 'Where's the two chaps from the other car. Is there another passenger cabin on board?'.

The crewman hesitated. 'What, Oliver Hardy and Stan Laurel? They're back down in their car. Must be worried someone's going to pinch it.' With that he was gone.

After what seemed like endless more pitching and rolling, he eventually heard the engine tone changing and felt the ship slowing. He looked out of the side window and could make out a small sandy bay appearing with huge breakers hitting up onto the beach and beyond that a low lying island. In the far distance he could make out a lighthouse. He collected up his bits and pieces and holding on as tightly as possible to the railings made his way back down to the car deck. It was still raining hard and the cold water spat against this face. He quickly made his way over to his van and jumped in, rolling up the window he'd left open. His seat was now soaking wet and he could feel the water seeping in through his trousers. He could feel the little ship working hard to dock up against the harbour side. It pulled back and forward several times, and he felt it hitting each time against the dock wall. Suddenly he saw a crew member throw out a rope, but it missed, and he pulled it back in. He tried again and once again it missed with the ship moving up and down on the swell. A third attempt and it was caught by an unseen hand on the dockside and quickly a larger rope was fed out. A second rope was thrown out and secured. A tap on this window. He rolled it down. 'There's no ro-ro here' the crew member who'd handled the rope explained. You need to step off and then we'll lift the van over'.

Out again into the rain, he was shown to a gap in the side of the boat, where a ladder was fixed to the dock wall. With the ship rising up and down with the sea, he gingerly stepped over onto the ladder holding onto it with one hand and his cane with the other. He took a step up the ladder, losing his footing on the wet run. At that moment a big hand from an islander grabbed him by the arm to secure his way and with that he part stepped and was part lifted off the Earl Erland onto West Hunday.

***

'Welcome to West Hunday Mr. Tulloch. Will you stand over there please while your car's lifted off.'

He was pointed to an iron shipping container on the quayside and was happy to take up some shelter from the rain although the wind still rattled around. He wiped his glasses against his sleeve and smelt the sea. His hands were freezing and he shoved them in his pockets. The wee ship sat against the harbour wall straining on its ropes. A small crane had started lifting the cargo off the ship one item at a time. What appeared to be a thin fishing net was used with a man siting high in a gantry above the ship operating the crane. A man and woman, both no less than his age, on the dockside caught ropes attached to the cargo net and with some dexterity pulled and pushed the cargo into place until it gently lowered onto the dockside.

One after one the crates and other cargo was unloaded and a forklift moved it along the dockside. Finally, the top of his VW appeared over the side of the ship. The ship itself rolled to the side of the dock under the weight and he could sense the rope and netting tensioning under the weight. Up and over the side of the ship the VW swung and it was lowered down. One of the islanders on the dock side grabbed a rope and pulled the van round to face inland. It landed with only the slightest bump. An old woman on the dockside gestured to him and he stepped back into the van and out of the weather and slowly started up the dock into West Hunday.

He did not see the two chatty men dubbed Laurel and Hardy step ashore. Perhaps they had come off before him.

***

West Hunday is the most remote of the Orkney Isles and lies about eighteen, nautical miles east of Westray on a line of latitude approximately equal to that of Bergin in Norway. It technically comes under the administrative authority of Orkney Council in Kirkwall but given its remoteness it has traditionally been largely self-governing, overseen by a council of crofters under the supervision of the local ruling family, the Bransons. The Orkney archipelago itself sits off the north of Scotland and is made up of approximately seventy islands of which twenty-one are inhabited.

West Hunday is only about seven miles long and at its widest about two miles wide. Technically it is two islands only accessible at low tide, but it is connected these days by a causeway built by Napoleonic prisoners of war. Low lying to the south, it is particularly exposed to the strong North Atlantic winds. There is not a single tree on the island and such bushes as grow there are gnarled and bent in the direction of the prevailing wind. The highest point on the island lies at its northern end where fifty foot high cliffs fall away into the sea. A lighthouse stands on the edge of the cliffs acting as a warning beacon for passing shipping.

It has a population today, reduced from about three hundred at its peak in the eighteenth century, of about fifty, the majority of whom are over retirement age. The island has however been occupied since pre-historic times as evidenced by a number of well-preserved standing stones, cairns and burial brochs. It formed a Norse strong-hold for several hundred years. Indeed its name derives from old Norse and means 'Dog Island'.

The islanders have traditionally derived their livelihoods from agriculture and fishing. In more recent years, however, this has been supplemented by the building of a state of the art bird observatory. The island has since proved a magnet for bird watching enthusiasts due to the number of unusual breeds regularly sighted after being blown in either from across the Atlantic or down from the Artic.

Thursday 6 April

The letter had arrived the previous day along with a collection of circulars advertising the usual entreaties for unneeded double glazing and unwanted credit cards. Fin had been distracted by his badly behaved Dandie Dinmont, Sammy, running through his legs and out the front door of his house as he opened the door to take in the mail from the postie, and he had left the mail on the hall table in his rush to retrieve the daft mutt. It was only the following day when he had returned from the bowling club that he had picked up the mail and glanced through the various envelopes. He was irritated by his failure to the deal with the mail the previous day, notwithstanding that it was unlikely to contain anything of interest. Bringing the mail through to the kitchen, he flicked through the usual junk. In amongst it, a handwritten letter jumped out. He couldn't remember when he'd last received one and couldn't think who might be writing to him. He picked it up and turned it over as if the reverse might give a clue as to who it was from. Turning it back over, he saw that it was addressed to him in a tidy hand, the letters almost printed, with a first-class stamp neatly placed in the corner. He tried to make out the post mark but couldn't find one. Looking around for his reading glasses, and eventually finding them on their usual loop around his neck, he carefully opened it with a butter knife and read it for what would be the first of several times.

5 April

Mr. Finbarr Tulloch
11/1 John Street
Portobello
Edinburgh EH15

Dear Mr. Tulloch

My name is Ophelia Macleod. I am afraid that you do not know me but I am your grand-daughter. Someone is trying to harm me and I do know where to turn. Please help me.

I will be at the Baillie in Stockbridge at 7 pm on 7 April.

Please do not tell anyone. I don't know who I can trust.

Yours sincerely

Ophelia Macleod x

PS My grandmother was Grace Harper from Musselburgh.

He turned over the letter. The back was blank. He looked again at the envelope, trying to find a post mark but it was illegible. He considered it for a moment, tore it in two and threw it into the kitchen bin. He was both angry and upset.

Later the same evening Fin was again sitting at the kitchen table looking at the letter, now sellotaped together. It was obviously written by some chancer after a hand-out, or worse still, some paranoid looney who really thought she was his grand-daughter. It was the PS that had troubled him. He'd known a Grace Harper in his youth just before he'd joined up, but she'd certainly not had a child by him. Their relationship, if you could call it that, had been no more really than childhood friends, certainly nothing serious. But that was almost fifty years ago. He'd not thought about her for years so how would anyone know about her and link her to him. He picked up the letter and looked more closely at the writing as if this would enable him to decipher some hidden meaning. Nothing came to him. He shoved in in a drawer, turning to Sammy. 'Well this is a rum one wee man, that's for sure'. He beckoned to the dog and it jumped up onto his lap with a toy fox in its mouth.

Friday 7 April

Fin Tulloch had been a widower for slightly over five years since the unexpected death of his wife Maggie, and as with many other single men of his age, he had developed somewhat into a creature of habit. Following his usual breakfast of porridge, made religiously with half a cup of oatmeal to three halves of water stirred always, as his mother has taught him, clockwise to keep the Devil away, and washed down with his first cup of tea of the day, he then put on his old TA camouflage jacket, picked up his favourite walking cane and took Sammy out for his morning constitutional along Portobello beach, letting him do his business and carefully bagging it up afterwards. Stopping to sit for a while with Sammy on the way back outside the Beach House café, he shared a scone and jam with Sammy and had another cuppa. He took out his Scotsman – concentrating first on the cryptic crossword and then, and in somewhat more detail, on the horse racing pages, working methodically through the runners and riders for the various meetings and underlining those deemed worthy of investment. Cutting back up to the High Street he made his daily visit to Malcolm at the bookies placing a two pound yankie on four horses, plus an extra pound on the nose on each of his selections.

Each morning had passed in a similar fashion since Maggie's passing and he felt no need to alter this routine on account of the arrival of the letter.

As on each other week day, following a lunch back home of a bowl of Baxters soup, always tattie and leek, and a bread roll from the local Co-Op, he gave Sammy a biscuit and left him in his bed to walk over to the bowling club on Lee Crescent, where, because a haar had drifted in from the Forth making play impossible, he spent a less than fruitful couple of hours in the bar chatting to his fellow non-players over a pint of Deuchars and a game of dominos and moaning about the current lack of form of Hibs FC.

Back home it was time for his afternoon dose of 'Pointless', a quiz on BBC 1 with Fin calling out to Sammy the answers and bemoaning the stupidity of the contestants and the general fall in educational standards in the country. That ordeal over for the dog, a quick tea of cheese on toast followed, followed by another brisk walk along the promenade, stopping to watch a few hardy swimmers taking to the water through the mist. Then, with Sammy fed, he pulled on a sports jacket and his ex-forces tie, patted Sammy good-bye, and climbed in his VW campervan to drive over to Fettes Avenue to join the usual suspects from his old colleagues for a Friday night drink at the Lothian and Borders Police Social Club.

Fin had been attending the social club twice a week since he'd retired from the police force. He liked it that the club had retained its name despite Lothian and Borders having been subsumed, in his opinion not to its benefit, into Police Scotland in recent years. He felt at home in the club and liked that people knew his name, most calling him 'Fin' and some behind his back, 'Old Fin.' It held a comforting familiar atmosphere despite Fin never having worked at Fettes. He was an 'A' Division man himself, having joined in the early 1980s and had spent his whole career up at St Leonard's, performing many roles over the years, mostly of a sedentary nature it had to be confessed. If his career had not been exactly stellar, he was at least consistent and he had risen slowly but surely from Constable to the rank of Sergeant at the time of his retirement just before his fifty seventh birthday. To be truthful, he lacked the ambition to go further and had been happy to spend the last ten years of his career on reception duty, shoveling around paper and in quieter periods reading the sporting pages in the daily papers.

***

Fin normally parked outside the Edinburgh Accies ground to walk back up to Fettes Avenue, but this evening what with building work ongoing and a rugby match in progress, the few available spaces were already all full. So instead he found himself driving on up into Stockbridge to look for a space, eventually finding one opposite the Mellis cheese shop. Stepping out of the van, he sighed. It would be a long walk back to Fettes. He crossed the road and noticed the Ballie on the next corner. Instinctively he felt into his jacket pocket and touched the letter. He could not remember bringing it with him. He idled for a moment and started back down towards the social club. He had gone only perhaps twenty yards or so, when he stopped saying out aloud 'What the hell'. A woman passing with a small child gave him a look and a wide berth. He turned around and started back the way he had come.

He was not sure what he expected to find as he walked down the stairs into the bar but the place was packed with a throng of folk who'd presumably just finished work. He looked around but there was no one who immediately fitted the bill of Ophelia. Then again, he had no idea what she looked like. He found a seat in a corner, laying his jacket over the chair to secure it.

'Can you keep an eye on my coat?' he asked a couple sitting next to him.

'Sure pop' said the girl.

The Ballie in its day had been a working man's bar thick with smoke but over the years it had been gentrified in line with its surrounding neighborhood. He did not think the changes were necessarily an improvement.

Pushing his way through to the bar, he held up a tenner. No-one paid him any attention. A youth in a suit used his elbows to squeeze in next to him.

'Four pints of lager' he shouted.

'Tennants do?'.

'Aye, that's fine.'

He was still ignored.

The youth's beers arrived. He lifted up three glasses in his arms. He tried juggling the fourth but couldn't quite make it. Turning, he spilt some larger onto Fin's sleeve.

'Watch it!' cried Fin wiping the beer off his shirt sleeve.

'Hold your horses old man' said the youth and he disappeared with his three glasses through the crowd back to his mates.

Fin starred into his back.

'What can I get you?'

He turned and a barmaid stood impatiently in front of him.

'A pint of IPA please' he said. The young woman behind the bar was wearing a Grateful Dead t-shirt. She looked bored but she took her time carefully pouring his drink and it looked cold and inviting with a thick head.

He handed her a tenner and received what seemed to be not nearly enough change.

'Who's is this?' the barmaid asked, pointing to the youth's final glass of lager.

'Oh, I think he's left' said Fin. Shrugging, she picked up the lager and poured it down the sink.

He made this way over to his table, lifting an evening paper off another as he went. He had to push by the youth heading back to the bar for his now missing drink. He took care not to spill any of this own.

He waited. Perhaps an hour passed with him nursing his pint and checking the disappointing racing results. The bar had by now cleared as people made their way home for dinner or on to somewhere more exciting in the city centre, and there were only a few folk scattered around. He swirled around the end of his drink and finished it off. What a waste of time and to add insult to injury he was now late for the club. Perhaps he should have worn a red carnation. He took the empty glass up to the bar. 'Thanks' he said, nodding to the barmaid. 'Cold out tonight', she said, just passing the time. 'Weather says there's a storm on the way.' Fin grunted an 'Aye' by way of acknowledgement and then added 'My name is Tulloch. I am supposed, errr.. to be meeting someone. I don't suppose anyone has asked for me.' The barmaid replied 'not that I know'. She then called out to the snug beyond the main bar. 'Isla, has anyone been asking for a Tulloch'. A voice called back 'no – what's he want?'. The barmaid smiled an apologetic smile. 'If anyone comes in asking for you I'll point you out'. 'Och well' said Fin 'in that case I guess I'll have another for the road and add a wee whisky this time to keep it company.' Fin retreated with his beer and chaser to the same seat in the corner and pulled out his newspaper again.

He sat nursing his drink and watching the other customers. He decided he didn't mind the bar as much as he'd originally thought, and possibly even quite liked it now it had quietened down. The beer was good and no music or television blaring was an added bonus. Slowly the second glass lowered. He spent the time looking around the room trying to pick out someone who could be his grand-daughter but no-one fitted the bill. It dawned on him that it could just be a rouse and back home burglars could be rifling through his possession at the very moment. Just as he was blaming himself for being so naive, a young woman pulled up a stool next to him and plompted herself down.

'You're Finbarr Tulloch' she said. It was not a question but a statement. Fin nodded.

'Would you like a top-up? she asked, eyeing his half empty glass. She didn't wait but was off up to the bar with it. He watched her as another pint of IPA was poured. She was dressed in cycling gear, multi-coloured lycra leggings topped with a garish yellow jacket. Short spikey blonde hair set off with a diamond stud through her nose. He was not good at guessing ages but would have put her at no more than about twenty. She was not what he was expecting in a potential grand-daughter.

Back again, she put another pint down for him and what looked like a vodka and Coke for herself. She took a sip. She pushed the other towards him.

'I take it you're Ophelia Macleod.'

'Becky' she said, and surprised him by reaching out her hand to shake his. She had a surprisingly strong grip for someone so small.

'Ok, Becky... so what are you after?' he asked.

'Listen, I know this all seems odd. It does to me too.' She lent in towards him and lowering her voice went on. 'I'm a friend of Offie... err Ophelia. I got a note to say they she was meeting her grandad here for the first time and asked if I could chum her along.'

'I don't know anyone called Ophelia' he said, pulling back to regain some personal space.

She looked a little taken aback. 'But you are Finbarr Tulloch'.

'I prefer Fin'.

'Well you must know her.' She had lent in again re-creating an intimacy between them.

'Listen, I'm sorry dear but I don't know anyone of that name, and I don't know you either. Thanks for the pint and all that, but just what do you want exactly?'

She shuffled in her seat and took another sip of her drink.

'Offie just told me to be here at seven. She said she was meeting her granddad and wanted some support. I've been sitting in the far corner over there for the last hour and a half, not that you noticed, but she's never turned up.'

She pointed over to the opposite corner of the bar where a young man with long blonde hair was sitting. He smiled back embarrassed. 'That's Magnus. He's just a friend' she added by way of unnecessarily supplement. She waved at him over and rather sheepishly he made his way over. He was also dressed in de-rigour cycling kit.

'Sit down Magnus' she said. 'This is Mr. Tulloch.' Magnus reluctantly drew up a chair. In contrast to the girl, he was tall, well over six foot.

'Listen, err….Becky isn't it…I don't know what this is all about, but if you and your friend are on the make you've chosen the wrong guy to try it on with.' He gave her what he hoped was a hard stare.

She gave him a thin smile and looked him straight back. He felt uncomfortable and embarrassed at the same time.

'Mr Tulloch, I've told you why I'm here. Offie asked me. There's no ulterior motive.' She reached into her jacket pocket and pulled out a crumpled piece of paper. She handed it over to him. It was a letter in the same neat handwriting as the one he had received.

5 April

Dearest Becky

Hello darling. Sorry for not keeping in touch but I'm in real trouble. I can't contact the police up here about it so I am going to try my granddad who used to be a policeman. Yes, I really have one, not that he knows! I am coming down to meet him at the Ballie at 7 on Friday night. It's sure to freak him out so could you meet me there too please.

I know I can count on my big sis.

Love.

Offie xxx.

Fin studied the letter and then took another drink of his beer.

Finally, he said 'I don't understand why If she's in trouble, she can't just call the police or her family'

'I don't know about the police but she has no family' she said.

'But you're her sister' he said.

'Not really. It's just what she calls me.'

He turned to Magnus. 'What's this all about?' but Becky answered.

'We don't know.'

'There's not much you do know is there.'

'That's not fair. I don't know why she hasn't contacted the police. But I do know this isn't like her. She's normally so level headed. If she says she needs help then I'm sure she does.' She looked down at her drink.

He softened his tone. 'Listen Becky, I'm sorry but I don't know your friend. I think she has the wrong person. I don't have a grand-daughter.' He pushed back his chair, leaving the remainder of this drink, and picked up his walking cane and jacket. He took a couple of steps towards the door, but she called out after him

'Then, why are you here. Tell me that.' He kept going, up the stairs and into the cold of the night.

With the drink, he decided to pick up his car in the morning. Instead, he walked up through the New Town to catch a bus home from Princes Street. He normally liked to sit upstairs despite his bad leg and watch the people below on the streets, but tonight he took the first seat available. He did not know what to make of the letters. He was sure that Becky had been genuinely concerned. What if he did have a grand-daughter? Surely, he would have known about it. He decided the best thing to do was to hand in the letter he'd received to the police and leave it in their hands. He would do this first thing tomorrow. He would also do some digging and see if there was any possibility he'd had a child with Grace. He had not seen her for over thirty years and had no idea where she might be. He struggled to think where to start.

Back home, he pulled down the dog's lead from the hook by the door and clipped it on. 'Well, Sammy, this is an odd one that's to be sure' he said, ruffling the little dog's head. The dog wagged its tail at him in reply. He closed the front door and he stepped outside for a last walk of the day, wrapping up his jacket against the weather.

Saturday 8 April

Fin first spotted Magnus as he stooped to pick up Sammy's mess at the turning onto the promenade. To be honest, it was not difficult. At that time of the morning the only folk down on the sea front were other dog walkers and a group of women in wet suits trying to launch a rowing skiff off the beach. So, a tall red long-haired bloke on a bike rather stood out. He meandered along the walkway, allowing Sammy to stop and sniff at the smells of other dogs as he went. Eventually, they reached the far end by the cafe and he bought himself a tea and a scone, sitting down at one of the outside tables to share it with the dog. From the corner of his eye he saw Magnus shuffling around about a hundred yards away. He waved over to him. Magnus maintained his charade for a moment and then reluctantly pushed his bike over, and took a seat next to Fin.

'Magnus isn't it?' Fin asked.

'Err…. yes' said Magnus, reaching down to pat Sammy.

'How did you know where to find me?' asked Fin.

'It wasn't difficult. I looked you up in the telephone directory and then watched this morning outside your house.'

Perhaps he's not such a poor tail after all thought Fin.

Magnus sat down. 'Thing is, Mr. Tulloch, Becks doesn't know I'm here but she's really worried about Offie. She's not heard from her for more than two weeks and now she'd received that letter.'

'Two weeks is not very long.'

'It is for them. They've spoken every day since they were children.'

'I'm sorry that but don't understand what it has to do with me.'

'Well, you're her grandad aren't you.' Magnus's voice was slightly raised.

Fin raised his in return. 'As I said last night I don't have any grandchildren. I realise your girlfriend is upset but you have me confused with someone else.'

'So how come you were at the Baillie? You must know her.'

'I received a note like you one Becky got, asking me to be there. It was curiosity that's all.'

'I don't think that's true' said Magnus.

They sat for a moment neither saying anything.

Breaking the silence, Fin said 'I honestly don't know her. Now, I'm busy...' He got up and pulled Sammy along. Magnus followed with his bike.

'I don't believe you.'

Fin turned and straightened up. 'Look, I don't give a feck about what you believe. Now stop harassing me or I'll call the police.'

Magus backed off a couple of paces, but still following him. At the turning onto the High Street he called out 'Fin, we can't just leave it like this.'

Fin stopped and waited for him to catch up.

'We need to talk. Becks and me will be grabbing a coffee after work up at Peter's Yard on Middle Meadows Walk. Why don't you join us about five o'clock. If you then think she is still talking crap we will leave it at that, and we won't bother you again.'

'Is that a guarantee?'

Fin stepped into the bookies with Sammy, leaving Magnus and his bike on the pavement.

Fin sat in the bookmakers looking through the racing pages but was too distracted to concentrate. His mind kept coming back to his meeting with Becky yesterday evening and then Magnus this morning. Magnus had clearly made an effort to track him down and he could not get out of his head how worried Becky had looked last night. He was sure she had been genuine.

'Are you using that paper?'.

An old man pointed to the newspaper he'd been staring at for the last twenty minutes.

'What… err…no, here you go.' He handed the old man the paper.

'Oh, for heaven's sake' he said to Sammy sitting by his side cleaning his paws. He stood up, picked up his cane and made for the door.

***

The drive down the coast to Musselburgh only took him twenty minutes but as always when he made the trip it took him back half a century to his boyhood. He parked up outside the gates to Loretto school and walked back towards Luca's. Although it was not much past twelve, there was already a queue at the ice cream counter but he went past it and asked for table in the café. Luca's had already been an institution by the time of his childhood and although it had been through a number of refurbishments over the years, it had never lost its atmosphere. Looking around it still had the same eclectic mix of customers. There a worker in this overalls with a plate of pie, beans and chips just delivered, two children busy scooping out ice cream sundaes and an old spinster in the corner nursing cream soda and a bowl of macaroni. A young girl in the Luca uniform brought him over his lunch, a big artery hardening fry up with all the extras. The Scottish diet on a plate.

'Is Nona in today?' he asked.

'She's back in the kitchen' he was told.

'Tell her wee Fin Tulloch's here and wonders if she'd have a moment for him.'

Fin was busy wiping up his egg yolk and beans with the last of his toast when Nona appeared. He had no idea how old she was. She'd seemed ancient when he'd come in as a child, then again maybe all adults appear that way to children. Despite being born and bred in Musselburgh she had the half Scottish, half Italian accent enjoyed by so many of her compatriots who ran the ice cream bars and fish and chips shops up the coast.

'How are you Fin? What brings you down to the honest toun, not enough crime for you in Edinburgh?'

'Now Nona, you know I'm retired.'

'Retired! How can you be retired at your age. Look at me. I'm in here every morning at six.'

One of Nona's sons, a man of Fin's age walked by, raising his eyebrows.

'And enough of your cheek Paulo.'

'Will you have a cup of tea with me Nona?' asked Fin.

'I can maybe spare you five minutes but then I have to get back to the soup.' She pulled up a chair next to him. 'Two teas' she called to the waitress, 'pronto!'

When he was a youngster, Nona had been good to Fin. She knew he was from a poor background and often an ice-cream float would appear in exchange for him helping to lift out the empty ginger bottles or for some other minor task.

'Nona' he said stirring his tea 'you remember the boys I used to run with back in the day. Ian, JimP and the others.'

'Aye, you were a bad lot that's for sure.' She said laughing at the memory. 'JimP of course ended up in the pokey. I though that's where you'd be going. I still can't believe you joined the polis.'

'JimP would be out by now, no?' he asked.

'Oh aye, he got released years ago. Used to live up on Campie Road.'

'Where's he now?'

'Didn't you know. He's been dead these last six months. Too many pies and not enough exercise. You should watch yourself' she added 'pointing down to his empty plate. 'Too many of those and your cholesterol will be through the roof.'

'Any what about the rest of them?'

'All scattered to the four seas, except Ian of course. I still see him walking that wee dog of his down by the racecourse.'

'Any idea when I might catch him?'

'It's after opening time isn't it.' She laughed again. 'He's be in the Ship. Anyway, why the trip down memory lane. You feeling nostalgic or something?'.

'There's no rule against looking up old school friends, is there.'

'You just be careful Fin. There's still plenty round here not be happy to see a copper, retired or not. Now, I need to get back to that soup or there will be none for the dinner service this evening.'

Fin tipped generously, bought an ice cream cone with a 99 flake in it and wandered up the High Street to the Ship Inn. The bar was quiet and he spotted Ian immediately. A bear of a man, he was busy propping up the bar making his beer last and smoking a roll-up.

***

'Well, well' said Ian in a loud voice as Fin walked over to him, 'I think I can smell pork.'

Fin ignored the insult. 'Hello Ian. No see for a long time. How's it doing wee man?'

'It's doing great Fin. Just great. I'm just relaxing here whilst they repair my yacht. I'm off to Monte Carlo in the morning.'

'I see you've lost none of your electric wit.'

'A pint for my friend here' said Fin to the bar man 'and a ginger beer and lime for me'. Ian raised his eyes. 'Looking after your figure Fin.'

'Driving' explained Fin.

'So, Sergeant Tulloch, I assume this isn't just a social call, what with you not bothering for the last twenty years. What do you want?'

'Wo there, Ian. Can't I just catch up with an old friend?'

'What, like you did at JimP's funeral.'

'Aye, I just heard about that. I'm sorry.'

'Leave it Fin. You don't give a shit about us boys since you moved up to posh Porty.'

'I don't recall seeing you at Maggie's funeral, so don't lecture me.'

'Touché' said Ian.

Fin took a drink to let their tempers settle.

'You remember the lassies we used to run with, back in the day' he said.

'Aye, we thought we were the bee's knees back then.' Ian smiled for the first time exposing black rotted teeth. 'Remember the denim and flares. We were some sight.'

'Aye, what were they called? I remember Beth, what a looker and then there was, what was she called, oh aye, Grace. Do you remember?'

'Oh yes Fin. I may be past it but I'm not senile yet. Everyone knew you had a wee thing for her. Mind you, yon Grace was a bonnie lassie, long hair and plenty up top. She ran with that edjit Tommy Flynn didn't she.'

'Is she still in the toun?'

'I've never seen her for years. Once Tommy got her up the duff they moved somewhere over in the west I think'.

Fin took another drink. He was just contemplating what a dead end this was becoming, when Ian added 'Of course Tommy was back within the year. Just abandoned her, poor cow.'

'Is he still around?'

'Aye, last I heard he lives in the sheltered housing scheme up on the Brae.'

'And what about you Ian, how are you.'

'I'm sixty and have the Big C, like you'd give a shit. That's how I am.'

'I'm sorry to hear that. Can I get you another pint' asked Fin.

'Go on then'.

'We should catch up again soon.'

'Aye, right' said Ian, looking down into the dredges in his empty glass.

***

When he entered the Swedish bakery up at the Meadows he struggled to find them among all the rich students and young trendies from the nearby office blocks. Then he spotted Becky waving at him from a table near the rear. There were two half empty coffee cups in front of them and they looked as if they had been there for some time. They were both still in their cycling gear.

Fin went up to the counter. 'A pot of tea please' he asked.

'And what sort of tea would that be?' the assistant behind the counter asked, his voice dripping with sarcasm.

'Just tea. The sort you add milk to'.

The man had a well-groomed beard topped off with a handlebar moustache. The word metrosexual could have been invented to describe him. 'I'll assume that's English breakfast' he said.

'I'd prefer Scottish breakfast' said Fin in an exaggerated Edinburgh accent.

Fin was handed an oversized spoon with a number on it and told that his tea would be brought over.

'I hope the tea's better than the service' he said, sitting down. 'Ok, why don't you two start at the beginning and tell me everything you know'.

Becky sighed. 'I've known Offie, that's Ophelia, since we were wee. We were in the same care home together up at Bruntsfield. I can remember like yesterday the first time I saw her. I must have been about nine and she would be about a year younger, but she was like a little bird. I remember her looking scared as hell when they brought her in. She didn't cry though. Not then, but I heard her later at night in the dark.'

'Too old for adoption and too young for much else we were. No-one wanted damaged goods of our age. Cute babies they were after. Just farmed out a series of foster homes we were. But somehow we always ended up back at the Pines.'

'The Pines?'

'Aye, that was the name of the care home. Just off the links.'

'What was Offie like?' he asked.

'The other kids thought that she was stuck up, what with that posh name of her's. But she wasn't. It was more that she was reserved. She found it difficult to trust anyone.' She looked at Magnus. 'Any chance of another brew Mags?'. He got up to join the queue at the counter. She then continued. 'He's not my boyfriend. Just someone I flat share with.'

'You've mentioned that.'

Fin's tea arrived. 'She's smart' Becky continued 'but I've always had to look after her if you know what I mean. Like I was her big sister or something. We went right through school together. James Gillespie's it was. The other kids looked down on us care home kids but we stuck together and we did OK. I got into design college and now work up at the Art College and Offie went off to Heriot Watt to study zoology. Super bright she is. Got a First and then went on to do a Masters in conservation or something like that.'

'We've always kept in touch. I don't think there's ever been more than a couple of days when we've not spoken.'

Magnus had returned with her tea and with a fancy coffee and cake for him. 'Yeah' he said 'close as two peas in a pod are that pair. Offie's never out of our flat.' Becky gave him a warning shot to keep quiet and he concentrated on his coffee.

'Anyway, this whole letter thing is completely out of character for her. There must be something seriously wrong.'

'When was the last time you saw her?' he asked.

'Just after the new year. She left for a uni placement up north. It's part of her course. But we still spoke by phone every day. I never knew she even had any family let alone a grandad.'

Fin had been supping his tea, taking it in. 'She never mentioned me?' he asked.

'No, sorry. I knew she'd been looked into finding out about her birth mother but she'd never mentioned anything about it. I thought she'd drawn a short straw.'

'You mentioned a placement. What do you know about it'

'It's at a bird observatory on a wee island called West Hunday I think. Way up in the Orkneys. Something to do with bird wilds and migration patterns'

'Have you tried speaking to them?' he asked.

'When I phoned they said she'd left for a few days to go travelling round the islands. But she wouldn't do that without telling me first; and even if she did, why has she not been in touch since.' He noticed that her hand was slightly shaking. Magnus took it but he shook him off.

She said. 'I'm really worried about her. I know it all sounds so peculiar but I don't know what to do.'

Fin thought for a moment. 'I could try reporting it but I can't see the authorities doing anything given she has only been gone for a couple of weeks. It's not exactly unusual for someone of her age to go off travelling.'

Becky looked crestfallen. She sat fingering a pendant around her neck.

'I'll tell you what' said Fin I can't promise anything but 'I'll do some digging. I used to work for Lothian & Borders and still have a few contacts on the force. Let's meet up here again on Monday morning at nine and we can take it from there.'

Becky tried to put on a brave face. 'I'm really grateful' she said, planting a kiss on this cheek. She grabbed his hand and wrote down a number of the palm. 'Call us if you find out anything sooner.' Once she had left Fin took out the letter from his jacket pocket and read it again, trying to decipher something in its lines. *'Someone is trying to harm me.' 'Someone is trying to harm me'. 'Someone is trying to harm me.'*

***

Fin Tulloch was brought in Musselburgh in the 1960s when it was still known as the 'Honest Toun', although from the years he had later spent in the police force serving its citizens he could attest to the fact that this epithet was not necessarily always accurate. His father had worked on a trawler based out of the then thriving port but was killed in a knife fight in a pub when he was only two, leaving his mother to bring him up alone. His mother cleaned at Loretto the expensive private school which dominated one end of the town. Fin had not benefited from a Loretto education but it had gifted him his unusual first name, borrowed by his mother from a boy at the school.

They'd lived in a Council tenement flat in Stevenson Street in the poorer end of the town. There were six flats in the close and theirs was on the first floor. Across the stair lived the Arbuckles. Ian Arbuckle was the same age as Fin and his wee brother Davie was a year or two younger. As he grew up Fin seemed to spend as much time in the Arbuckles' flat as his own. Their door was always open and Mrs. Arbuckle seemed not to care about feeding an extra mouth at tea. When they were little, their playground comprised the shared green outside, pretending to be soldiers or cowboys and indians. At that time, it still housed an air raid shelter from the war and all the boys in the street used it as a den. As they got older they ventured out around the town.

He had not been a big boy but had proved himself able with his fists early on as he ran with the Arbuckles. They had spent their days bunking off school and stealing penny sweets from Woolworths. Their evenings, when they managed to put together a few shillings, had been spent down Luca's, initially, when they had the money, scooping out red cola ice cream floats, and then when they hit their teenage years smoking single Woodbines and trying to look cool for the girls. His lack of stature had however counted against him and his strike record with the girls had been poor. That was until he met Grace.

He'd been aware of her for a while. He had seen her in Luca's sitting with a group of girls from the posh houses down near Loretto's. They hung out with boys from the same area, Tommy Flynn included. Tommy was a tall good looking boy and fancied himself as a bit of a footballer. That was where the trouble started. Somehow, Fin has been drawn into playing in a match to be held on the racecourse one July evening during the school holidays. He was not a player but his team were short of boys and he had no option. Tommy was on the other team, made up of boys with proper boots most about a year and six inches taller.

When they arrived for the match, Fin's team, led by Ian, wore a mixture of t-shirts and black gutties. The boys from the other team wore a matching kit. Jumpers had been laid out for the goals and a crowd of boys had turned up as supporters, with some girls also looking on from a distance. The match was uneven from the start. Despite their lack of kit, Ian's team ran rings around Tommy's and were soon two goals to the better. That's the thing with football. Size and fancy boot and kit counts for nothing. Soon the tackles started to come crunching in as Tommy's lot started to lose the rag. Elbows were also flying and Fin took one right in the face, bringing a deep bruise up under his eye.

About twenty minutes in, the ball came to Fin in midfield. He passed out to Ian on the wing who drifted past an opposing player and then hit it back into the open for Fin to run on to. Fin was flying forward towards the ball. He caught Tommy out of the corner of his eye but was already on the ball. He pulled it back with one foot and nutmegged it through Tommy's legs, opening up the goal. Casually he then swept it past the keeper for a three-nil lead. His mistake was to celebrate as if he'd just scored at East Road against the Jam Tarts. Turning to run back to his half, he was dismantled from the back by a furious Tommy Flynn. 'Nobody does that to me, yer fuckin twat' he shouted and then he spat into his face. Well, that kicked off a huge melee and soon all the players and some of the supporters were laying into one another. It was only when the blue lights from a police car showed that they all scattered in every which direction. Fin only just got away before the coppers were on top of them, losing a shoe in the process for which his mother leathered him when he got home.

It was a couple of nights later and Fin was helping out back at Luca's shifting some cases of empty bottles ready for collection the next day. Finished, Nona had a cream soda float waiting for him and he took it gratefully through to a stool in the café. He was busy mixing the ice cream into the ginger when he noticed the table of girls watching him and laughing and talking amongst themselves. He tried to ignore them, but found his face reddening. Then they were standing. They had to pass him to get out of the café, and he felt them one by one squeezing past. The last was Grace Harper. She stepped by and then turned back to him. 'I saw you at the footba the other day. I'm sorry for what Tommy did. He was out of order.'

'That's OK' he said and at that moment Nona appeared. 'Would you like another Fin' she asked 'and what about your friend?'

Fin looked embarrassed but Grace said 'Thanks, that would be nice. I'll have the same as him' and she eased up onto the stool next to him.

'So you're called Fin. That's a strange name. Tell me about it.'

And he did.

Everyone knew that Tommy Flynn was a bit of a psycho and everyone also knew that Grace Harper's was his girlfriend and that he'd be toast if Tommy and his gang appeared. Fin kept a wary eye on the café door as they chatted ready to make a break for it round the back if needed. Still, if Nona had offered another drink, he'd have risked sharing it with her.

***

For Fin Musselburgh had been somewhere to escape from, and after leaving school at the first opportunity he had at sixteen joined the army serving as a squaddie in the Royal Highland Fusiliers. He stayed in the army for ten years, climbing to the heady heights of Private and had then left to carve out his equally stellar career in Lothian and Borders Police. He had spent his first few years on the beat patrolling the mean streets of Musselburgh before being side-lined into a desk job at St Leonard's. He would like to have boasted of a career threatening injury in the line of duty but in fact he had been hit on a pedestrian crossing by a woman distracted by her child on the way to dropping him off as a day boy at Loretto. He'd walked with a slight limp ever since and had taken to using his walking cane although it was questionable as to whether it was more an affectation than being really needed.

Fin's had married Maggie within a couple of years of leaving the army and had settled into the humdrum of domestic life, but this was abruptly terminated when his wife had suddenly died of a heart attack five years ago within a couple of months of his retirement from the police service. They had had no children but he had taken solace in the current Sammy and a series of Sammys before him. He was not unhappy in his current routine of dog walking, losing on the horses, lawn bowling and day time quiz shows; or at least had thought he was not unhappy. Now he was not quite so sure.

Sunday 9 April

Fin was a classic technophobe. He did not own a computer let alone a fancy iPad. He knew however that you could use one down at an internet cafe at the bottom of Leith Walk so after taking Sammy for his morning constitutional down by the beach, he made his way along there only to find it not yet open. After waiting fifteen minutes outside in the rain a young girl in jeans and a worn t-shit finally appeared and let him in.

'You're keen'.

'Never too early to learn.'

He'd bought a cup of tea and was allocated a computer. He sat looking at the screen for a couple of minutes. The girl brought over his tea.

'Errr… can you show me how to turn it on.'

She laughed. 'Sure, what are you trying to do?'

'I'm thinking of taking a bird watching holiday in Orkney. There's a bird observatory on an island called West Hunday and I'm trying to find out about it.' She pulled a chair up next to him and showed him how to log in and make use of a search engine. There were only a small number of entries about West Hunday giving the basics on geography and tourism, as well as a specific site for the bird observatory. His eye was drawn to one entry about an Iron Age broch, a huge dry-stone structure built on a rocky foreshore of the island before the birth of Christ, near which an enormous stone slab with striking Norse symbols stood. He remembered a similar design on the pendant around Becky's neck.

He flicked through the various sites making notes of the email addresses and telephone numbers for Logannair and Orkney Ferries as well as the number for the bird observatory.

He then typed into the search engine 'Ophelia Macleod'. About six returns pinged up. The first was for something called Facebook and clicking on it the screen showed a string of people called Ophelia Macleod or something similar. The first was for an actress in Phoenix and the second for a housewife in Cape Town. The third however was for an environmental conservationist in Scotland. He clicked against the small photograph and a series of further pictures appeared, showing a young woman with shoulder length red hair. A tattoo was just visible on her neck, poking out of the top of her t-shirt. In one she was alone smiling up at the camera and in another she appeared in a small group outside, standing to the right of another couple of girls all wearing waterproof jackets. It was labelled 'West Hunday Bird Observatory Census Survey – February 2017'. He asked the counter assistant if it was possible to print off a copy and for fifty pence he obtained a colour print. She gave him a strange look as she handed over the print. He looked at the photograph for a considerable time trying to see something of Grace Harper in the young woman but no memory was sparked.

Next, he tried typing in Grace Harper's name. This was much worse. There were dozens of entries. It was obviously a much more common name. He spent about fifteen minutes scrolling through the entries but could find nothing that seemed to link to the Grace Harper he knew. He was about to give up when he had a flash of inspiration. He smiled as he tried Grace Flynn. Surely this time, but as the screen opened he saw that there were again pages and pages of entries. Why couldn't she have been called something more unusual. He logged off. Traditional policing methods looked a more likely way forward.

***

Fin was relieved to see that Bob Malcolm was on desk duty when he arrived at St Leonard's.

'Morning Fin. What brings you in today?'

'I was hoping for a word with Willy down in Records.'

'Well, you're in luck. He's on duty. I'll ring down and ask if he's free.'

Willy Ewing appeared in reception a few minutes later. 'Hello boss. To what do we owe the honour.'

'I was wondering if I could treat you to a bacon roll in the Pantry' said Fin.

'Sounds ominous. You must be after something. It might cost you a slice of haggis as well.'

The rolls were good, the bacon crispy and the McSweens haggis good and spicy. They sat at one of the small tables in the tiny café.

'How are things in Records these days?' asked Fin.

'Not too bad Fin. How's retirement? I hear you are still pestering them down at the Social of an evening. Are we here just for a jolly or is there something I can do for you?'

'I need a favour Willy. I need you to run a couple of names through the PNC and see what comes up.'

The constable sighed. 'Now you know I can't do that.'

Fin persisted. 'Come on Willy. Remember all the time I covered your ass when you took your sickies. Just a couple of names.'

Willy sighed more loudly and after a long pause said. 'See if I was not retiring myself in a couple of months. Go on then.'

Fin gave him Ophelia's and Grace's name and also asked him to check against West Hunday Bird Observatory. Willy said he'd call him back on his mobile once he had anything and then ordered a second roll. 'Mr. Tulloch here is paying' he said to Hughie behind the counter.

***

Fin eyed Sammy looking up at him. He was not used to being left for so long. He was also hungry and looking for his tea. Fin poured half a jar of dried food into the dog's bowl and watched him wolf it down. He then gathered up his lead for another trip around down the promenade. There was no sign of Magnus this time, or perhaps he was simply getting better at keeping in the shadows. Once back at home, Fin made himself his own tea, cheese on toast with spots of Lea and Perrins and plenty of pepper, and then sat down for this afternoon's edition of Pointless. The show was interrupted by his phone half way through. It was Willy Ewing from Records.

'First thing first. None of this, I repeat none of this has come from me. 'Understood.'

'Understood' confirmed Fin.

Willy went on. 'OK, I ran a check on the two women's names and there's nothing on record for either'

'And' said Fin, knowing that Eric was holding back the best bit.

'I also ran one on West Hunday and, guess what, it's a Red Flag.'

'What does that mean?' asked Fin.

'It means brother that its way above my pay grade. A Red Flag means you need an enhanced security clearance to see what the entry say' explained Tom. 'I could be in deep shit just for looking if anyone picks this up'.

'What? Like a Specialist Crime investigation?' Fin asked.

'Yep. It can cover everything from organized crime, VAT fraud up to full-blown terrorism Fin. It is not something you want to be getting into. Leave well alone.'

'Advice noted.'

'You owe me.' Willy Ewing hung-up.

Fin sat back but could not concentrate on the remainder of the quiz and turned the TV off.

***

They weren't bad, at least not most of them. It was more that they'd outgrown school. A couple of the lassies in his year had already had bairns and more would be on the way. They used to sometimes see the boys from Loretto in town in their pink blazers, their careers as lawyers and doctors all mapped out for them, but they might as well have come from a different planet.

You could see it in the dead eyes of the teachers, just grinding out the years to retirement. Any aspiration they'd ever had to make a difference had long left them. The worst of them was Wee Nick. Rumour had it that he'd been a joiner who'd found a job in the real world too hard, so he re-invented himself as a woodworking teacher. Beyond parody he'd then been promoted over the years all the way up to Dep. Head.

Wee Nick used to patrol the corridors with a tawse hanging from his waist. He must have only been about five foot but he marched around the school with pride picking out boys randomly to give out six of the belt to for minor or made up infractions of school rules. Fin had been the subject himself of several such beatings. Made to hold out his hands in front of him as Wee Nick raised the belt over his shoulder and brought it down with full force, one leg raising off the ground in the process.

By the time however Fin and his pals were approaching sixteen they were all half a head or more taller than Wee Nick and he had taken to picking on the younger children. One of those was Ian's brother, Michael. A couple of years younger than Fin and the others Michael did not yet have the physical presence to warn off Wee Nick.

It was morning break and the boys were kicking a ball around the school yard. In those days, the girls spent their break times in a separate playground although this seemed to have done little to stem the pregnancy rate. No-one could remember who kicked the ball but it shot like a cannon into the side window of the car, shattering the glass. A silence fell over the playground for a second or two and then shouts of laughter as the kids realised it was Wee Nick's mini that had been hit.

Someone must have called him because he fairly much came running down the school steps into the playground. The crowd of boys opened up and he ran over to his pride and joy. 'Which of you fuckers did this?' he shouted. He looked around eyes blazing. For some reason Michael was holding the ball. God knows why.

'Did you do this you wee bastard?' shouted Nick.

Michael stood frozen to the spot.

'I said do you do this?' spat Wee Nick.

'No sir.'

'Liar!' cried Wee Nick. He grabbed Michael by his collar and wheeled him around.

'Arms out!'. Everyone knew what was coming.

Trembling, Michael put one hand on top of the other in front of him. Nick raised up the belt and down it came. There was a crack as it hit Michael's hand. He cried out.

'Shut up' cried Nick and again he raised the belt high above his head. Down in came but this time Michael pulled his hands apart and the belt whooshed down into the empty space. Stumbling back up, Nick shouted 'OK, that means six extra.' He took hold of Michael's hand and forced them together.

A wet patch had formed at the front of Michael's trousers and a small pool of wee was puddling out from the bottom of his leg.

Wee Nick raised up the belt again, but as it got to the top of the arc, Ian stepped in and grabbed his arm. He pulled the tawse out of his grasp. Wee Nick stood their astonished.

'How dare you' he shouted. Ian threw the belt away and took Michael's hand. 'Come on, we're going home.'

'He assaulted me. You all saw it. He assaulted me' shouted Nick.

It was later the same day we were told that Ian had been expelled. His hopes of going on to college were in one moment crushed.

***

The incident with Michael took place only a couple of weeks before the end of the summer term. Two weeks on and Wee Nick's car had been repaired and stood in its place at the front of the school. Football had been banned.

It was a Friday and as usual Wee Nick and the male teachers had gone off for a pie and a pint to the Railway Tavern.

There were perhaps a dozen boys involved, Fin included. They crowded round Wee Nick's mini and on a shout of 'Up' hoisted it into the air. With so many hands, it seemed remarkably light. Off they marched with the wee car. At the door into the school, they turned it on its side and pushed it in, the noise of the car scrapping on the floor. It banged down onto its wheels. The stair case at the end of the assembly room was wide and marble tiled. Emboldened by getting the car so far, they hoisted it up again and started up the stairs. The going was tougher but more hands appeared and soon it was up on the first floor balcony.

'Oh, what do you think you are doing?'. It was Mr. Rodgers, one of the PE masters.

He stood looking at the car and the crowd of boys.

'Nothing sir' said Fin.

Mr. Rodgers looked again at the mini.

'Give me two minutes' he said and he walked away. So, it was not only the pupils who hated Wee Nick, thought Fin.

One last effort and they hoisted the car up and it tumbled over the balcony. For a split second, it was in the air and then it hit the floor with a tremendous bang, pieces of metal, glass and dust flying off in all directions.

A huge cheer went up and then dozens of boys scattered in all directions.

***

Fin learned later that Wee Nick had left the school over the summer and reverted to his old job as a joiner. He'd worked for a number of years in Musselburgh but always found it difficult to get jobs.

Monday 10 April

Becky and Magnus were in their usual seats when he arrived at the Swedish bakery. This time, though, both were in their work clothes and looked older and more professional. The bearded hipster was on duty behind the counter and Fin ordered his usual pot of tea. The assistant did not ask what type he wanted. He sat down opposite Becky and carefully balanced his walking cane against the side of the table.

They looked at him expectantly. 'I've done some digging and I'm sorry but nothing is showing up.' He folded his arms.

'What do you mean nothing's showing up?' asked Becky.

'I asked an old colleague to run Ophelia's details through the police computer and there is nothing suspicious showing up against her name.'

'What! Is that it?' stormed Becky. 'All you can be arsed to do is run her name against your records. You're saying there's nothing more we can do?' Magnus reached out for her arm but she shook him off.

'I'll tell you what. If you do not hear from Ophelia by Monday next, you should report her as a missing person. Leave it then to the police. They're the experts.'

Becky was almost out of her seat. 'That's bullshit Mr. Tulloch and you know it is. This is your grand-daughter we're talking about.' She had raised her voice and people from neighbouring tables were looking away embarrassed.

As calmly as possible he replied 'I've already told you. I do not have a grand-daughter. Your friend has obviously been confusing me with someone else. I'm really sorry about all this but there's nothing I can do.'

Becky did not look persuaded. More quietly she said 'But surely there is something further we can do. There must be.'

Magnus interrupted. 'Come on Becks. Mr. Tulloch's done as much as he can.' He started to stand up but Becky remained seated.

'I tell you. This isn't like her. Something's wrong. We need to be doing something.'

'I'm sorry' said Fin 'but I just can't help. Keep in touch but I am sure everything will be OK'. He handed over a piece of paper with his mobile number.

Becky looked like she was on the brink of tears. She jumped up, grabbed her jacket and stormed out.

'Sorry Mr. Tulloch' said Magnus 'she's just upset. Offie means such a lot to her.'

Fin watched them go. He felt all the eyes in the bakery were looking at him. He knew he was being a shit and was upset for Becky, but he really couldn't see what he could do. He would call them tomorrow and if Ophelia had not turned up by then, he'd report it himself to St Leonard's.

***

The sheltered housing on the Braes comprised a small estate of well-maintained bungalows. Parking up the van in a resident only bay, he saw the glow from a television in the window of the first unit and buzzed its door. After what seemed like an endless delay, an intercom clicked into action and a voice said 'We don't allow hawkers here' and then went silent. He pressed the buzzer again. There was another lengthy delay and then the intercom clicked on again. This time he was too fast. 'I'm looking for Mr. Thomas Flynn. Do you know which number he's in?'.

'Who are you?'

'Police' he lied.

There was a pause and then 'Number twenty seven.' The line went dead. 'Thank you' he said into the nothingness.

Tommy Flynn's bungalow was at the end of the road. Unlike its neighbours its front garden was a mess with the lawn uncut and the flower beds untended. It appeared to be in darkness with a curtain drawn against the front window, but when he tried its bell, a dog started yapping. 'Haggis, shut the fuck up, will ya.' He heard keys rattling and the door opened a crack on a chain. An unshaved face peeked out in the gap. 'What the fuck do you want?'

'Police' said Fin. 'We're investigating a missing person.'

There was a rattling behind the door. 'Haggis, will you keep down!' and then it opened up to show an overweight man in a Hibs top. He was standing on crutches, this right leg missing below the knee. 'Diabetes' said Tommy Flynn, sensing the question. He looked nothing like the Tommy Flynn he had once known.

'Can I come in?' said Fin.

'Where's your ID?'

'Listen, if you prefer we can go down to the station. Up to you.'

Tommy Flynn did not answer but stepped back in the bungalow, an ugly little dog behind him growling at Fin. He led them into a lounge in semi-darkness and slumped down onto an easy chair. There was a filled ashtray to one side and a couple of open cans of cider on the other. He did not ask Fin to take a seat. Fin pulled out a notebook and pen.

'What is it you want to know?'

'You're Tommy Flynn?'

'Aye, what of it.'

'We're investigating a cold case from the 1970s.'

'Oh aye?'

'It concerns a Grace Harper. Do you remember her?'

'I should do. I was married to the bitch wasn't I.'

'What year was it you were married.'

'1977 – same year as the Queen's jubilee.'

'And you lived here in Musselburgh?'

Tommy Flynn smirked. 'Like fuck we did as you know fine, Finbarr Tulloch! What, you thought I wouldn't recognize you after all these years. I'd know a little shit like you anywhere. Small town this Tulloch. Ian was on the blower to me the moment you stepped out the Ship.'

'Ok Tommy, let's cut the charade. I want to know where Grace moved after you split up and what happened to her bairn.'

'Well, you can go fuck yourself' shouted Tommy.

Fin calmly knocked over the ashtray with his cane. He pocked about in the ashes. 'Diabetes, my arse. Once a junkie always a junkie. Would you like me to let the Hoosin. Association know what you've been smoking? You'd be out on the street double quick.'

Tommy starred at him with a look bordering on hatred. Fin pulled out his wallet and waved a couple of tenners at Tommy. 'Now where did you say you lived?'

Keeping an eye on the notes, Tommy said 'She had an auntie up near Cupar in Fife. When we split up she and the bairn moved up there.'

'Where near Cupar?'

'Christ, I can't remember.'

'Try harder.' Fin put the two bank notes back in his pocket.

'Err… Brunton I think it's called, it's somewhere off the road to St Andrews.'

'Now that wasn't so hard. Nice to catch up Tommy. We must have a footba game together some time.' Fin laughed. He was on his feet and making for the door.

'Err… come on….' said Tommy, trying to get up.

'Oh, here you are' said Fin and he threw the two banknotes on the floor. 'Buy your dog a new collar.'

'Go fuck yourself' called Tommy, but Fin was already out the door and on his way to his van.

***

After the evening at Luca's Fin saw Grace a few times more than summer around town but she was always with her friends. She would smile at him but he was too shy to speak to her, what with her friends giggling in the background. The nights started to draw in. Grace would be going back to school for her Higher exams. Despite his erratic attendance record Fin had done well enough in his fourth year exams to join her, but he was feeling pressure to start bringing some money into the house. His mum was already working all hours and he felt guilty idling his time away at school. He had hoped to secure a job on the boats like his dad but by then the fishing industry was in decline and lay-offs rather than hirings were the favour of the day. So, he spent the summer days moping around the town centre with his pals and hanging out at Luca's in the evenings.

The army recruitment centre was on the High Street in those days. It still is. Its window was full of pictures of combat jets and young men having a good time. It was drizzling the day he passed, and he had taken shelter in its doorway to light up a Woodbine. 'Phishing doon' again. He turned and a man dressed in uniform stood beside him. 'Oh.. sorry' he stepped back out into the rain. 'Don't worry wee man, I'm just opening up. Don't I know you, you're Maggie Tulloch's son, no?'. Fin nodded. 'Come in, I'm just putting a brew on.'

Fin had signed up within the hour. He knew that the recruitment sergeant was spouting bullshit but he was happy to buy it. There was nothing here for him. It was not the promises of fun in exotic locations that sold it to him, but more the fact that he'd get his bed and board provided and have something to send home to his mum. He'd expected his mother to be furious when he told her later than night but she just seemed tired and resigned. He was sent a letter and given a date to turn up to Glencourse barracks outside Penicuik in a month's time. In the interim he continued his usual routine of sitting around the house during the day whilst his mother was at work and sloping around the town with this pals in the evening.

Grace was alone at the bus shelter when he saw her across the road. She waved and he crossed over. 'Where are you going?' he asked. 'Oh, nowhere,

I'm just hanging about.' He sat down next to her, but could not think of anything more to say.

'I heard you'd signed up for the army' she said.

'Aye.'

'When do you leave?'

'In a couple of weeks…. When are you back at school?'

'Next week.'

They sat in silence for a while.

'It was funny at the football' she said, then added 'have you recovered?'

'Oh, aye, it was nothing really.'

'Tommy's like that. Got a bit of a temper on him.'

'Why do you go out with him then?'

'Do you want to go into Edinburgh tomorrow. Saturday Night Fever's on at the Dominium.'

'Aye, OK'.

'See you here at six then.' It was as simple as that.

***

The drive up to Cupar took Fin across the Forth Road Bridge. Sammy sat up in the passenger seat next to him looking out onto the new bridge being built as they rattled over the existing one. If there was something Scotland was good at it was building bridges. Fin had struggled to find Brunton on the map, but eventually located it just off the Dundee road. It was a pleasant drive and soon they were off the motorway and on the road to St Andrews, passing through neat and tidy countryside, with grass already cut and bailed.

The turning up to Brunton was poorly signed and Fin almost missed it, swinging the van round at the last minute and depositing Sammy off his seat and onto the floor. 'Sorry wee man' said Fin. The small road up to Brunton took them up a hill with ploughed fields on each side, past a small picturesque church and down into a valley, with the river Tay lying just beyond. Brunton itself was just a hamlet with a few cottages spread arranged higgerty-piggerty around a burn running through it. As he turned down into it a big dog fox shot across in front of him and he had to slam on his brakes again, making Sammy fall off his seat again into the floor well. 'Sorry wee man, not your day is it'. He drove slowly through the village to the other side and then did a u-turn, parking up next to the burn.

Stepping out Sammy was pulling at this lead, raring for action among the new smells, but Fin held him tight concerning that he may run off after the sheep in a nearby field. Pulling the dog back to his side, he made his way back through the village. It was very quiet. No doubt, it acted nowadays as home for commuters into Dundee and most folk would be at work. He saw then though a red Royal Mail van trundling down the road into the village. It pulled up and the postman stepped out with a handful of letters. 'Excuse me' called Fin. The postie waved a friendly greeting and came over. 'I am wondering if you knew perhaps where a Mrs. Harper or Flynn might live.'

'Sorry. It doesn't ring a bell.'

'Ok, thanks'.

The postie started to walk away, but then turned back. 'Perhaps you could try the Fitzwilliams. They've lived in the village the longest so might know.'

'Which one is their house?'

'Over there at the old manse on the back road' and the postie pointed to a larger house sitting on the outskirts of the village.

When Fin made it up the former manse, he found a man of about his own age busy cutting back weeds on the front drive.

'Excuse me, are you Mr. Fitzwilliam?'

He looked up from his knees. 'Yes, how can I help you?'

'I understand you have lived here for a long time. I am looking for a Mrs. Flynn, or perhaps a Mrs. Harper, and I wondered if perhaps you knew them.'

He looked at Fin, thought for a minute and then said 'I'm sorry but I can't help.'

'Perhaps you might know someone else who might be able to.'

'No. Nobody of those names has ever lived here.'

'Are you sure? It would have been in the late 70s.'

The man struggled up to his feet. 'Yes, I'm sure.'

'Well, thanks for your help. Have a good day.'

He pulled Sammy back down the path, wanting to ask more but deciding now was not the time.

Drawing back down to the main road, he pulled in at the church he'd seen on the hill. 'You'll need to say here' he explained to Sammy, turning down his window to let some air in.

He walked over to the front of the church but the door was locked. Going on he came to a small grave-yard overlooking the surrounding fields. A magpie was sitting on a fence but took off as he approached.

'Hello Mr. Magpie, say hello to your wife.' He felt foolish although only Sammy was there to hear him.

There were on a few grave stones and he wandered amongst them reading the engravings. Some were so old that they were barely legible but standing slightly alone was a more recent stone marking a grave with some fresh daffodils in a planter. Its simple inscription read 'Georgie Fitzwilliam – Beloved daughter of Grace and Michael' with the dates '1978-1997' below. He took out his phone and photographed it.

Getting back in the van he turned back up to the village. He pulled up at the old manse and stepped down with his cane in his hand. He walked quickly up the drive and pressed the bell on the front door. There was no answer. He tried knocking and again no answer. There was a noise from behind. He turned to see the postman bringing up a couple of letters.

'I think you've just missed them, only Mr. and Mrs. Fitzwilliam passed me on the Dundee road.'

'Oh, thanks.' Fin took out a scrap of paper, wrote a quick message and posted it through the front letter box.

***

Back home, Fin was tired from the long drive, but before settling down he made a couple of calls. The first was to Orkney Ferries to check the timing for the next ferry to West Hunday, The weekly boat left on Friday morning. He booked a passage for him and the van. The second was to the bird observatory. He reserved a week in their bunkhouse with the promise of a cooked breakfast and evening meal.

Lastly and most importantly he popped across to the spinster next door. Mrs. Maclean. She'd always held a candle for him and yes it would be a delight to look after Sammy for the week whilst he was away.

Tuesday 11 April

He got off the bus outside the Balmoral Hotel and walked over the street into the Georgian spender of New Register House. Slightly intimated by his surroundings he approached the desk and explained that he was looking to check the register of deaths. He was asked to fill out a form and then to take a seat. Just as he was beginning to regret not bringing a newspaper with him to pass the time, a young man appeared with a photocopy of the relevant entry. He took it to a reading desk and checked the details. Georgina Kate Fitzwilliam died in May 2003 aged only 22. She was unmarried. The place of death was entered as Melrose and the cause of death as opioid intoxication. The name of the father was given as William Fitzwilliam and the mother as Grace Fitzwilliam (nee Harper). He starred at the form and found himself touching brushing away a tear coming to his eye. He felt his chest tightening and the tears started to flow. The girl sitting next to him asked if he was okay and offered him a tissue. He tried to smile and shook his head.

He had to get out of here and into some fresh air. Pushing back his chair he made his way out onto West Register Street and ignoring the hordes of tourists forced his way forward and into the Guildford Arms where he took refuge in the gents toilets to compose himself. Freshening up by throwing some cold water onto this face, he returned to the bar and ordered a whisky. It was only just gone eleven but he needed something to get his emotions under control. He poured in some water off the bar top and took a mouthful.

Taking a seat, he pulled out the death certificate. There was no doubt. Grace had had a daughter. He thought of driving straight back up to Brunton and confronting the man who'd said he'd never heard of her, but looking at the certificate again, he saw that it had been signed by a doctor with a Melrose address. Melrose was also given as her place of death. Perhaps that should be his first port of call. His thinking was interrupted by his mobile.

'Hello, Fin Tulloch.'

'It's me. Becky. Have you found out anything?'

'I'm afraid not Becky, but I am planning a run down to Melrose. I think there may be a link. Do you want to join me?'

'What, Melrose in the Borders.'

'Aye. I need to go home first to check on my dog, but I could pick you outside, day, Doctors at mid-day.'

'I'll be there.'

***

She was waiting at the corner by the entrance to Doctors bar when he arrived.

'Hi. Meet Sammy. Don't worry, he doesn't bite.'

He pushed some papers off the passenger seat and she climbed in next to him.

'No offence Fin, but I don't think I've ever been in a car as manky as this.' She wiped some dust off the seat.

'I like to make an effort' he said dripping sarcasm.

She raised her eyes.

Changing the subject, he asked 'Do you know why it's called Doctors?'

'No, pray tell.'

'It where all the doctors used to drink when the hospital was up this part of town. They used to have a bell on the bar counter they'd ring if there was an emergency. Not that I would have wanted to be operated on by a surgeon who'd been out drinking all night.'

'You're a font of wisdom.'

They cut across town to take the road south to Peebles.

'Have a look at this.' Fin handed her the death certificate.

'What is *opioid intoxication*?'

'A heroin overdose' he explained.

'What, in Melrose?'

'That's what we're going to find out.'

They drove on, passing Glencourse Barracks where he'd spent much of his army career, then out through Penicuik and into the Border's countryside.

'How did you meet Magnus' he asked, trying to pass the time.

'It was Offie who introduced him. He's a post grad in the department where she's doing her masters. We needed an extra person for the flat and he moved in just before Christmas.'

'He seems a nice guy.'

'He's OK. Can be a bit intense if you know what I mean.'

'Well it was good of him to come along to the Baillie with you.'

'I think he feels a bit responsible. It was him who secured Offie her placement at the West Hunday bird observatory.'

'Oh, how did he manage that?'

'I'm not sure. Some contact at the uni I think.'

They drove on through Peebles turning east along the Tweed into Melrose. Fin parked up in the market square. 'Do you mind if we take Sammy for a stroll first' he asked. 'I don't like him to be locked up in the van too long.'

Out of the van they walked down past the ruined Abbey and to the river, crossing over the iron suspension bridge. Fin let Sammy off his lead and he was immediately down and into the water. 'That's dandies for you. Can't keep them out of the water.' Becky threw a stick and the dog dived further in to retrieve it, bringing it back and dropping it by her feet.

Fin laughed. 'Now you've done that, he's going to pester you the whole way.'

It was a cold but bright day and looking back the town looked beautifully set below the surrounding hills.

Turning back to the town, Fin asked Becky. 'Why did you write the letters?'

'What do you mean?'

'Why did you write the letters? I'm not daft you know. I realised straightaway that it would have taken a lot longer for a letter to get all the way from Orkney to Edinburgh and no post mark? Did you just put it through my letter box?'

She was quiet for a moment and then said 'Magnus delivered it.'

'Why?'

'I know it sounds very dramatic but I thought you would be more likely to take an interest if you thought it was a direct cry for help from your grand-daughter. You know, rather than her weird friend.'

He mulled it over. It had worked. Perhaps she was right.

'No more games from here in Becky. Okay?'

'Okay.'

***

Back in town, he asked in the first shop they came to where the doctor's surgery was located. Rather worryingly, he was told that there were three. The nearest was just by the entrance into the rugby stadium, a five minute walk, and after leaving Sammy in the van, they made their way there. It was an old fashioned surgery with a list of the GPs names on brass plates outside. Looking down the names there was no sign of a Dr. Hill, the person who had signed Georgie Fitzwilliam's death certificate. 'Let's try inside' said Fin.

The waiting room was busy with the usual collection of ailments waiting to be treated. He went up to the receptionist's window and tapped it. A less than welcoming woman looked sternly up from the magazine she was reading. 'You need to sign in at the machine' she said, pointing to an automated check-in machine.

'I'm looking for a Dr. Hill'.

She gave him a hard look. 'You need to sign in at the machine.' He made a mental note to himself not to fall ill in Melrose.

'Do you have a Dr. Hill or know in which surgery she's based?'

'There's no Dr. Hill here.'

'You should ask for your money back.'

'Sorry'.

'From the charm school. You should ask for your money back.'

She scowled at him.

They turned to leave. An old woman waiting to be seen said 'You looking for Dr. Hill, son? She used to be my GP. She's retired these days.'

'You don't happen to know where she lives' he asked.

'Right next door, the house with the red paintwork.'

'Thank you very much. You've been very helpful.' He smiled at the old lady and then gave what he hoped was a killer stare at the receptionist.

The woman who opened to door next door must have been about seventy.

'Can I help?'

'This is a rather strange request but we're interested in the death of a young woman in 2003. Her name was Georgie Fitzwilliam.'

She looked at them both. 'You'd better come in.'

She made them some tea as they sat in her kitchen.

'I remember her well' said Dr. Hill. 'It was a very sad case. She was a lovely girl but she'd started on drugs while at boarding school in Edinburgh. St. Margaret's if I remember. She was in and out of rehab all through her teens, finally ending up as a heroin addict down in Pilton.'

'How did she end up in Melrose?' asked Fin.

'There used to a rehab centre down here run by a charity. It housed young women from all over Scotland. I acted as the GP to some of the residents whilst they were there. It's all closed now of course.'

She took a sip of her tea, offering a biscuit to Fin and Becky. 'I remember vividly the night she died. I got a call from the centre saying one of the girls was not well. When I got there, it was mayhem. The other girls were hysterical. She was lying on the bathroom floor, a real mess. I couldn't believe how she looked. I'd seen her just a month or so before and she seemed quite with it. I thought she was recovering.'

'And it was a heroin overdose?'

'Yes, all of the usual paraphernalia was there, the needle was still in her arm.'

Becky was looking white and fiddling with her pendant.

Fin said 'I understand she was from near Cupar in Fife?'

'I'm sorry' said Dr. Hill. 'I can't remember. It was such a sad case. The centre was closed not much later. Of course, what made it doubly a tragedy was that Georgie was a mother.'

'A mother?'. It was the first time Becky had spoke.

'Yes, didn't you know. It was a centre for young mums with drug problems.'

'Do you know what happened to her child.'

'I imagine she would have been taken into care.'

'Oh, it was a little girl?' asked Fin.

'Yes, she had a little toddler. She was found by her mum's body if I remember.'

'You've been very helpful Dr. Hill. We'd better get going. I've got an appointment back in Edinburgh.'

Dr. Hill said 'You didn't say why you were looking into her death.'

'We're trying to track down her daughter' said Fin.

They were both quiet on the drive back up to Edinburgh. Eventually, with the City in sight Becky asked 'Do you think Georgie was Offie's mum?'

'Yes, I do' said Fin.

She dropped her off at Doctors promising to be in touch.

***

Fin was waiting at the bus stop for Grace a good half hour before six. He sat nervously fidgeting on the bench, fearing she was going to stand him up, but at last she appeared around the corner just as the bus was coming into sight. 'Hi Fin.' She looked older tonight and was dressed up. Fin immediately regretted not making more of an effort, but she seemed not to notice.

They sat up top at the front of the bus for the journey into town. Grace chattered on about her day at school but Fin did not take any of it in. He did however think she smelled good sitting tight against him.

Arriving at the cinema, there was a long queue. He worried that the cinema may have been full by the time they reached the ticket desk, but eventually it was their turn. 'Two for Saturday Night Fever please' she asked. Armed with their tickets they made their way up into the auditorium. The usher clipped their tickets and Grace walked past, but there was an arm on his shoulder. 'How old are you son?' 'Sixteen'. 'Sorry it's an X, can't let you in.' He wanted the ground to eat him up. 'You go on in' he said to Grace, but she was having none of it. 'Come on' she said and she marched out from the cinema, Fin in tow.

'I'm sorry Grace' he said 'I hadn't thought.'

'We're not beaten yet' she said, and she led him down the alley to the side of the cinema. At a fire escape door, she stopped and using a stick lying by the door, managed to prize it open. 'Shuh..'she whispered 'it's a trick I learnt'. She took his hand and led him inside into the dark. The corridor opened out at the front of the stage and, giggling, they stumbled on in the dark up to their seats.

As the film started, Grace took hold of Fin's hand. He could not remember the film, but remembered holding her hand throughout. He desperately wanted to lean over to kiss her but didn't have the nerve.

Rushing out of the cinema with the crowd at the end, they ran to the bus stop for Musselburgh only to find that they had just missed the bus. 'Oh my God, my dad will kill me if I am not back in by ten' she said, but she was smiling. She cuddled into him in the cold.

'Come on' she said 'let's get some fish and chips.' He hesitated, knowing that he only had enough money for the bus fare home. As if sensing this she cuddled in and said 'My treat.' They enjoyed their fish supper, with plenty of salt and sauce, sitting at the bus stop. Eventually one arrived and they climbed on board, this time making for the rear seats at the back. Sitting down, she lent over and kissed him. He did not want the journey back to end, but of course it finally made its way back to the depot in Musselburgh. Getting off, he stood hesitating. She said 'Thanks for a fun night.' She lent in, kissed him on the lips and was off running down the street to the posh part of the toun.

***

Fin dropped Becky back at Doctors and then made his way back down to Portobello. He fed Sammy and then settled down to the afternoon quiz. Half way through, he said to the dog 'Come on wee man. Let's go for a walk.' They made their way down to the promenade. A couple of wee kids with buckets and spades were playing in the sand in the late afternoon sun as their mothers drank coffees from the beach kiosk. He sat watching them and think of Georgie and her little girl.

Wednesday 12 April

Fin was waiting outside New Register House when it opened. He knew the routine. He searched against Ophelia Fitzwilliam. Dr. Hill had described her as a toddler so he'd assumed she could not have been more than five at the time of her mother's death. There were no entries. He then tried Ophelia McLeod, the name under which the letter had been signed. He would have to ask Becky why she'd used that. Surely if Offie was married, Becky would have told him. Again, there were no results.

He asked the assistant to try a third name. She looked slightly annoyed but entered the details. This time, there was a positive match and he ordered up a copy of the birth certificate. He was asked to wait and again regretted not remembering to bring a newspaper.

The assistant handed over the copy and he paid the small fee.

Rebecca Fitzwilliam was born In Edinburgh in February 1995 to Georgina Fitzwilliam making her just over two at the time of her mother's death. He father's details were blank. He sat starring at the certificate for some time. He tried calling her on her mobile but there was no reply. 'Shit' he thought, 'I don't even know where she lives.'

No wonder she had been so quiet at Dr. Hill's.

Leaving the records office he made his way on foot, clicking his cane in time all the way, up the Bridges and along by the Sheriff Court to Lauriston Place where the College of Art stood. 'I'm looking for a Rebecca Fitzwilliam' he said to the receptionist. She checked down a staff list and pointed him in the direction of the Graphics Department. He found it down a corridor in the basement. Going in, he asked for her by name again. The girl he'd approached looked blank and then said 'Oh, do you mean Becky Macleod'. He nodded. 'I'm afraid she's not in today.'

'Do you know her address?'

'I'm afraid we can't give out that sort of information'. She saw his disappointment 'But you could try up at the Edinburgh Wheelers. She goes out on Wednesday mornings cycling with them. There's just across the Meadows.'

Edinburgh Wheelers was a cycling shop. Looking in its window, the price of the bikes on display were shocking and more than he'd have been willing to pay for a car. 'I was hoping to catch Becky Macleod. I was told she might be out on a cycle ride.' The youth behind the counter explained that the riders were due back in half an hour or so and pointed to a trendy café to the rear of the store.

He spotted Magnus and Becky as soon as the cyclists pulled up. They came in with the remainder of the group looking fit and chattering away.

'That looks like hard work' he said.

She turned, surprised to see him, but quickly recovering her composure. 'Hi Fin. How did you know I'd be here?'

'Oh, it wasn't difficult' he said, not expanding further. 'Will you join me for a coffee?'

'Yes, that would be nice, but it will to be quick as I need to be at work soon.'

Magnus whispered to Becky and then made his excuses. She sat down opposite Fin, still flushed from her ride.

'I wanted to ask you a little more about Offie'.

'Fire away'.

'You said she was about eight or so when she first arrived in the care home. Do you know where she was before then. I mean, if her mum died when she was only a toddler then there must have been a few years when she lived elsewhere.'

She thought and then said 'I'm afraid I don't know. She's never mentioned her time before coming into care. Is it important?'

'Probably not. I'm just trying to get a full picture.'

'I don't see the relevance to her disappearance. Is there no news on that?'

'Nothing I'm afraid. I assume you've still not heard from her.'

'No'.

'I'm afraid that I need to be away for a week or so. It's something I can't avoid. I'll keep in touch though with my contacts on the force and let you know immediately if I hear anything.'

She looked crestfallen.

'Becky, I'm sure she'll be OK.'

'Yeah….right.' There was a touch of irritation in her voice.

'I'll call you when I get back.'

She nodded. He stood up, pulled on this ex-army jacket and made for the door.

***

Fin's next stop was St. Leonard's. Bob Malcolm was on desk duty again.

'My God Fin, twice in as many days. Are you trying to re-join?'

'I want to report a missing person.'

Bob Malcolm may have been surprised but didn't show it. He asked Fin to wait while he found someone to take a statement from him.

Fin sat waiting for a good thirty minutes. Eventually, a young woman PC he didn't recognise said that she could see him. He was taken into a small cubicle.

'Right, Mr. Tulloch is it. I understand that you want to report someone missing.'

Fin gave her the basic details but leaving out his trips to Fife and Melrose. He handed over a copy of the letter he'd received and gave her Becky's contact details.

'Why didn't you come in before?'.

He didn't have a good answer. He simply said 'I thought she would turn up.'

The PC looked at him over her glasses.

'Does she have any mental health issues?'

'Not that I'm aware but then I don't know her.'

'So, what's she said in the letter to you is not true?'

Fin did not see any benefit in saying that Becky had written the letter. He simply said 'No, it's not true.'

'Do you have a photograph?'

He dug out a copy of the one he'd printed at the internet café and handed it over.

She bundled up her notes and the documents he'd provided. 'Okay, thanks for coming in Mr. Tulloch. If there is anything further we need from you, we'll be in contact.'

'And you'll let me know as soon as she's been found.'

'We can only do that with her consent. Some people simply want to go missing you know.'

She was out of her seat and guiding him out of the cubicle. She'd spent at most only ten minutes with him.

Out in the reception area, Bob Malcolm asked 'Hope that was useful Fin.'

'Aye, thanks Bob.'

He walked out into grey day. He wanted to believe an investigation would be activated, but was not convinced it would amount to any more than going through the motions. He'd read that over a quarter of a million people went missing in Britain each year. It was difficult to see Offie being prioritized.

***

Fin spent a good part of the afternoon loading up the campervan with provisions for the trip. It was dusty inside the back of the van and it took him some time to clean it up. It had sat in the driveway for most of the last five years since he'd lost Maggie. Before then they had enjoyed their holidays with Sammy and his forebears meandering up and down the north of the country, although never as far as Orkney. With Maggie's passing though, he had lost interest and the van had been largely left to gather dust with a tarpaulin dragged over it. Save for his recent trips up to Fife and down to the Borders it had not been out of Edinburgh in the last five years.

Once the van was loaded up, he took Sammy down along the promenade for a final run on the beach before he handed him over to Mrs. Maclean for temporary safekeeping along with his bed and a supply of food for the next week. It was a sunny afternoon with a light breeze blowing on-shore and he bought himself a 99 cone from the ice cream van on the front, getting the man to drip some raspberry sauce on top. He sat on a bench along from a mother with her baby in a pram breaking bits of cone off for Sammy who sat up begging and gazing out over the water to Fife. Surely, he didn't couldn't have a grand-daughter and not know about it. He watched the woman take the baby girl out of the pram and jiggle her up and down on her knee. The baby made happy gurgling sounds as her mother bounced her up and down.

***

When he'd left for basic training at Glencourse barracks, he'd been no more than a long haired callow youth. To be honest, once it was completed he was much the same, although his hair was considerably shorter and he was a lot fitter. His recollection was of a lot of PT and running about, often lugging about a huge log across a frozen obstacle course. The highlight, if it could be called that, had been a night tab over the hills, starting out in pouring rain and ending in a blizzard.

The rest of the boys in his platoon were much the same as him, a few a couple of years older, but mostly just a group of wide eyed innocents recruited from the surrounding mining villages and depressed central belt towns, all looking for a way out of the miserable lives led by their parents and siblings. It would be nice to say that during this period he developed some life-long friendships but to the frank he'd forgotten most of the boys as soon as he received his first posting.

He was only about two months into his first posting to Catterick when his section commander, a young man only a few years his senior, called him in. He asked him to sit, shuffled his papers before spurting out. 'I'm sorry Tulloch but I've received a message to say your mother has died.'

'Oh, thank you Sir' was his stupid reply.

He learned later that she'd collapsed while cleaning at Loretto and had been dead by the time she reached the hospital. Apparently, she'd had a few previous episodes but had kept them to herself.

He didn't cry at the funeral. It was the usual get together of old fags of misery-inducing relatives he didn't know, or, if he did recognise them, didn't like. The day was cold and wet and it was obvious that the minister at the Crematorium had never met his mother and knew nothing about her. He went through the formalities saying what a loving mother she'd been and lots of other crap he'd failed to take in. He spent the night drinking in the Ship with Ian and co and then returned to the barracks as early as possible the next day. He didn't bother with the distribution of her estate, leaving the rellies to fight over the little that she had. He had his memories and they were enough. He didn't return again to Musselburgh for the next two years.

He hadn't meant to end up back in Musselburgh. He'd agreed to go up with a few of the boys from his company to Edinburgh for a pop concert. He wasn't even into music but it was a weekend away on the beevy and he'd been having a bad time with his new company commander, a public school prick of the first order, and needed to let off some steam to avoid decking the guy.

Thinking back he couldn't even remember the band that had been playing. Goodnight Mr. Mackenzie or something like that. They'd been drinking most of the day so by the time the band came on they were really up for it and even Fin was on his feet bopping around with the rest of them. The boys were becoming more and more boisterous and security at the club was keeping a weary eye on them. One of the squaddies decided it would be a good idea to take his top off and it was at that point they decided to step in. Two big bouncers came crashing through the crowd.

'Right you, outside. Now!'.

And it kicked off. Who's knows who threw the first punch but boots and fists were soon flying. Fin was laying in with the best of them, the local boys teaming up with the bouncers.

A harsh whistle announced the arrival of the polis. A couple of big guys came wading in, truncheons drawn.

Time for a quick departure thought Fin, and he made for the emergency exit onto the back lane outside. He went tanking up the lane towards Princes Street, slowing down as he reached the main thoroughfare. He slowed to a walk as another police car, siren blaring, rushed by. He felt bad for abandoning his colleagues but it was every man for himself in that situation.

He thought he heard his name being called. He walked on, hesitated and looked back. There at a bus stop was Grace. He walked back up to her.

'What are you doing in Edinburgh.'

'Oh, just up for a gig.' He was looking over her shoulder towards a police man and a bouncer walking towards him.

'Are you in trouble?'.

'Nah, just a wee bit of bother in the club.'

A bus had drawn up at the stop.

'Come on. She took his hand and pulled him onto the bus with her. 'Two for Musselburgh.'

And that was how he ended up back in the toun. They got off near Loretto school. She hesitated as they stood on the pavement.

'Where are you staying?'

'I'll find somewhere.'

She hesitated again. 'Why don't you stay at mine.'

'I don't think your mum and dad would be too happy about that.'

'They're away at the moment.'

***

He was back again just six months later. What brought him back this was an invitation to attend a wedding – between Tommy Flynn and Grace Harper. How she tracked him down he had no idea. By then he was as squaddie up at Inverness and he hadn't exactly been keeping in touch with anyone from the town. If it had come from anyone else he'd have chucked it in the bin but an invitation from Grace drew him back.

The train journey south had been long and slow. He was through his six pack of lager by the time they hit Glasgow but fortified himself with a double voddie and coke in Queen Street Station. By the time he stepped out of the train at Waverley and looked up at the Edinburgh skyline he was uneasy on his feet. Another beer in the station bar waiting for the connection to Musselburgh saw him in need of a kebab. He wandered down the High Street looking for somewhere open and found himself at a Chinese takeaway. Sobering himself up he stepped inside and placed an order for some Foo Yung. The Scots woman serving eyed him up and down and asked 'Are you Maggie Tulloch's boy?'.

He shook his head.

He'd arranged to stay the weekend at a bed and breakfast up by the racecourse and found himself pitching up the worse for wear just before midnight to be met by a less than welcoming landlady. After missing breakfast the next morning he made his way down to Luca's but Nona wasn't in and there was no-one in that he knew from his past so after a quick bacon and egg roll, washed down with a mug of tea, he found himself wandering around the town killing time.

Inevitably, he ended up at the Ship just as it was opening. He bought himself a pint and took it to a corner, watching the sport playing on the wall-mounted telly. There were a few familiar faces already in the bar but he was happy to keep his own company.

'My God, if it's not Fin Tulloch.'

Fin looked up, not recognising the weasel of a man in front of him.

'Davie…. Davie Arbuckle. For Christ sake don't you ken me?'

Fin looked into the gaunt face. Sure enough it was Davie. But he was a shadow of himself, puffing away on a dog-end.

'Oh, Hi Davie, Sorry, I was away with the birds.'

'What are you doing back here?'

'I'm supposed to be going to a wedding, although now I'm here I'm not sure I can face it.'

'Is that yon Grace Harper's. I hear she's getting hitched to Tommy Flynn. Poor bitch. He's a real bastard that one.'

Fin did not say anything.

'So, how's yourself. Still in the army.'

'Aye.' He could see that he was not going to be getting rid of Davie. 'Would you like a drink.'

Davie gave a thin smile. 'Aye, why not. A pint of eighty shillings would touch the spot.'

Davie sat down next to Fin. The first thing Fin noticed was his body odour. The second was his leg twitching manically. He had to pick up his pint to stop it from spilling.

'Are you expecting someone?' asked Fin. Davie was looking to the door.

'Eh… no.'

'What are you working at?'

''Working. That's a joke. There's no jobs here Fin. You did good to get away when you did.'

Another look to the door.

'Here, Fin, I don't suppose you could lend me a tenner. I can pay you back later.'

Fin pulled a note out from his wallet and gave it to Davie.

Another look to the door.

A gaunt youth walked in, looking about as shit as Davie.

'I need to have a slash' said Davie. He was up and off to the gents. The newcomer followed him in.

Fin had had enough of Davie. He would go back to the B&B and hang out there until the service. But first he needed a pee himself. As he pushed open the door, it was as if he had taken a freeze frame camera shot. There stood the youth handing a wrap to Davie and Davie handing Fin's ten pound note to the youth.

'What the fuck!'. The youth jumped back. Davie stood stock still, looking confused by Fin's entrance.

Then Fin saw the blade in the youth's hand. 'I don't want no bother' he said, but the youth stabbed his arm forward. Instinctively, Fin kicked out his boot catching the youth on his leg. He grabbed his arm and twisted it behind his back. The knife fell to the floor. Fin punched the youth in the stomach and he fell back onto the urinal trough, smacking his head on the porcelain. Fin grabbed the youth by his hair and bashed his head hard against the urinal. There was a trace of blood trickling from his mouth as he lay face first in the trough.

Davie was on this knees on the floor picking up the tab the youth had been handing to him.

Fin checked himself in the broken mirror above the dryer. He then undid his zip and pee'd into the urinal his stream landing on the gaunt youth's head.

Pulling his zip up he said 'Come on' to Davie and he manhandled him out into street past some puzzled looking customers no doubt wondering what all the din had been about.

Fin pulled Davie down a side street way from the Ship.

Davie was shaking. 'Shit Fin.'

'I take it he was your pusher.'

'Just some blow. Why did you burst in like that?'

'I needed a piss.'

'Well, you'd better make yourself scarce. He works for Tommy Flynn.'

Fin took out his wallet and handed Davie a bundle of notes. 'Here, take this. You'd be advised to make yourself absent for a few days as well.'

'Thanks Fin. I'll pay you back.'

***

Back at the B&B he took a long shower and packed up his bag. He paid the landlady, Mrs. Paton and asked her to order a taxi to take him over to Waverley Station. The black cab pulled up outside after a short wait.

'Waverley is it?' asked the driver.

'Aye'.

They were just passing Luca's when Fin said 'Can you pull up here for a minute.'

With a shrug the driver pulled over. Fin pulled out a five pound note.

'Change of plan. Can you pick me up here at 10 pm. I've got some busy I need to sort first. There's be another tenner in it for you.'

'You're the boss.'

Fin went back into Luca's and asked if Nona was now in. She appeared after a few minutes from the kitchen. Kissing Fin on both cheeks she cried out 'Finbarr Tulloch? I hear you've been in town a whole day and not come in to say hello to your auntie Nona.' Her eyes were smiling as she scolded him.

'I came in first thing to see you but I was told you were still in bed' he pretended.

'Oh, that devil of a girl. In bed indeed. I don't have time for bed. I'm here chasing after all my lazy sons.'

Turning serious he asked 'Nona, can I ask you a favour. Can I leave my bag here? I'll be back by ten this evening to pick it up.'

'That's no problem Fin. I'll put it in the back office.'

'Thanks Nona, but first of all I need to change my clothes. I've a wedding I need to attend.'

She rolled her eyes.

He changed in the back office. 'Aldo' he said as he passed one of Nona's sons 'if anyone asks I've not been in in.'

'Understood Fin.'

***

He sat at the back of the church, sweating and self-conscious in his dress uniform. A few glances were cast in his direction but no one spoke to him. It was an upmarket affair with the men all in morning suits and the women flaunting the latest designs. He watched Tommy Flynn who stood nervously at the front fiddling with the flower in his lapel. He took some bitter pleasure in seeing that Tommy's hair already starting to thin and he'd had to resort to a comb over. He recognised Tommy's best man as one of the boys from the town but couldn't put a name to the face.

Then the music started up and a moment later she was there, standing at the doorway to the church perhaps no more than ten feet away from him. She looked gorgeous in a simple cream dress and he felt his mouth drying as she walked by. He couldn't remember what hymns they sang or anything else from the service other than Grace. He was as mesmerized as he'd been on their trip to the cinema all those years before. She was just too beautiful.

The service ground on and eventually with the register signed, a new piece of music broke out and the bride and groom started their walk back up the aisle. As they reached his pew she looked over to him and smiled. He managed to smile back. Tommy Flynn was not smiling as he caught his eye.

The reception was in a local hotel and he had been seated at the official sad table in the corner with the odds and sods of single aunts and ugly nieces they'd failed to match up elsewhere. As soon as the speeches were finished, he managed his escape to the bar and ordered a pint of Deuchars.

Grace's father was already there with a beer in hand and to Fin's eye already a little the worse for wear.

'You must be Fin. Grace insisted on inviting you.'

Charmed I'm sure thought Fin. 'It was a lovely meal Mr. Harper.'

'My name's Ally. What's life like in Oliver's Army?'

'Beat's being back here I guess'.

Ally Harper gave him an unfriendly stare.

In for a penny in for a pound, thought Fin. 'I thought Grace would have been off to University instead of getting hitched at her age to a loser like Tommy.'

'Aye, well, she didn't have much choice.'

Fin took a deep swallow of his beer. 'Sorry?'

'Didn't you know. She's up the duff.'

'Are you sure. She'd doesn't look it.'

'Aye, I'm sure. Susan went along with her to the hospital.'

They were interrupted by a group of the boys from the town bursting into the bar. 'Outside' shouted one 'fight in the back yard.' Fin and Grace's father were carried along with the crowd. Outside there was already a circle of men and a few women gathered around two men threshing about on the floor. Fin immediately saw that one was Tommy Flynn. He didn't recognise the other but he was clearly handy with his fists and was all over Tommy, blood spurting from his mouth and down his white shirt. 'Give it to him' screamed one of the girls. He watched for a moment from as Tommy's assailant pummeled into him. Tommy was on the ground and the other man standing over him. He gave Tommy an almighty kick to the body and raised his boot up to stamp on his face. Instinctively Fin stepped in and pushed the man off balance, his boot landing away from Tommy's head. The man turned towards Fin his eyes glaring.

'Come on, he's had enough' said Fin. For a second, the man considered his options, but taking note of Fin's uniform, spat at Tommy lying on the ground and stepped back.

'Fucking cunt' he shouted.

'OK, it's over'. It was Ally Harper. The crowd had already started to disperse with the excitement over. Tommy had made it onto his knees and was holding his face with one hand. Ally Harper produced a handkerchief and handed it to him. 'For fuck sake Tommy, what do you think you're up to. It's your wedding for Christ's sake. Get back inside and tidy yourself up.'

Tommy looked up at Fin, but didn't say anything. Instead, he got up and half staggered to the back door of the pub. Alone, in the yard, Fin said 'What's was all that about.'

'No idea' said Mr. Harper. 'Probably some dealer he owes money to. Come on, my pint's waiting for me.'

Back inside, Ally bought Fin another pint. 'Thanks for stepping in, not that the stupid prat deserves it. Stupid bampot thinks he can control it. But I tell you, it's the one controlling him.'

'What's he taking?'

'I've no idea. But half the boys in town are on smack so I'd be surprised if he's any different.'

'And what about Grace' Fin couldn't resist asking.

'I honestly don't know but if she sticks with that daft junkie, it's only a matter of time. I'd better get back to the wife. This will have been enough to end her.'

Fin bought another pint for the road. Taking a pull on it, he eyed Ian coming in. In contrast to his brother he was well dressed and looked as fit as a fiddle.

'Hello Ian. You've just missed all the excitement.'

Ian lent in close to Fin and whispered into his ear. 'Never mind all that. See that pusher you decked in the Ship earlier. I've just heard he died. You need to get out of here fast before the polis, or worse still, his colleagues, are on to you.'

'Thanks for the nod Ian.'

Fin fished the end of his pint with a gulp. He made for the door but out of the corner of his eye he spotted Grace coming towards him.

'Hello Grace.' He lent in and gave her a kiss on the cheek.

'Hello Fin.'

There was a pause.

'I just wanted to thank you for stepping in to help Tommy.'

'That okay.'

He couldn't think of anything to say.

'Err.. I've got to be going.'

She looked so disappointed. 'But it's so early.'

He smiled apologetically. He saw her eye flicker. Sensing someone behind him he turned and there was Tommy Flynn right behind him.

'Fin Tulloch isn't it. I heard you'd joined up.'

'Aye.' He could feel Grace's discomfort.

'Just to say thanks for stepping in out there.'

Fin didn't say anything.

'Mikey, get Mr. Tulloch here a whisky.' A youth by Tommy's side made off to the bar.

'Grace, I think your mum's looking for you.' Tommy was playing the big man.

'Oh, right. See you later Fin.'

As soon as she was gone, Tommy lent in closer and said 'I heard what happened earlier in the Ship. With you stepping in out in the yard, we're quits but I want you out of this town tonight and I don't want to see your ugly face again. Capisce?'

Under his breath, Fin replied. 'Capisce. Who do you think you are, fucking Scarface? I'll tell you what you are. You're a total fecking loser Flynn.'

The boy was back with Fin's whisky. He took it and slowly poured it down over Tommy's shoes. With that he made for the door.

Wednesday 12 April

He set off at six in the morning for the long drive up the A9 across the highlands and up the coast road across the moors of Caithness. This was the first time he'd driven the VW up to the north of Scotland since Maggie had died and the familiar sights brought back to him the happy times they'd spent holidaying up here. The weather deteriorated as he drove, with the wind and rain rising, turning to sleet and snow as he passed over the Drumocher pass, the little van struggling up the long climb. He stopped for a bacon roll and cup of tea just north of Inverness and arrived at the ferry terminal just along the coast from John o' Groats just after three in the afternoon. The boat did not leave for Orkney until five and he was tired from the drive. He thought of stretching his legs along the pier but by then there was a gale blowing. The ferry when it appeared was a huge red catamaran and after it had loaded a number of trucks Fin found he had to reverse the campervan on board. He was sweating as he eased it into a space tight against an articulated truck.

The trip across the Pentland Firth to St Margaret's Hope on Orkney took about an hour. The ferry swayed up and down across the swell as Fin watched large white breakers crashing against the foreshore of unnamed islands. The islands that loomed into sight were very different to the mainland. They were bleak and treeless and from the distance of the ferry appeared devoid of life. Turning into a large bay, the waves lessened, and with practiced skill, the captain swung the ferry around and it slowly reversed into the dock at St Margaret's Hope taking shelter out of the wind. Up and off the ramp of the ferry doors, he followed the road signs up to Kirkwall, taking care over the narrow Churchill Barriers where waves were topping out over the side of the road. He'd heard they were built by Italian prisoners of wall to protect shipping in Scapa Flow during World War Two and being up here for the first time he could appreciate the back breaking work this must have entailed. He passed by the little chapel the prisoners had built and which the islanders now carefully preserved in their memory He was relieved to finally see the spire of St. Magnus cathedral appearing over the brow of a hill by the Springbank distillery and after a short time found the guest house by the shore he'd booked for the night. He parked up the van for the night and tapped in gently on the bonnet as he got out. 'Good job old girl.'

***

Fin did not return to Musselburgh for another three years. When he did, it was for another funeral. This time around it was a burial and they had chosen a fitting bitter January day with a harsh wind blowing in rain and sleet from across the Forth. The church was large and cold, and the little funeral party barely filled the first three rows of pews.

'David was a young man with so much to offer, struck down in his prime' rattled on the priest.

Bollocks, thought Fin, Davie was a stupid junkie with nothing to offer the world.

Davie's mum sat in the front row, comforted by Ian. Davie's dad had full blown dementia and was at home with a carer from the Council, provided for the day.

Eventually the priest stopped droning on and the coffin was hauled back into the hearse for the trip up to the graveyard. Up here, perhaps because of the weather, there were even fewer in attendance and Fin found himself having to take a cord in the absence of enough men. As the body was lowered down, Ian said 'What a fucking waste.'

Back up at the Arbuckles afterwards, Davie's mum busied around Fin trying to feed him sandwiches. 'Are you here for Davie's birthday party' asked his dad.

Ian took him into the kitchen and poured him a glass of whisky.

'Not what you expect for your wee brother is it? Dead of fucking AIDS by the age of 25.'

'He was a good man' said Fin, failing to think of anything better to say.

'Nah he wasn't' said Ian 'He was a fucking waster of a junkie. The world's better without him.' Fin could see the tears in Ian's eyes.

'Do you remember when we played in the air raid shelter out back when we were little. Is it still there?'

But Ian wasn't listening. 'It's the fault of that bastard Tommy Flynn. He'd better watch his back from now on.'

'What do you mean?' asked Fin.

'Tommy fucking Flynn. Lives in that big house up by Loretto and drives around like he's in Miami Vice. Biggest pusher in East Lothian. Not that the useless fucking polis seem to be able to do anything about it.'

'I thought he was a junkie himself.'

'Nah, his dad paid for some rehab over in the States and he managed to kick the habit. Spent his time over there learning the tricks of the trade and now he's the biggest distributor these parts.'

Fin drained his whisky and Ian topped up his glass.

'And what about Grace?'

'Another fecking junkie. Ditched her, didn't he and them with a wain and all. I tell you, give me half a chance, and I'll swing for him.'

Ian's father stumbled in. 'Are you going out to play with Ian and Davie' he asked Fin.

Ian gently took him by the hand. 'Not today dad. Why don't you have a rest in your room.'

Then to Fin 'There's too many folk in here for him. Old bugger's all confused. I tell you Fin. You're better off out of here. Stick to the army.'

***

Fin served a full ten years as a squaddie in the Royal Highland Fusiliers including a tour of duty in Iraq. He had been fed and watered by the army, taught how to polish his boots and how to fire a gun. He was totally unprepared for civilian life.

For a month or so following demob he dossed on a sofa in a friend's house in Manchester before his friend's wife got bored of his mess and kicked him out. He then slept on a series of sofas before managing through an old army contact to get some part-time work bouncing in the Glasgow club scene. It was there that one night one of the other door men said he was applying to the police. 'They're desperate at the moment.' So was he, he thought. So, he fired off application letter to the Met and several other forces. The only one to bite was Lothian and Borders and so just shy of five years after last leaving he found himself again on a train pulling into Waverley station.

The interview panel did not go well.

'Can you tell us the name of the Chief Constable for Edinburgh and the Lothians?'

'Err..no'

'Why do you want to join the police?'

'Errr… I need a job.'

And so on.

After just ten minutes, the lead interviewer asked the inevitable 'Is there anything you would like to ask us?'

'Err… no thanks.'

'Well thank you, Mr….Tulloch. We'll be in touch.'

Just as he was about to stand up, one of the three on the panel, who'd been silent up to that point, said 'It says on your application form that you were in the Royal Highland Fusiliers. I served with them. Where were you based?'

And with that stroke of fortune Fin knew he was in.

Fin found the police in truth not that much different to the army. There was a basic training of sorts followed by a probational period on the beat There was a clear hierarchical structure and you knew where you stood. He liked that. He was soon settled in at St Leonard's. Within a year he'd met Maggie and no more than a year after that they were married and had moved into the house on John Street where he still lived. When they'd found that Maggie could not have children, the first in a long line of Sammys arrived. Later, they bought the campervan and he enjoyed the routine of police work and holidays up north. The years passed slowly and happily until the day five years ago when Maggie went for a routine scan and their whole world was torn asunder.

***

It was ironic that Fin found himself undertaking one of his first solo beat patrols in Musselburgh. For some reason he could not now remember, Musselburgh had found themselves short of staff and had to pull in a few bodies from St Leonard's. The chief had somehow known he had been brought up there and he'd therefore been a natural choice.

He felt very self-conscious walking up the High Street and past the Ship Inn. He saw a couple of faces he knew from school but he seemed invisible to them in his uniform. Eventually he reached Luca's and popped inside. Nona as always was therefore, busy behind the ice cream counter. It was a warm summer's day and there was a queue reaching out the door. Seeing him, she shouted out a greeting.

'Hello Nona. I hope you are well.'

'I can't afford to be ill Fin. I've too much hard work to do.' She pulled a strained face. 'What would you like to eat today?'

'I'm on beat patrol in the toun for a few days so I thought I'd just pop in to say hello.'

'Oh, you can't just do that. You'll have a cup of tea surely.'

'I'm supposed to be working Nona, but maybe I could take a break for five minutes.'

Nona ushered him through to the café and sat down beside him. 'Lucy' she called to one of the girls 'a pot of tea for me and the constable here.'

The tea came, strong as tar as Nona liked it. She poured him a cup and without asking added a couple of tea spoons of sugar. She wanted to know all about his new job. 'I always knew you would make something of yourself, Fin. You'll be the chief constable one day, mark my words.'

As they chattered on he noticed at the back of the café a table of four men talking loudly.

'Who are they?' he asked Nona.

'Don't you recognise him? That's Tommy Flynn and three of his stooges. A real bad lot.'

'Why do you let them in then?'

'What, and find the café burnt to the ground.'

He looked over. Tommy Flynn had put on some weight since he'd last seen him. He was wearing a flash suit and expensive shoes and looked every bit the successful local gangster. He must have seen Fin coming in but obviously didn't give a shit for the uniform.

'And what about Grace. Do you still see her?'

'Did you not know? They split up not more than a year after they married. She moved away and took the child with her.'

He finished his tea and then, promising to Nona he would pop in again, made this way out to the street. There, parked on a double-yellow line, was a large Merc its windows tinted black. He called in the registration and asked for an ID check. 'It's registered to a Thomas Flynn. Oh, and the insurance is out of date.'

***

It was two days later and Fin was again on a foot patrol along the High Street, this time accompanied by another PC, Lesley Paton, also on secondment from St Leonard's. Reaching Luca's the shiny new Mercedes was parked up in the same position as before.

'Are there no bloody traffic wardens in this town' said Lesley.

'I'm sure there are' he replied, 'but I suspect they want to keep a hold of their kneecaps.'

'You know whose it is?' she asked.

'Let's see if they are in Luca's' he said, knowing full well they'd be sat at their usual table. Sure enough, there they were.

'Does one of you gentlemen own the black Mercedes parked out front?'

'What of it' said Tommy Flynn without looking up. His boys remained silent.

'It's parked on a double yellow line. You'll need to move it.'

'We'll just finish our coffees and then we on our way.'

'You need to move it now.'

Tommy Flynn looked up for the first time and clocked Fin.

'I know you. You're that bam who used to run about with Ian Arbuckle when you were wains.'

'Well, now I'm the bam telling you to move your car.'

Tommy slowly looked up again at Fin. 'As I said, we'll finish our coffees and then we on our way.'

'In that case I'll just have to go outside and call a tow-truck.'

Tommy was on his feet, followed by a couple of his boys. 'You touch that car, and you're fucking dead.'

Trying to remain calm Fin said 'PC Paton, did you just hear this gentleman threaten a police officer?'.

The tension was cut by Tommy. 'Come on boys, we're off.' He pushed past Fin mouthing 'scum' in his face. But Fin was too quick and tripped him, sending him splashing down onto the floor.

Lesley's truncheon was drawn and she pointed it at Tommy's compatriots. 'Get back!' she screamed at them. They hesitated for a second but obeyed. Tommy struggled to his feet again and Fin immediately stepped in to put him in an arm lock. There was a hushed silence from the other customers in the café.

'You lot' he said to the boys with Tommy 'we're just taking Mr. Flynn here outside for a quiet chat. Now behave like good boys and you won't get into trouble.'

Fin pulled Tommy's arm up his back and frog-marched him out on the pavement followed by Lesley. He forced his face down on the bonnet of the Mercedes and slapped on a pair of handcuffs. Lesley was already on the phone calling for a back-up car.

Swiveling Tommy's around, Fin reached into his trouser pocket and pulled out the Merc's keys. 'Nice car, Mr. Flynn. You won't mind if I have a look inside.' Allowing Lesley to take hold of Tommy, he opened up the car and rummaged through the front. It was immaculate. He then clicked open the boot. Going around to the back, he looked inside.

'What do we have here?' He reached inside and brought out a small paper wrap. He dangled it in front of Tommy.

Tommy sputtered 'You bastard. You've just planted that.'

'I am arresting you on suspicion of possession of an illegal substance.' He then lent in out of earshot of Lesley and whispered 'This one's for Davie'.

The back-up car had by then arrived and Tommy was bundled in the back.

Tommy and Lesley started on foot back towards the station. 'Did you put that wrap in this car?' she asked.

'Of course not, and even if I had I don't think many of the folk around here would be sad to see a scumbag like him get his comeuppance.'

They went back into the café but Tommy's boys had already left out the back.

'Come on' said Fin to Lesley 'I'll treat you to an ice cream.'

■■

When Tommy's house was searched an industrial scale cocktail of drugs was found, lifting his charge from possession to dealing. With him in custody one of his boys stepped into this shoes within a few weeks. The bigger players in Edinburgh were not unhappy with this outcome. Tommy had never been the smartest tool in the box and now he'd become a liability. His twelve year sentence was seen as harsh when handed down but then again who has any sympathy for a drug dealer.

Fin's pedestrian crossing accident took place only a couple of weeks after Tommy's arrest at Luca's and after a month recuperating at home, he was moved off the beat to take up a desk job at St Leonard's. He was not disappointed.

Part 2 – The Island

Friday 14 April

Driving up carefully from the pier head and across a rattling cattle grid with the windscreen wipers struggling against the rain Fin took in his first view of West Hunday. To his left was a broad bay with breakers crashing up onto a sandy beach and ahead of him stretched a single track road over a causeway and up to the brow of a rise on which he could make out the ruins of a castle. The landscape was of small fields of farming land broken up with stone dykes, some set to grass and others ploughed neatly into long lines on what appeared to be a run-rig system. The wind swept across the fields and buffeted the VW. A few small birds were being blown across and up the road. There was no sign of human activity but he could see a line of black cattle in this distance sheltering against a stone wall.

A small sign to the left pointed off up a rough track to the bird observatory. He rumbled up over the potholes fearing for the VW's suspension and parked up in front of a spectacular curved building built of glass and stone. It was not what he had expected. Someone must have a spent a fortune building it. A pity, he thought, it was not extended to the track up to it.

The wind pushed the van door back as he struggled out, making him drop his cane on the ground. He struggled down to pick it up and then hurried through the rain to the entrance into the observatory. There was a heavy oak door and above it, carved into the stone lintel, were two interconnected triangles. Pushing at the door he was relieved to find it open. Finally out of the wind and rain, he shook off his coat. He was in a hallway. It was dark with no lights but as he stepped forward lighting came on automatically. The hallway lead into a large circular lounge with an open fire place in the centre and with windows providing a panoramic view across the bay. He was pleased to see a bar built into one corner. Unfortunately, no-one was manning it. He thought however he heard voices and retracting his steps he was led by the sounds down a corridor. The voices were coming from a room to the right. He called out a hello and pushed open a swing door. He was in a modern kitchen. A couple of girls were busy chopping vegetables. Each wore a long plain dress with polished black boots laced up. They both had their head covered with a scarf. It was like stepping back a century in fashion and seemed very incongruous against the high tech back ground of the kitchen. Whilst each girl was small one was thin whilst the other very visibly pregnant and he felt his eyes drawn to her belly.

'Sorry to interrupt' said Fin. 'I'm Fin Tulloch and I've booked a room in the bunkhouse for the next week.'

The taller of the two girls stuttered 'I'm..mm… Frigga. I'll…ger..g.er. get.. the master' while the other looked shyly to the ground.

At that moment the kitchen door burst open and in stepped one of the most striking men Fin had seen. He was dressed in a long black robe with a collarless shirt but what caught Fin's attention was his piercing light blue eyes set in along thin face topped with white hair flowing down to his shoulders.

'Eric Branson' he introduced himself, grabbing Fin's hand and shaking it vigorously. Sensing Fin's uncertainty he added 'Don't worry about my appearance. I've just returned from our Sunday church service.'

Fin tried to remove his hand but found it enveloped in a huge grip. He felt it squeezed as Eric Branson gave him a broad grin.

'We weren't sure if the ferry would be cancelled. Must have been a bumpy ride.' He smiled again. 'I'll show you your room'.

Eric lead Fin out of the kitchen and down a corridor which led to an outside door to the rear of the main building. Braving the weather, he guided him over to an attractive bothy building again built of local stone and, bending low, took Fin in through a low door. 'Mind your head'. Fin noticed the inter-connected triangles above the door.

'We built the bothy out of an old smithy that used to be here. Your room's the furthest down the hall. It's called Loki' he said, opening up a door to reveal a well equipped room with two single beds. 'You'll have it to yourself unless we get any unexpected guests. Dinner's at seven in the main building and we do a call-in at nine.'

'Thank you very much. It's a very impressive set-up. Is anyone else staying at the moment?' asked Fin.

'There a party of four up from London staying in the main building and a new couple arriving on this afternoon's plane, wind permitting, but apart from that you have it all to yourself at the moment' said Tom. 'I'll let you settle in and perhaps if the weather improves this afternoon you can take a walk up to the nets?'

Fin was not sure why he'd want to do that, but said 'Thanks. I'll see how it is once I have unpacked my stuff.'

'Give the girls a shout if you want them to make you up some soup and bread for lunch.'

With that Eric left Fin and marched back out into the weather, apparently oblivious to the rain and wind.

Fin's room was immaculately clean and boasted an ensuite bathroom. He'd stayed in a number of bunkhouses in his day but nothing as good as this.

He decided to see if the rain would ease off before he carted his kit over, leaving it in the VW in the meantime. Looking around the bothy, there were three other rooms all closed and a kitchen area to one end with a small table.

He opened a couple of cupboards in the kitchen to see if he could find any tea making kit but they were bare. He was tempted to have a peak in the other bedrooms but decided to leave them be.

With the rain slackening for a moment, he made it back over to the main building where voices chatting again led him back to Frigga and her friend. Tapping on the door before popping his head around its corner he said. 'Hello again. I was told you might be able to rustle me up some soup for lunch.'

'Is …le…le..leek and potato OK' stammered Frigga.

'That would be lovely' replied Fin.

Frigga showed Fin through to a dining hall with a single long oak table. While she heated his soup he cast his eye over various leaflets and books lying around the room. Almost all of them focused on bird and bird watching with advertisements for powerful binoculars and other apparatus. There was also a white board with the latest sightings listed. Yesterday showed White-billed Diver and a Siberian Chaffinch. Fin had heard of neither. He routed around and found a map of the bird hides on the island together usefully with various other places of interest listed, including a light house at the north of the island and a village on the west side. He pocketed a copy.

When the soup arrived it was thick and tasty and accompanied by some warm home-made bere bread. Duly fortified he decided to venture out, and after pulling on his army surplus jacket and a dry pair of trousers, he set off in the VW down the track from the observatory feeling positive but with no idea what he was looking for. There was a little easing in the wind but the wee van still swayed from side to side as he drove up the single track road. He passed along the narrow causeway with sand from the beaches on either side blown up onto the roadway, then up past the ruined castle and on until he reached a crossing with a war memorial. There he risked venturing out, pulling his wollen hat down over this forehead. The memorial was in the shape of a Celtic cross but with other imagery he could not identify carved into the stone. He took out his mobile phone and took a photograph.

Looking down the list of the fallen It was difficult to comprehend how an island so small could have lost so many of its men. There must have been at least two dozen names. To the right of the memorial a single lane road led down to an airfield. He knew that there were flights twice a day except for the Sabbeth, and he watched as a small Islander plane buffeted against the wind as it came in to land. He could hear its engine straining against the head wind and it seemed to be coming in sideways, but at the last minute its nose was pulled round and it landed with a bump. Taxi-ing up the grass runway it pulled up outside a small building where a man head to toe in waterproofs came out to meet it with a trolley. He saw two people, a man and a woman, stepping out and their luggage being unloaded from the rear of the plane onto the trolley. There were two large rucksacks and long tubes. The man kept back making sure the tubes were treated with care. He assumed they contained telescopic sights or some such and these were bird watchers. He was passed by large black SUV with WHBO on the side that swept up to the airport building. He saw Eric Branson step out, now dressed in a tweed suit, and wave a greeting to the newcomers.

There was a road on the opposite side of the war memorial which from the map he'd picked up at the observatory Fin knew led down to the island village but he drove on up to the north of the island. The road was surprisingly straight and narrow and rose gradually upwards. There were a few wet bedraggled sheep in the fields, presumably ready for lambing. Above him swirled various birds in the wind but his knowledge and eyesight was too poor to identify them. The drive up to the top of the island only took a few minutes but the island took on a different characteristic up here, more rugged and darker. Ahead lay the cold North Atlantic and he could pick out white elephants crashing over skerries off shore. It was easy to imagine a huge wave submerging the whole of the island. At the end of the road, there was another cattle grid and then an untarmacked track which led up to the lighthouse. Even from this distance it was an ominous sight and stood over the land like a giant. He had read that it was the tallest lighthouse in Scotland and had been built by Stevenson over two hundred years ago after the original light had been destroyed in an enormous winter storm. He was stopped half way up the track by a closed gate ahead of him with a sign across it reading: *Private Property. Keep Out. By order of the West Hunday Estate.*

He parked up the van which rocked gently in the wind. A wide links area of grass spread out in front of the track down to the rocky shoreline. Fin got out of the van taking care with his walking cane. The wind was blowing much stronger up here than he'd expected from sitting in the van and he struggled to keep his balance as he made his way down a slope onto the grass. A few straggly sheep, their winter fleeces ruffled in the wind, scattered as he approached. He pulled up his coat tight and pressed his face into the wind making for a wooden hut sitting just above the rocks. What first brought people to this place he wondered. It was difficult to understand how anyone could have made a living but he knew that the Orkneys had been a magnet for settlors from the Iron Age onwards. As he approached the hut he felt the bite of the salt spray from the sea and his cheeks freezing against it. The door into the hut was held by a heavy bolt but it readily pulled across and he stepped inside, welcoming the calm inside. The hut itself slightly rattled in the wind but it was well build and fitting out with benches and a small kitchen area. Its only narrow slit window faced towards the sea. There was a whiteboard pinned up but nothing written on it. He peered out through the window onto the beach and rocks below but could not see any wildlife. Even the birds were hiding today. He stayed a few moments to dry out, watching the rhythm of the waves breaking over the rocks, then tightening up this coat and pulling his hat firmly down onto his head, made his way back to the VW. It rattled into action after a couple of turns of the ignition key and he did a three point turn, praying not to stick in the wet grass, and turned back towards the south of the island. Passing by the airfield it was in darkness. He was just thinking how tough you'd have to be to live here when a dog skittered across the road in front of him. Goes for the animals too he thought.

***

When he made his way over from the bunk house just before seven, the dining hall was already full with about a dozen people chatting. Eric Branson stood out in his tweed suit speaking to an older man in a kilt and Argyll jacket. The remaining group was mixed. There were four middle-aged men who looked to Fin's eye like a bunch of aged hippies in Fair Isle jumpers and he took them to be birders. Standing to one side were the couple he'd seen coming off the afternoon flight and finally there were three girls of about Becky's age talking amongst themselves. The long table had been set for dinner and the group began to take their seats. Fin sat at one end opposite one of the young woman.

'Hello, I'm Fin' he introduced himself.

Avoiding eye contact she replied 'Anya' she replied in an accent he could not place.

'Are you a bird watcher?'.

She smiled at him. 'No, I'm one of the helpers at the observatory.'

Eric Branson interrupted by knocking a thick bottomed toasting glass on the wooden table. He announced to the group. 'Please be seated.' Turning to the old man in the kilt he added 'Father, would you like to say grace'. The old man struggled up and leaning on his chair mumbled what passed for grace. He sat back down with a thump. Eric then called out 'Come on Frigga, we've good some starving folk in here.' There was some muffled laughter. Fin suspected some of the diners had heard this routine before. Frigga and the other girl he'd seen earlier helping in the kitchen then appeared carrying plates piled high with tonight's fare. Hobson's choice was clearly the order of the day. Fin's food arrived and he was pleased to find a plate full of roast beef, potatoes, Yorkshires and vegetables before him. A classic mix of the carbs and protein needed to fuel a day around West Hunday. Anya piped up 'Its Aberdeen Angus raised on the island. You'll taste the sea off it.' She spoke in low voice and paused, sensing Fin's hesitation, adding 'Don't worry, it tastes good' and gave him a shy smile. She looked down to her dinner. She was clearly not a one for chit-chat and that was about as much as she said throughout the meal.

Another young woman sitting to Fin's side lent in and said. 'Don't worry about Anya. She's such a chatterbox.' Anya gave her a frown. She spoke English in what Fin thought was German accent. 'I'm Lydia by the way. Not the best of days to arrive but should be great to see what blows in on the wind.' Fin was looking a little blank but tried to nod in agreement. 'Oh, I assumed you were a birder' said Lydia.

'I'm afraid my knowledge of birds doesn't stretch to what's in my back garden' said Fin.

'What brings you up to West Hunday then?' asked Lydia. It can't be our lovely Spring weather. She laughed at her joke. She had a surprisingly deep laugh.

'I'm doing some research on my ancestors. My surname's Tulloch. It's is an old Orkney name and I'm here to check out a few of the islands.' Fin's cover story held at least some modicum of truth, with a number of Tullochs having been listed on the war memorial he'd passed earlier.

Lydia seemed satisfied with his answer. 'I'm a volunteer here. Chatterbox Anya is another and down there at the end wearing the fetching red fleece with the bird poo on the shoulder is Yulia.'

'Where are you guys from?' asked Fin.

'Oh, from all corners' said Lydia. 'I'm from Germany, Anya there is Polish and Yulia's all the way from Russia. She's immune to the cold.'

'Wow, that's some mix. And no boys?'

'No' said Lydia, making a fake frown. 'Just birds. No boys.'

Lydia turned to chat to the woman sitting on her other side. The rest of the meal was spent with Fin listening to Lydia talking birds with the new couple.

Fin had the impression that Eric Branson had been listening carefully to his conversations with Anya and Lydia.

A choice of puddings followed the main course and Fin was then asked by Frigga if he would like a coffee in the lounge. But when he made it through to the lounge, the bar was already in operation and a number of the other guests and the volunteers already had beers in front of them.

Frigga brought him his coffee, but noticed him eyeing the bar. 'Well, can we t...t...tempt you with a beer Mr. Tulloch?' she suggested.

'Why not' said Fin 'what's good?'

'At this time of the year, try a Corncrake. Its brewed in Kirkwall.'

Fin took a bottle and asked Frigga to put it on a tab. Not half bad he thought as he took a slurp, if not up there with a pint of Deuchars.

Fin was onto his second Corncrake by the time Eric announced the call-in. All the birders trouped back through to the dining hall where a screen had been set up. For fear of being alone in the bar, Fin took his beer through and pulled up a chair at the back of the room. Eric Branson spoke to the group. 'Hello, for the benefit of newcomers, I am Eric Branson and this is my father Rolf who has the honour to be the current laird of West Hunday.' The old man barely managed a nod in acknowledgement. 'This is our daily call in of bird sightings. We split the island into four quarters, south, east, west and north monitored daily by our volunteers and we try to record all bird sighting in these areas. This is then fed into the national database. You are all invited to contribute, particularly if you spot anything unusual. Shall be start. Right, who was on zone 1 today?'

The young woman with the red fleece from dinner raised her hand and then quickly listed her sightings. It was all double-dutch to Fin. *510 Golden Plover, 95 Purple Sandpipers, 8 Pink-footed Gees at Hoy Loch*. Fin tried to pay attention but it was clear this was a language he did not understand. They went through the other three zones in similar fashion and by the end they must have listed about fifty species and hundreds if not thousands of birds.

Including the three volunteers, and the Bransons, that made a host 'family' of five plus the two girls in the kitchen. There was no sign of a Mrs. Branson to either Branson senior or junior. To these there were added six visiting birders, the two from today's plane and the four others who had the look of folk who had been here for a few days. They all had the look of seasoned bird watchers. Laurel and Hardy from the ferry had not made an appearance.

Once the count was over, the group split up, a few retiring to their rooms but most back to the bar. Fin decided to give Mrs. Maclean a call to see how Sammy was faring without him but couldn't get a signal. Laughing, one the volunteers manning the bar told him that it was difficult enough in the best of weather to find a signal but given the storm it would be nigh-on impossible. 'Try again tomorrow' he was told 'you might have better luck then'.

Fin consoled himself with another bottle of Corncrake.

'Arrived today?' asked one of the four birders.

'Aye, have you been here for a few days?'

'We came up on Monday. Some bloody journey it was. Delayed flight from Heathrow to Aberdeen and then another from there up to Kirkwall. Had to stay overnight. Still the flight over from Kirkwall to the island was amazing. Absolutely spectacular. The sea is such a beautiful turquoise green.'

'And has the bird watching been good?'

'Yeah, we've all managed to tick a few off our lists. Some luckier than others, eh Derek.' He prodded the man sitting next to him.

'Some of us have it Steve and some don't.'

Derek joined in. 'It is really interesting island. Like going back to the 1950s. I didn't think anyone lived like this any longer. Have you see the two poor girls in the kitchen? My daughter would die if she had to dress like that.'

'Mind you' piped in Steve 'some of the islanders are fricking weird. I suspect they've been here too long.'

His friend piped up, laughing 'do you remember that old timer we came across up at Hoy loch?. Just lying on the grass looking up into the sky. I thought he was dead when I saw him. Then, when we got closer, we realised he was just out of it. We had to get Eric to come and give him a lift home. He kept rattling on about *bread of Christ* or something.' Both men snorted with laughter at the memory.

They offered Fin another beer but he made his excuses and retreated back to the bunkhouse to turn in for the night. The fresh sea air had taken its toll and he had a lot of ground to cover tomorrow.

Saturday 15 April

Fin was used to his comfortable double bed and the narrow single bed in the bunkhouse had not exactly been kind to his back; but he had still managed to sleep through his normal time of waking. Opening his eyes, light was streaming through a dormer window into his room and he could make out blue sky above. He stretched out and a twinge of pain shot through his bad leg. Swearing quietly, he got himself up and rocked his leg back and forth to get some motion into it. A present from Musselburgh is how he thought of it. He ventured into the bathroom and starred into the mirror above the sink. An unshaved old man looked back at him. He still had a full head of unruly hair, mostly turned to grey, but otherwise he struggled to connect himself with the face in the mirror. He splashed some water on this face to see if that would clear the image but the same old man starred back.

Dressed, he ventured out into the courtyard and found that the wind had died down to a breeze and the sky was a bright blue with only a strip of white cloud on the horizon. Venturing round to the front of the observatory he looked out across the bay with the blue green sea gently lapping against the beach. Tiny birds were playing in the stone wall in front of him. The difference from the day before was stark. There were a few puddles of water on the path back up to the main part of the observatory but otherwise it was as if the storm had never happened. A voice called out 'Morning Mr. Tulloch' and he turned to see Lydia waving as she rode away down the track on a bicycle that looked like it had seen better days.

In the dining hall for breakfast he found no one there. There was however at least an unused place setting for which he was grateful. Frigga stuck her head around the door. If anything, the clothes she was wearing today were more from the 1850s than the 1950s. Again, her head was covered with a scarf. He wondered if they were home-made.

'Mm.. morning Mr. Tulloch, hope you slept well. Would you like t…t….tea or coffee?' 'I slept very well thanks Frigga. Perhaps a little too well looking around there. Tea would be lovely please' he said.

'Tea it is' Frigga smiled 'and would you like the full Scottish'.

'If I am not too late, that would be great' said Fin 'just what the doctor ordered.'

Frigga tootled off and was back in a few minutes with a pot of tea. 'Where is everyone?' asked Fin.

'Oh, after a storm, all the birders are out at the crack of dawn checking if anything usual has turned up. Just last week we had a red winged blackbird, the first sighting this side of America.'

'You know your birds then' he said.

'You can't help it around here. Comes with the territory. Of course, it's sad. Poor wee thing blown over the Atlantic and lands here. This will be its resting place.'

'You mean it will die here.'

'Yes, away from its own.'

She looked troubled as she retreated to make up his breakfast.

When his food arrived, it was a plate full of square sausage, black pudding, haggis, egg and all the works, it was brought in by the second girl he'd seen in the kitchen. 'I'll bring you some toast in a moment.' she said presenting him with this plate.

'Thanks. I don't think I caught your name' said Fin. It was Frigga who replied, coming in with the toast.

'That's our Fulla' explained Frigga after the girl left. 'My wee sister'.

'That's an unusual name' said Fin. 'Is it an Orkney name?'

'Oh, we don't see ourselves as Orcadians' explained Frigga. 'We're a Norse island and we look back to our Viking ancestors for our names.'

'How long have you two worked here?' Fin asked.

'We've worked here each summer since the observatory opened. Our family's from the island you see.'

He thought it impolite to mention Fulla's pregnancy so instead asked 'And what about the Bransons. How long have they had this place?'.

'Oh, I'm not sure. The Bransons have always been the laird. They own the whole island you know.'

Fin tucked into his breakfast. Fulla appeared again with more toast, enough to feed four, and by the time Fin ventured out on foot into the sunshine he felt ready to face whatever West Hunday had to throw at him.

***

No-one had mentioned Ophelia but then again why would they. She was just another volunteer who gone off sightseeing round the islands for a few days.

Fin set off up the island road with a day sack on this back and his walking cane tapping along beside him. This time and on foot he was aware of the huge number of birds of myriad varieties in the surrounding fields. He reached the causeway over to the larger of the two islands and started off across it. The remnants of the hulk of a boat lay in the water on one side its mast sitting out at an angle. On each side of the causeway huge boulders had been piled to protect it from the power of the sea.

From the far side of the causeway the road rose gently up to the remains of a castle, the thick stone walls still standing but the roof caved in. A couple of bicycles were propped up against the gate to it. Fin made his way up to the entrance and inside. There was a large open roofed interior with grass now growing on the ground. A huge smooth stone lay in the centre. Off to one side were the remains of what would have been smaller rooms including stone steps down to a lower level. A metal grill blocked off access.

The walls were several feet thick and crumbling. Stones fallen over the years lay around the sides. Arrow slits were built in at places. Carrying on round to the back of the castle he came to what must at one time have been a walled garden. It was filled with gnarled bushes and long grasses all leaning to the east from years of prevailing wind. The broome bushes were covered in tiny yellow flowers. There was a wide grove down the centre and at the far end of this a large fine mesh net had been propped up. He could see Anya and Yulia busy at the net but he could not make out what they were doing. 'Hi' he said. 'Shuuh' came the reply. He went closer and saw Yulia untangle a small bird. She held some small pliers and with great dexterity clipped a tag around the bird's tiny leg.

'You must have done that a few times' Fin said quietly.

'A lot of times' the girl said, 'we ring the migrants as they drift in off the storms. We can then track where they turn up on another reserve.'

Fin watched for a while as the girls worked away.

'Have you been here long' he asked.

'About three months' Yulia replied 'I'm on a six month university placement.'

'Oh, so you're half way through. What are you studying' asked Fin.

'Ecology in Prague.'

'That's a long way away. How did you hear about West Hunday.'

'The observatory has a very good international reputation. It has links with lots of similar places across Europe.'

'Would you like a cup of tea' asked Anya. I'm just about to make us one.' Fin was please to find her less quiet today.

While Anya went off to get the tea, he sat down on the grass and watched as Yulia worked, catching the birds from the net, weighing them and applying identifying rings to their legs. She was very skilled.

'Do you not get bored up here with the lack of boys?'

Yulia gave Fin a serious look. 'No, we're kept pretty busy although I do want to do some travelling to other parts of Scotland once may placement has finished.'

'Perhaps you can visit Edinburgh. That's where I live' he suggested.

'I'd like to do that' she said. 'We had a volunteer from Edinburgh but she had to leave.'

'That's a pity. Did she not like it here?'

'Oh, she loved it.'

'Why did she leave then?'. He knew he was pressing it.

After a pause she said quietly 'I'm not sure.'

Changing the subject Fin said. 'Maybe there be some boy volunteers soon.'

'Maybe' said Yulia. She laughed politely.

Anya returned with the tea. 'Would you like to put a ring on one of the birds' she asked.

'Thanks' said Fin 'but I don't think I'd trust my clumsy big hands.'

The tea was good and strong. 'Yulia said that you'd had a volunteer from Edinburgh. That's where I live.'

'Yes, Offie left a few weeks ago. I'm not sure when she'll be replaced.'

'Oh, is she not coming back.'

'I don't think so.' She was concentrating on ringing the tiny bird in her hand.

 I've pestered you too enough. I'll leave you to it but perhaps we can have a chat at dinner'.

'But you've not finished your tea?' said Yulia.

'Too much tea and I'll need a wee.'

'That's what the walls in the fields are for.' Both girls giggled.

***

Fin walked back down to the road. The sun was by now high in the sky and he found himself frowning to keep the brightness out of his eyes. He wished he'd left this coat back at the observatory and brought his sun glasses instead. He reached the war memorial and this time turned right down a track towards the western shore. He could see the lighthouse in the distance and beyond that the flat sea stretching out to the horizon. A small plane buzzed overhead. He assumed it was the morning flight from Kirkwall. He passed a half fallen down cottage with some rusted out cars without wheels propped up on bricks by the side of the road. A small Massy Ferguson tractor came up behind him and he stepped onto the grass by the roadside to let it squeeze past. He waved at the driver as it passed and the farmer acknowledged in response. As he walked on a flurry of small birds rose from the stone dyke to the side of the road and rested on the other side. This was repeated for some time as the flock chased him down the road. In a field to his right the tractor was busy unloading a silage bale and ripping off the plastic sheeting with its front fork. A group of cattle circled around it impatiently mewing loudly in anticipation of their lunch.

He could see the roofs of buildings lying in a dip further on and he made towards them. From the map he'd lifted from the observatory the night before we knew this was marked as the village and he was interested to see what was there. He came up over a small rise in the road and the view opened up to show a row of about a dozen or so cottages set around a small bay with a habour in front. An old stone church stood at one end and a little bit beyond that another larger building. It was very picturesque on a day like today with the village arranged on one side of the road and a pebble beach falling away down to a sandy beach on the other side. A couple of crabbing boats had been pulled up onto the shoreline.

He walked on into the village past a traditional red telephone box. Looking inside there was no phone although a directory lay on a shelf. The cottages on the front were all white washed with large stone slabs for roofs and tiny black windows. Their doors were all painted with bright colours and, although the paintwork was largely flaked, the overall effect was to create a picture postcard effect. He had hoped for a shop to buy some water but there was none. He'd have to make do with the lukewarm tea in his flask. No-one seemed to be around, although smoke was rising from two of the cottage chimneys, and he wandered on through the village, stopping at the harbour. It was in a poor state with the harbour walls broken. Some rusty rings to tie up boats were fixed to the stone work but it must have been some time since it was last used.

He walked on up to the church. It was a plain looking building with a small square tower. There was a faded carving of three inter-linked triangles above the door, the same as he'd seen at the observatory. It opened up to reveal an amazingly elaborate interior. He had expected Calvanist starkness but instead every wall and column seemed to be covered with carvings of faces and symbols. He recognised amongst the carvings classic green man faces spouting foliage from their mouths. He knew these were pre-Christian in origin and symbolized life from death and he wondered if perhaps the other carvings also pre-dated Christianity coming to the island. There being nobody about, he braved taking his phone out and shot a series of images. On a pillar in one corner he was surprised to see the shape of what looked like a swastika carved into a wall.

At the front there were statues of, he presumed, saints although he could not identify any of them, and a Madonna and child by the alter. The alter itself was adorned with a cover in the pattern of the three interlinked triangles above the doorway.

He noticed a stone slab on the floor of the nave. On it, partly rubbed thin by centuries of footsteps, was inscribed 'Sir Rolf Branson, First Lord and Protector of West Hunday'. He discovered some other slabs also with the names of various member of the Branson family recorded. This was clearly very much their place of worship and their island.

Stepping out into the bright sunshine, he wandered around the grave yard. Again, the weather worn tombstones were decorated with swastikas, interlinked triangles and other symbols with which he was unfamiliar.

Squinting his eyes against the midday glare he made out the figure of a man coming towards him along the road. He wandered back down to the church gate to meet an old man with an unkempt beard. A small terrier was running about by his side. Again, he looked to be dressed from a different age, in rough black trousers and a waistcoat over an uncollared shirt that once upon a time must have been white. Fin noticed that his boots were almost falling to bits.

'Morning, lovely day isn't it.'

'Aye' said the old man, grinning at him.

Fin said 'I've walked up from the bird observatory' as if needing to explain why he was here.

'Aye' said the old man, still grinning manically.

'Do you live in the village.'

Another aye. Looking more closely at the old man, Fin saw that he was dribbling. He wandered if this was the same person the four birders had come across the worse for wear at one of the hides. Then, another figure appeared from down the road from the village. Another man of more Fin's age was walking briskly down the road towards them. He was dressed much the same as the first but wore a dirty frock coat over his waist coat.

'Good morning' said Fin.

'Good day' said the second man. 'Dinnie worry about Willy here. He's away with the fairies this morn.'

Then to the old man 'Willy, dinnie you pester the gentleman here. Get on your way now.'

'Oh, there's no problem at all' said Fin, embarrassed by the intervention. But the second man ignored him. He picked up a stick and threw it on down the road. 'Go on Rosie' he called and the terrier ran after the stick, with the old man following.

The second man said to Fin 'You'll be a bird watcher then'.

'Yes' said Fin, thinking a white lie was simpler than a lengthy explanation 'Do you live here?'

'I was born in yon cottage' said the old man pointing down the road. 'I've lived in the same place over sixty years. I used to be the school master but I'm retired now.'

'How many folk live on the island these days?' asked Fin.

'Perhaps about fifty or so, although some work on the mainland during the week and only come over for the weekend. Used to be over three hundred on the island. There were two shops and a public house. Nowadays it's mainly old folk.'

'But you've still a school here though' said Fin.

'Aye, that's it there' said the old man, pointing to the building lying further along the road. 'We're down to only three children of school age and when the youngest one goes over to the big school in Kirkwall that will be it. The Council will close it and it will be the end for the school and perhaps for the island'.

Fin had read of this sort of issue facing lots of the Scottish islands. The populations were getting smaller and older and the younger folk rest for jobs down south to escape the harsh lifestyle of their fathers and mothers.

'I was looking around the church. It's got some amazing decoration.'

'Aye, we're very proud of it. The oldest parts are more than eight hundred years old.'

'I've never seen anything like it.' He pointed to the three inter-twinned triangles above the church door. 'I've seen that carving in a few places. Do you know what it signifies?'

'That the Valknut, the knot showing the transition from life to death.'

'So, it's a pagan symbol. That's fascinating..' but the man interrupted, clearly displeased. 'It's Norse not pagan. Before Christianity came to West Hunday we were a Norse people and followed the Norse customs.'

'Apologies' said Fin. 'I didn't mean to offend.'

'Dinnie fash yerself. It's an easy mistake for an outsider to make.' He gave Fin a thin smile.

Fin said 'Well, I'll press on. I want to get up to the lighthouse and back by dinner time.'

'You'll not get into the lighthouse' said the old man. 'It's closed to visitors.'

'Oh, that's pity. Why's that?' asked Fin.

'The laird's busy renovating it. They've been working on it for a few years'.

'That's a pity. Thanks for the background to the carvings. Most appreciated.'

Fin raised his cane by way of acknowledgment and walked on. He walked on past the school, a single storey modern building with a tarmacked playing area, but shortly beyond the school the road petered out into a rough grass track. It was very muddy from the previous day's rain and it was not long before he was forced to turn back. He walked back through the village. He was hoping to see the man he'd spoke to, but he was no-where to be seen. Passing the farmer's field all the silage had disappeared and the cattle were spread out over the field chewing the early spring grass. He trudged on back up to the war memorial. He looked through the names. There were Tullochs, Rendalls and Sinclairs, the same names as had appeared on the tombstones in the church yard, but he could not see any Bransons. The benefit of the ruling class. The lighthouse stood inviting in the distance but his leg was starting to trouble him and he decided instead to make his way back down to the observatory. Half way back down the road towards the causeway he thought he saw in the distance Eric Branson's SUV down by the ferry pier. He pulled out his binoculars for a closer look. A man he assumed was Eric was leaning against the car and talking to two other figures. He was too far away to be sure but he thought it was Laurel and Hardy from the ferry.

When he got back down to the bay in which the observatory stood, he decided not to go straight back but to take a stroll instead along the beach. He struggled over a rusted farm gate and down onto the soft white sand. Leaning back against a stone dyke he opened up his day pack and took out his flask. He poured out some tea into a metal cup, adding some sugar he taken from the breakfast table to sweeten it for an energy boost. It tasted good if not hot and he dunked in a digestive biscuit. The tide was in and the water shimmered crystal blue in the light. Holding up his hand to shield himself from the sun, he relaxed and took in the view. There was a small fishing boat bobbing around on the horizon with men working on the stern but otherwise all was quiet. After a few minutes he thought he saw a dark shadow moving in the water. He looked again and a head, not unlike Sammy's, bobbed up above the water. It was a seal. It watched him for a moment and then dived down. A minute of so passed and the seal reappeared, again watching him, but this time closer into the shore. Then he saw another head appear and then another. Now there were perhaps four or five seals watching him. They did not seem afraid but, rather, curious. He whistled and they picked their heads up. He idly watched their heads bobbing with the soft swell of the water. Occasionally they would dive down only to reappear after a minute or so in a different position. This went on for some time until eventually the animals lost interest and disappeared out of view. The sun was warm on this face and he suddenly felt tired from his walk and the sea air. He decided it was time to go back up to the observatory for a rest ahead of dinner. Packing up his flask he started to make his way back along the beach, the going tough in the yielding sand. Suddenly there was a flash by his shoulder that took him by shock. Instinctively he waved his cane above his head. He looked up but couldn't see anything in the sun. With a whoosh, a black shadow fell across him and he crouched down. This time, he saw what it was – a bonxie dive-bombing him. He picked up pace as best he could and made his way up off the beach the skua gradually losing interest. He was glad finally to reach the observatory and to take a rest on his bunk bed, the rest quickly turning into an afternoon snooze.

***

He woke with a start. He must have been asleep for a couple of hours. He quickly threw some water over his face and rushed over to the dining hall. There a slightly different crowd tonight, the four birders from last night having departed and been replaced by two newcomers. He took his usual seat. There was no sign of Sir Rolf tonight but the three girl volunteers were all present as was Eric Branson. As before there was no sign of the two men he'd seen earlier down at the pier with Tom.

'Did you have a good day?' Eric asked him.

'Excellent thanks Tom' he replied. 'The island has a wonderful atmosphere and it was such a fine day. I spent some time up at the old kirk. Such a fascinating building. I didn't realise the island had such strong Norse connections.'

'Yes, we are Norse first and foremost. Most of the families on the island have lived here for generations and can trace their roots back to their Viking ancestors.'

'I'm hoping tomorrow to get up and about the north of the island.'

Eric said 'Sounds good, but we can't promise you the same weather. It blows in and out.' He noticed an empty space opposite Fin. 'We seem to be one short.'

'Is your father not joining us tonight' asked Fin.

'Arr.. no' said Eric 'he's a little under the weather but we have another guest off this morning's plane. Lydia', he asked one of the volunteers, 'could you pop up to her room perhaps. Don't want the food to go cold do we.'

Lydia pushed back her chair to get up but at that moment a young woman came into the room and sat down opposite Tom. Fin twitched and felt himself involuntarily taking a deep breath. It was Rebecca.

Eric said 'Arr.. there you are Miss. McHaig. Super. Now we're all present and correct, I hope everyone's hungry. Let's thank the Lord before we eat' and he lowered his head and recited the Selkirk grace. With an amen, he banged the table and Fulla and Frigga, presumably waiting outside for their cue, made their entry with a huge joint of lamb ready for carving.

'Hi' said Rebecca, looking Fin straight in the face and offering him some bread 'I'm Becky. Are you here for the birding as well.' Fin looked her in the eye and after a pause he was sure must have been noticed by the table said 'No, I'm just sightseeing. You must have arrived on the morning flight?'

'That's right' replied Becky, 'it was a spur of the moment decision.'

'I like to plan these out' he said 'I always think it is so risky deciding to do things off the cuff.'

'But then you can lose out' she replied.

'Well I hope you have a rewarding time' he said. 'Do you like the bread. I believe it's made from bere barley. Is that right Eric?'

Eric Branson, busy carving up the leg of lamb, said 'Yes, grown right here on the island the way it always has been.'

Fin now had his dinner in front of him and he was grateful to be able to start eating, both because he was hungry and more importantly because he was struggling to think of something more to say. Surely their little charade was obvious to everyone. He was sure he was sweating. Becky however seemed immune from his concern and had already started up a conversation with Yulia and Anya and they were laughing as she recanted a story for them about her bumpy flight over to the island.

Fin concentrated on his dinner.

'You're quiet tonight Fin', said Eric from the end of the table. 'Have you been worn out with our wonderful weather?' He gave him a big grin. 'Perhaps I can introduce you to Mrs. Gillespie here' he said indicating one of the two incomers. 'She's a birding widow so you'll have something in common. Maybe, you can couple up tomorrow' he added 'Clive here can then have a free day in one of the hides.'

'Yes' that would nice, said Fin, nodding a smile to Mrs. Gillespie 'wondering how he would manage to ditch the poor cow in the morning. 'What's the weather due to be like?'

Eric said 'The forecast is good, but it's never terribly reliable so I can't guarantee it.'

After dinner, there was the usual split of folk with Fin making for the bar. He waited for Becky to join him but she sat with the volunteers chatting away. After a couple of Corncrakes to add to his bar tab, he decided to put in for the night and took his leave.

Back in his room he tried again to call Mrs. Maclean to check on Sammy but as with last night there was no signal.

He was already in his bed when there was a tap on the door. 'Just a minute' he called, 'trying to pull a t-shirt over his head'. With it half on, Becky stepped in and closed the door looking down beside him struggling with the garment. 'Well, well, Mr. Tulloch, so your investigations turned nothing up did they? Just decided to have a wee holiday up here did you? Bullshit! You know full well something's up. Well I'm here now as well and us two are going to get to the bottom of it.'

'Listen Becky, there is no 'us two' about it. I want to see you on the first plane off here in the morning. I'm not sure what's going on here, but I do not want you around blowing things for me. You'll just hold me back.'

'Hold you back. What you and your gammy leg. Don't make me laugh. I'm staying right here.'

Fin sighed. 'Listen, let's discuss it in the morning. In the meantime, whatever you do make sure no-one knows we know one another.'

'What you do take me for? An amateur?' she said.

Fin gave the smallest of smiles. 'Aye, a fecking amateur like me. Oh, and you'd better call me Fin rather than Mr. Tulloch.'

'Ok Fin, but from now on I want us to share what we find. I'm sure something bad has happened to Offie and I need to find out what it is.'

She was out the door as quickly as she came in.

He sat on his bed thinking. It was bad enough when he only had himself to worry about. Now, he was responsible for Becky too. He would need to persuade her to get off the island as soon as he could.

Monday 16 April

Through early for breakfast, Fin was surprised to find Becky already there, sitting with Mr. and Mrs. Gillespie, and tucking into a bowl of porridge. 'Hi' she said. 'Mr. Tulloch is it?'. A career on the stage clearly beckons, thought Fin. 'Please call me Fin' he replied. 'I'll do that' she said with a smile. Eric Branson arrived with Yulia and Anya in tow. He assumed that Lydia must already have left for the day on her bicycle.

'Mr. Tulloch' said Eric 'You're keen to check your ancestry, is that not so? A good start would be Old Billy Halfway. He'll be able to tell you all about the Tullochs.'

'Oh, call me Fin please. Is Billy… sorry I didn't catch his surname, related to them?'.

'No, he's a Tulloch himself. The oldest one on the island. In days gone by you see, there were so many of them you couldn't go by folks' surnames but instead you referred to where they lived or perhaps what job they had. Billy lives at Halfway, so he's called Billy Halfway. There's also Bill Ness and his son Bill Pierhouse. There all Tullochs.'

'Right, I get you. I can see that would make sense on such a small island.'

'Aye, there are only really four family names across the whole island. There's the Tullochs, the Rendalls and the Sinclairs, and of course, the Bransons. We've all been here for generations.'

'Is it right the Branson family owns the whole island?'

'Nobody owns West Hunday Fin. We are simply its guardians and holding it in trust for future generations'.

'That's a nice way to look at it' said Mrs. Gillespie.

'Anyway' said Eric 'I thought perhaps Mrs. Gillespie here might be interested in going up to Billy's with you. He's a real character. That would then allow Yulia and Anya to take Mr. Gillespie and young Miss. McHaig here up to the nets to check out the morning's activity.' Before Fin could reply, Mr. Gillespie jumped in 'That would be great. You'd like that wouldn't you dear.' Mrs. Gillespie did not look overly excited but nodded her agreement.

'If I could trouble you' said Eric 'I need to let Billy have this.' He handed over a small parcel.

'Sure, no problem' said Fin, putting the parcel in his inside pocket.

So, after breakfast Fin cleared away the mess from the front seat of campervan, helped in Mrs. Gillespie, dressed in her best holiday gear, and off they trundled up the island following the sketch Eric Branson had provided to show where his Billy Halfway lived, which was basically half way up the island. Eric assured them that he had spoken to Billy the evening before and he would be expecting them.

'So, are you up here for a few days' asked Fin.

Mrs. Gillespie sighed. 'Yes, Clive drags me along to these types of God-forsaken places about twice a year trying to tick of his list. I get me revenge though and make him come with me for a week to Tenerife. It's good for you to pass the time with me, otherwise I'd be stuck down at the observatory all day failing to get any WiFi.'

'His list?'

'His list of birds he's not seen. That's what it's all about you know. Ticking off different breeds. It would be simpler if he'd taken up train spotting.'

'Sorry, I'm not a birdwatcher myself. Can't tell a sparrow from a starling.'

'Good for you' laughed Mrs. Gillespie 'Me neither. Mr. Branson said that you were researching your ancestry?'

'That's right. The Tullochs are an Orkney family so I thought I would see if I could do some digging.'

'It sounds like a bit of a long-shot. Should you not have started at the National Registers?'. Mrs. Gillespie did not sound persuaded by his story. 'Oh, look' she said 'a lighthouse. How charming.'

Fin decided it would need to tread carefully with Mrs. Gillespie.

Billy Halfway's cottage lay on the far eastern side of the island along a rutted track. At first sight it looked completely dilapidated but as they got closer they saw a thin line of smoke rising from a chimney. There was a rusted-up tractor outside the cottage, its front wheel missing and sitting on a pile of stones and various other rubbish strewn around. A broken down wall enclosed what at one time must have been a vegetable garden. More rubbish has been dumped amongst the weeds along with dozens of broken lobster creels. Billy was clearly not one for throwing anything away. The cottage itself had a traditional stone slab roof, with ropes stretched over and weighted down with boulders and fishing floats. The paintwork had seen better days with a couple of panes of glass bordered-up.

Fin knocked on the door but there was no reply. He tried peering through a window but could not see anyone, other than a clutter of cups and plates on a kitchen table. He was about to walk around to the back when suddenly a large black dog came running up barking loudly. Mrs. Gillespie yelped and jumped behind him with surprising speed.

'Dinnie worry yersel. He'll naw do you any harm' a voice shouted followed by an ancient and stooped old man from around the side of the cottage. 'Mitch, come here!' The dog turned at his master's voice and stopped barking, but keeping up a low growl and a narrowed eye on the two strangers.

Like the mean yesterday at the village, he was dressed in a white uncollared shirt with a waist coat. He wore a cap and boasted a long white beard. When he opened his mouth to smile at them his few remaining teeth were black and rotten. He was carrying a shotgun down by his side.

Mrs. Gillespie instinctively took a step back, keeping her eye on the gun.

'Och, don't worry. I just back from rabbiting.' He hung up two dead rabbits by a hook on the side of the crofthouse.

Fin stepped forward. 'Good morning. I'm Fin Tulloch'. He shook the old man's gnarled hand. 'This here is Mrs. Gillespie. We're both staying at the bird observatory and Mr. Branson said you might be able to help me with some research I'm doing.'

'Aye, he mentioned that. I'm Billy. You'll come away in and I'll make you some tea.'

Old Billy lead them into his cottage. Fin, although not a tall man by today's standards, had to bend his head to pass under the door. It was dark and smokey inside with the small windows letting in only a little light despite the brightness of the day. They were in a single room with a rough stone floor. At one end of the room there was a curtain covering what Fin knew from books he'd read was a box bed, although he'd never seen one in use. At the other side of the room, separately by a large kitchen table, was an old caste iron range. Billy busied over to it and put a pan on top of the range to boil.

'Will you no take a seat' he said to Mrs. Gillespie pointing to a kitchen chair and wiping a cloth over it. The dog had already curled up on the sole armchair but was still growling quietly.

Mrs. Gillespie sat down, keeping close watch on the dog.

'Have you always lived here Billy?' asked Fin. Billy was busing puffing on a roll-up. He pointed with the cigarette to the corner, scattering ash all over the floor.

'I was born in that bed over there' said Billy, pointing to the curtained box bed. 'I've never been off the island since, if you except my service in the war.' The Second World War assumed Fin, although from the look of Billy, it could equally have been the Boar War.

'And you've never put in an electricity supply' asked Fin, noticing the gas light on the table.

'Never had the need. I've a generator in the shed at the back, but no need for the mains. Of course, you'll know that there's only been a mains supply on the island the last twenty years or so once they'd laid the cable. Even now, it still fails all the time. More hassle than its worth. I make do with my range for heating and I take my water from the well the way my father did.'

He brought the tea over, giving the table-top first a wipe with the same cloth. The tea was black with a scum around the top. He then bent down and with the same cloth wiped the floor. 'Bloody Mitch. Always pishing on the flair.' He produced a rusty tin and offered Mrs. Gillespie a biscuit. 'Err, I'll pass' she paid 'I've just finished my breakfast.' Old Billy broke a biscuit in half and threw one piece to the dog, which it gobbled up, dunking the second half in his tea. He sat with this legs crossed, the top one twitching away.

'So, Mr. Tulloch, you're here to find out about your ancestors. What makes you think they came from West Hunday?'

'I'd understood it was an old Orcadian name. I am not sure there's any specific linkage to the island, but I'm keen to learn about the family's history.'

Old Billy looked carefully at Fin's face. He took another drag on his cigarette. 'I cannie see any of the Tullochs in yer, but then again, perhaps living on the mainland so long might have changed the way yer look'.

He took out an ancient dusty leather book from a drawer in a dresser and opened it to a hand-written family tree. 'This shows the Tulloch family all the way back to 1700. There's no records I know before then. The first Tulloch was Dag Tulloch who was a crofter and smithy here shown on the 1723 parish census. At that time the family lived down in Wester Hope but by the next census in 1760 they're shown as being up here in Ness. There's family still living there to this day.'

'Why would they have moved' asked Fin.

'There's no record of that but the laird would have had the right to move them on' said Billy.

'You mean the Bransons.'

'Aye, the Bransons bought the island from a Stuart after the 1745 rising. Well I say 'bought'. More accurately, they'd fought on the King's side against the Jacobites whereas of course the Stuarts fought for Prince Charlie so I suspect there would not have been such option but to let them have it. Anyways, the Bransons have been here ever since and still hold sway over the island.'

'Does that include your cottage?'

'Aye, this cottage goes with the croft. I'm just a tenant and the laird could kick me off here any time he chooses if I fail to work the croft to the required standard.'

'That's terrible' said Mrs. Gillespie. 'After all the time your family have lived here.'

'That's just the way crofting works. As long as you work the croft the laird cannie nowadays move you on, but once you're too old like me to work the land, you're at his beck and call. Not that I'm complaining like, you'll understand. The Bransons have not been bad for West Hunday. They've put a lot of money into the island over recent years, what with building yon observatory and the renovation work up at the lighthouse. The problem with an island like this is the lack of young folk. They all want the bright city lights these days.'

'Yes' said Fin 'I heard that there were only three children now at the school.'

'Aye' said Old Billy 'they're the twins, must be seven by now. There a rum pair. They're Tullochs you know. Moira and Bill Hosta. They live on the farm on the right as you go into the village. Oh, and wee Col. His father has one of the crabbing boats. Still, there's a couple of babbies on the way I hear so perhaps things are looking on. Anyways, you want to learn about the Tullochs no. I'd suggest you go up to the kirk. There a set of island records there with all of the names listed.'

Billy took another puff. 'The young laird said that you'd have a package for me.'

'Oh yes'. Fin reached into his pocket and handed over the parcel Eric Branson had given to him yesterday. Billy's face brightened as he took it. 'That's the boy.'

He added 'If you and your wife would like to join me for some lunch you'd be very welcome. I'll be heating up some broth'

'Oh, said Mrs. Gillespie, we're not married.'

'Never mind' said Old Billy 'hopefully he'll make a good woman of you one day'. Mrs. Gillespie blushed a crimson read. 'No, you don't understand' she said digging a deeper hole 'I am married but not to Mr. Tulloch.'

Fin stood, saying 'Thanks very much for you time, Billy. We'll pop down to the church and see what we can discover down there.'

'Well, it was good to meet you. I hope you find something useful in the records. Now, if you'll excuse me I've got work I need to be doing.'

Billy was up on his feet ushering them out the door.

'Good heavens' said Mrs. Gillespie as they set off in the VW, 'I think he got quite the wrong impression about us.'

'Never mind' said Fin laughing 'it will give him plenty to gossip about for the rest of the day. Now, let's try to find these island records.'

***

The church was quiet inside with not a soul about. He spent a few minutes looking over the stone slabs engraved with the Branson family names whilst Mrs. Gillespie examined the elaborate carvings.

'I had never expected to find anything like this on such a small island' she said, lighting a votive candle and placing it before the statue of the Madonna.

'Yes, it shows the power and wealth the Branson family must have had at one time to build this.'

'No, this was here centuries before them.' She went on 'The carvings are all pagan in origin. I think Norse.'

'I was told off earlier by a gentleman when I used the that word.'

'What, pagan? Well, they're certainly not Christian. I suspect that when the church was originally founded, the islanders still retained a lot of their pagan customs. Look up there' she pointed to a wall carving, 'do you see the thing that looks like a swastika?'

He nodded. She looked pleased to correct him. 'It's no such thing. It's a Norse symbol signifying the four seasons.'

'How you know so much?' he asked.

'I studied Anglo Saxon history at university. There's more to me than being married to Clive you know.'

'I thought all these islands were Presbyterian' he said.

'Oh, that came much later. I think there's a few islands still Catholic. Perhaps being so remote, the Reformation did not quite make it this far.'

'It is amazingly well preserved' he said admiring the interior.

'Do you think they might have preserved some of their Norse beliefs?' she asked but he hadn't time to answer as they were disturbed by the church door opening. The sun burst in followed by a man wearing the traditional island garb.

'Hello' he said. 'You'll be Mr. Tulloch. Billy Halfway said you'd be here. I'm Bill Ness. Old Billy said you'd were for after looking at the parish records as you're a Tulloch yourself.'

'If that would be possible' said Fin 'I would be really grateful. I'm trying to trace if any of my ancestors came from the island.'

'There kept in the vestry. Come on through and I will see what I can find.' He led them through to a small room at the back of the church. Pulling out a large black key he opened up an ancient wooden cabinet. There were several volumes stretched across its shelves

'Here you are. Just shut the vestry door when you're finished and I'll lock up later.'

Fin spent the next half hour or so on the charade of trawling through the parish records looking for fictitious ancestors. Mrs. Gillespie seemed quite happy about this and chatted on about the interior of the church. They then wandered around the grave yard looking at the tomb stones. What struck him was how many recent ones there were and how old the people had been when they died. Each grave stone was decorated with some form of Norse engraving. Eventually he suggested a return to the observatory for a bite of lunch.

'Are you sure you have everything you need?' she asked 'only you haven't made any notes.'

'Yes, thanks. I might pop back another day if I need some details.' She was worryingly observant he thought.

As they drove back down the road from the ruined laird's house towards the observatory, Eric Branson rushed by them in his SUV, waving but forcing Fin to pull over onto the grass verge to avoid a collision.

'You'd have to wonder what anyone would be in a hurry for here' he mumbled under his breath as he pulled back onto the road.

***

Fin and Mrs. Gillespie had just finished enjoying a hearty bowl of leek and potato soup with a warm crusty roll when Eric Branson arrived back with Becky and Mr. Gillespie. 'How was the birding' asked Mrs. Gillespie of her husband 'did you see anything interesting.'

'A pair of Garganey on the loch but nothing else of note dear' said Mr. Gillespie, 'but there's always tomorrow. How was your morning?'

'Oh' she said, I had a very interesting morning with Mr. Tulloch and the lovely weather was an added bonus. Old Billy is a real character and I certainly know a lot more about West Hunday than I did this morning. The church is absolutely awesome. You'll need to check it out.'

'Yes dear, that sounds good.' Mr. Gillespie did not sound convinced.

'And what about you Mr. Tulloch' said Eric Branson 'did you discover anything about your relatives?'.

'Billy was very helpful I thanks' said Fin. 'He obviously knows a huge amount about the island and was able to point me in direction of the island records held up at the church.'

'It's an amazing building' said Mrs. Gillespie. 'I'm surprised it's not more famous. I'm sure it would be a real tourist draw.'

'I think the islanders would prefer to keep it how it is' said Eric. 'They have a deep traditional faith.'

'Do the church authorities not mind about all the..' Fin struggled for the correct word '…. non-Christian symbolism.'

'All faiths are essentially the same' explained Eric. 'We are look to understand life, death and renewal. Why cannot one learn from another?'

Becky butted in 'What's your plan for this afternoon?'

'Oh, I think I might just take it easy and have a walk along the beach.'

'If you're doing that, then I might trail along' she said. 'I'm all birded out for one day.'

'Great' said Fin 'I'll see you out the front in an hour or so once I have had a wee rest. That'll give you time for some of Frigga's lovely soup.'

***

Fin was waiting for Becky at the front of the observatory when she appeared. 'Did you have a good morning pretending to learn about your ancestors?'

'Riveting, did you enjoy learning about ornithology.'

'Well, the thing is Fin. I have a real interest in bird watching. I imagine you know diddly sqwat about your ancestors.'

'And where does your ornithological knowledge come from?'

'From Offie actually. We used to go out together birding when she was at uni. I got quite into it in fact. We loved to go camping up at the RSPB centre at Loch Leven.'

'Did Offie give you your pendant? It looks Orcadian.'

She instinctively twisted her finger around it. 'She bought it for my eighteenth in a wee shop in Stockbridge that sells jewelry made in Orkney. I liked it so much I bought her the same one for Christmas last year.'

Fin and Becky had been strolling down the track from the observatory in the afternoon sun and were now at the gate down to the beach. The tide was out again, and although the weather was not quite up to yesterday's standard, it was still very pleasant with a light on-shore breeze, soothed by the sound of the waves softly breaking onto the beach. They walked together down to the shoreline and Becky took off her boots and rolled up the legs of her jeans to paddle in the sea. She picked up a stone and flicked it across the smooth surface. 'Hey, three bounces!' She flicked some water up at Fin.

'Hey? Watch it madam.' He thought how young she was.

She flicked more water at him. 'Does Eric Branson not weird you out?' she asked. 'He sure gives me the creeps. And what about those two girls? It's like they straight off Amish central casting.'

'How far on do you think Fulla is?'

'I've no idea but at least six or seven months by the size of her.'

They walked on a bit. Fin pointed out into the water. 'Look there. Do you see?'

'Oh yes' said Becky excitedly, 'it's a seal. Look! There's another one.'

'Yes, there just like nosey dogs aren't they. Can you see their whiskers? You could spend all day watching them.'

'Did you know the islands are full of them up here, since they've restricted the in-shore fishing. No competition you see and no culling.'

'There two types aren't there. Do you know which is which?'

'Yeah, that's a 'common'. They differ from the 'greys' as their heads are smaller. The greys have the big Roman noses. They call seals selkies up here. They used to believe they could turn themselves into human form. They would then mesmerize young men with their beauty and entice them onto the rocks. Of course, they wouldn't let them go and the men would turn into selkies themselves.'

'Yeah, I know a few girls who've treated their guys like that. What have you found out?'

Fin recounted his couple of days on the island. He felt he was starting to see the pieces of a jigsaw but was not yet sure how they went together.

'So, you haven't heard anyone mention Offie?'

'No, nothing yet. Perhaps now you're here you can try to get something out of the volunteers. I don't want you doing anything rash mind you.'

'Don't worry, I'm not stupid.'

'I know you're not Becky, but something's not right here and I don't want you taking any risks. Let's wander back. We don't want anyone becoming suspicious over what an old man and a young girl have got so much to talk about.'

They turned to make their way back along the shore line. In the distance a man stood in the middle of a ploughed field. He was holding a cubbie and sowing seed. 'Look over there' said Fin. 'That will be bere barley he's sowing. They call in 90 day barley up here because it grows so quickly. That's what the bread at the observatory is made of.'

'He looks a good age' said Becky.

'Aye, there's no young folk I've seen up here apart from the volunteers at the observatory.'

'It must be a hard life being a crofter up here. How do you think they manage?'

'I've no idea. It seems almost feudal to me. It's all if time's stood still and we were over a hundred years back. But I guess it all that the folk here are used to. I doubt some of them have ever been off the island.'

'It's the youngsters that amaze me. I can't believe they want to stay here.'

'Well I guess it's all they used to.'

'I suppose so, but what do they do to pass the time? No shops, no television, no WiFi. I would go nuts living here.'

'Well I think Fulla found something to do to fill in the time.'

***

At dinner Sir Rolf was still missing but Eric put in an entrance and afterwards conducted the daily bird count in his usual flamboyant manner. 'We've a new couple of new faces here tonight. 'Rebecca' he pointed out Becky to the room, 'any interesting migrants or visitors to report young lady?'

'I'm afraid not' said Becky, 'but I'm hoping to get out and about tomorrow, weather permitting'.

'Well, we'll looking forward to hearing from you then' said Tom smiling at her.

Mr. Gillespie had bought Fin a beer for looking after this wife in the morning and Fin felt obliged to take a seat next to them. Mr. Gillespie then spent the next hour or so boring for Britain by relaying his time in the bird hide. No wonder she wanted to come with me thought Fin. He felt obliged to reciprocate with drinks for the Gillespies and was relieved when Mrs. Gillespie made her excuses and departed for her room. 'I'd better step out myself' said Fin. 'I need to speak to someone at home. 'Oh, don't bother' said Mr. Gillespie, 'there's no signal at all. Eric said it's likely to be down for some days. Something to do with the weather.'

'Never mind' said Fin 'I'll still give it a go.'

When he stepped outside into the dark, he found Becky rolling a cigarette. 'I didn't know you smoked?'

'Purely herbal'.

'Be careful. I've known friends to start with a little weed and then get sucked in.'

She sighed. 'Thanks for the advice grandpa. What's your plan for tomorrow?'

'I'm going to catch the morning flight over to Kirkwall. I want to do some digging there to find out more about the observatory. I'll catch the evening plane back so should be back in time for dinner. What's are you up to?'

'Lydia has offered to take me on her bird census. She's on zone 4 up the top of the island.'

'That's good. See if you can learn anything about why Offie left, but be careful.'

'I'm not daft Fin.'

'I know you're not.'

She took a puff on her joint and offered it to him. He shook his head.

'I need to take a more in-depth look up the north of the island myself.'

'Perhaps we can have a run up tomorrow evening then' and with that she stubbed out her half-smoked roach and disappeared back into the observatory.

Fin watched her go. He has an uncomfortable feeling that it was not only his eyes in the dark that there watching.

Tuesday 17 April

Fin's planned trip to Kirkwall evaporated as soon as he woke in the morning. There was no blue sky this morning but instead a thick haar which had drifted in off the sea overnight and now covered the island like a blanket. Stepping out from the bunkhouse he could hardly make out the bay below the observatory. A change of plan was called for, but, first of all, he needed a hearty breakfast to power him up for the day.

He tapped on Becky's bedroom door as he went past but there was no answer. Over at the observatory, he was again last in for breakfast. He asked where everyone was and was told by Frigga that they were all already out for the day. She asked if she could make him up a packed lunch today and he said that would be good. He decided over a bowl of thick porridge and jam and his first cup of tea of the day to drive up to the village and then see if he could walk along by the side of the coast to the lighthouse.

Parking up by the church, he stepped out and was struck by the strong sea smell, the absence of any wind holding it over the island. The mist still shrouded the coastline and although it was not yet raining the cloud was very low in the sky and the sea an ominous grey. It was also colder without the sun from the day before and Fin shivered in the chill of the morning air. He couldn't believe the change from the day before. Looking up and down the village road there was nobody to be seen.

The tide was the furthest in he'd seen it, coming right up to a thin strip of shingle and making a low rattling noise as the waves rolled over. The going was tougher than he'd anticipated as he crunched across the stones and he welcomed the occasional interruption of larger slabs of stone from which presumably in the past the roofs of the island cottages had been quarried. The slabs were however wet and slimy with thick strands of kelp across them, and he struggled to hold his balance across them with his cane as he dodged between rock pools. Around the top of the island rocks led out to a spit and as he got closer he saw it was covered with seals. As Fin approached a number bumbled off the rocks into the water although some braver individuals stayed put and starred him out.

Fulmers nested under the stone dyke which separated the shore line from the neighbouring fields, whilst cormorants and shags sat idling on the sea rocks. Fin pushed on, resting only briefly for a swift cup of tea from his flask. The going remained tough and he decided to branch inland cutting across the fields. He soon regretting the decision as his boots sank into the wet ground and his trousers became soaked off the long grass. Eventually he reached the island road and he was able to walk along on the tarmac.

He was relieved when he finally reached the very top of the island. Looking out he thought he could make out the shadow of a large tanker off-shore but the mist was too think for him to be sure. Otherwise there was just an endless expanse of grey. He carefully crossed over the cattle grid he'd passed on his first day and then down across the links to the shore line. There was slightly more breeze up here and he hoped that it might allow the haar to lift.

He walked along the shore-line and the bird hide in which he'd sheltered eventually appeared out of the mist. He pushed the door open but it was cold and empty inside. Looking around there was no sign of either Becky or any of the volunteers. He pulled the door shut. He pressed on along the coastline though the haar for a few hundred yards and without warning came upon a fence. It must have been about six feet high and it reached down across the rocks and towards the sea, disappearing into the mist. Following its line inland he came to a sign reading '*Strictly Private and Confidential – Keep Out*'. He followed the fence further inland until he reached the gate across the track he'd encountered on his first day. It was closed but a padlock lay to one side. He hesitated for a moment but muttering to himself 'Nothing ventured, nothing gained' pulled it open and started up the track. The lighthouse tower stood directly in front of him at the top of the hill, its highest third invisible in the low cloud. After a few hundred yards he reached its base. It was made of brick with the top half whitewashed black and white. It was not difficult to appreciate what a wonderful engineering achievement it had been for a tower of this height to be built over two hundred years ago in such a remote spot. And for it to be standing today as good as it was when first constructed was truly remarkable.

On the coast side of the tower the ground led up towards the cliff top. There was a concrete path leading up to the cliff edge but in the mist he could not see to where it led. On the land side there was a small cobbled courtyard containing what looked to be two cottages, presumably accommodation for the keepers, and what was likely to be a store house for the coal originally needed to power the light. The light would however now be automated and the keepers' cottages would no longer be required. A SUV with WHBO on the side was parked up by the side of the courtyard. It was eerily quiet. Fin walked across the courtyard, taking out his camera to snap a few photos, trying to look in full tourist mode. There was a solid looking door at the base of the tower but, pulling against its heavy handle, he found it locked. He wandered over to the first of the cottages. He peered into its window but a blind across it was drawn. He tried the door but again it was locked. He started towards the second cottage but was interrupted by a shout.

'Hay you' a voice shouted. 'What do you think you are doing?'

Fin turned to find a man approaching him. It was the one he'd christened Oliver Hardy from the ferry, the first time he'd met him on the island since.

'Sorry, I was just having a look around.'

'You're not allowed here. Did you not see the signs?'

'I'm sorry. What signs? You can't see anything in this fog.'

Oliver Hardy was walking towards him. He stood perhaps a foot over Fin, a real monster of a man. 'I'm afraid you'll need to leave. The public is not allowed up here while we're doing works.'

'I was hoping' said Fin 'to climb up to the top of the lighthouse to take a few photographs. Is that not possible?'

Oliver Hardy was now looming over him. 'There's no access to the tower. Come on – I'll take you back down. You're parked in the village, yes.'

'Err.. yes… thanks…how did you know.'

'Small island…..' The man gestured to the SUV. There was clearly not going to be any discussion. As they turned towards it, Fin saw the curtain of the first cottage twitch and the face of a man peering out for a second, Stan Laurel from the ferry.

Oliver Hardy opened up the passenger door of the SUV for Fin to get in. It was immaculate inside. Clearly whatever renovation work they were doing was not making a mess.

Reaching the gate, Hardy got out, pulled it shut and clicking closed the padlock.

'Do you work for the observatory?' asked Fin.

'Uh?'.

'I noticed the logo on the side of your car.'

'Oh, yeah.' Hardy did not expand.

The man drove him back down to the village in silence, parking up next to Fin's campervan.

'I'll leave you here. Please avoid the lighthouse in future. It's not safe for visitors up there and we wouldn't want you getting hurt.'

'Thanks, and sorry for the trouble' said Fin.

Fin stepped out. The SUV drove past, reversed into the church entrance and then came back past him at speed. He held up his hand to acknowledge Oliver Hardy, who was busy speaking into what appeared to be a mobile phone.

Opening up the VW he was surprised to find that his hand was shaking and he struggled to get the key in the door. In the driver's seat he sat for a moment gazing out to sea. At least he thought he knew where to find the two men from the ferry. Oliver Hardy was well built and looked like he was familiar with the inside of a gym, but for sure he was certainly not a builder. He had been too well dressed and had worn what looked to Fin's untrained eye to be an expensive watch. He had been polite but with an underlying degree of menace. He was not someone Fin looked forward to meeting again.

He sat was a while more and then drove back down to the observatory. He was becoming increasingly worried. Worried because he was out of his depth on an island in the middle of nowhere with no police presence and worried for Becky. Back in his room he tried his phone and still no signal. He thought back to the man at the lighthouse having no problem with his. He flicked through his photographs from the lighthouse, but couldn't decipher anything of interest.

***

He ate his packed lunch in the bunkhouse kitchen, hoping that Becky would be back. With no sign of her, he ventured up to the observatory and found Frigga in the kitchen. He asked her if she'd seen any of the volunteers.

'I'm afraid they all took pack lunches with them today. I'm not expecting any of them back before dinner, although I think that Mrs. Gillespie's in her room I think if you'd like some company.'

'I might try her later thanks' said Fin. 'I don't suppose there's any chance of a pot of tea.'

'Go on through to the lounge and I'll see what I can do.'

When he went through to the lounge he found Mrs. Gillespie sitting by the bay window.

'Hello there. Is Clive out birding?'

'Yes, though I don't know how he's going to see anything in this weather. What have you been up to?'

'Oh, I tried having a look around the lighthouse but no joy. What about yourself.'

'Just here today. Mind up there's been lots of excitement.'

She kept him waiting. 'Go on.'

'Panic stations all round. Frigga was rushing around trying to find Mr. Branson. And when she did, he was running outside and zooming away in his car. I can't believe the speed he went.'

'What do you think it was all about.'

'No idea, but I hear Frigga saying something about an alarm being triggered.'

They were interrupted by Frigga appearing with some tea and shortbread.

'Could I trouble you for an extra cup for Mrs. Gillespie' he asked.

'Oh, don't bother about me. I'm all tea'd out.'

'How do you find the volunteers?' he asked Frigga as she poured the tea. 'It must be difficult with them coming from so many different places.'

'Oh, they're Ok' said Frigga 'they all speak English, some better than me.'

'Do you ever get any locals?'

'Not from Orkney but sometimes we get one from a Scottish college. There was one girl who's just left from....' Frigga trailed off as Eric Branson entered the room, out of breath. 'A quick word please Mr. Tulloch.' He paused as Frigga left.

'Johnny from up at the lighthouse called to say he'd found you wandering around up there. I have to tell you it's really not safe at the moment. We're carrying out major renovation works and some of the buildings are in a dangerous state. So, if you could make sure you avoid that part of the island I'd be really grateful.'

'I'm sorry' said Fin 'I shouldn't have ignored the signs. It's a magnificent structure all the same.'

'Yes' said Eric 'it was built at the turn of the nineteenth century and is one of the tallest lights in the country. We're hoping to create some new holiday accommodation out of the keepers' cottages, but there's still a lot of work to be done.'

'It's a pity it is not possible to climb up to the top of the lighthouse. The views must be fantastic.'

'Yes, they are' said Tom. He paused and then added 'Do you have any plans for this afternoon. If not, Lydia is monitoring the birds down at the hide at Hoy loch and I'm sure she would be happy with some company. The weather looks like lifting so hopefully there should be some good stuff on show. I could give you a lift up there if you wish but you might need to make your own way back as I need to pick up a new guest from the evening flight.'

'Thanks' said Fin 'that sounds good. By the way, I keep trying to get a telephone signal to dial home but I'm having no joy. Do you have any idea when it might be working again?'

Eric Branson laughed. 'I am afraid that's a recurring problem of island life. Perhaps tomorrow. Anyway, I just need to tidy up a couple of things here. Shall I see you in outside in half an hour?' and with that he was gone.

Mrs. Gillespie waited until Eric was out of earshot and then said 'that was you told.'

***

Eric was waiting for Fin in his SUV. It was immaculate like the one at the lighthouse. He bumped off at speed down the track, testing the SUV's suspension.

'Have you lived your whole life on the island?' asked Fin.

'No, when I left university I worked for a bank in the City of London for a few years, but to be frank I couldn't stand it. It was like being a worker bee in an enormous hive. When the economy hit the down-turn I was made redundant and I was happy to come back home. In truth, my heart had never been away from here. I have a duty you know to this island. My father's time will pass soon and I'll need to step into his shoes. We really just hold it in in trust for the next generation.

'I haven't seen your father for a few days. I hope he's not ill.'

'I'm afraid he's not very well. He's nearly ninety you know. At his age, it's better for him to be kept warm inside. He's up at the lodge.'

Fin said 'How many generations of Bransons have there been?'

'My father's the ninth laird and I'll be the tenth' explained Tom. 'My son, if I have one, will be the eleventh.'

'That must be a big responsibility' said Fin.

'It is' said Eric 'the population's getting older all the time and it is becoming more and more difficult to persuade younger folk to stay on the island. The observatory has helped to bring in visitors but we need to be careful it does not change our way of life.'

They had almost reached the path down to the hide and Eric pulled up short of it.

'You see Mr. Tulloch, it's a balance. I want to preserve the beauty and simplicity of the island but I also need to make sure it is a living, thriving community. Now, if you follow the path down to the loch-side you'll see the hide by the reeds. Have a great afternoon and good birding!'

***

Fin wandered down the path. As he did a crowd of robins scattered before him. The weather had cleared slightly from earlier in the day and the top of the lighthouse in the distance was now in view. The same pungent odour as this morning was hanging in the air, presumably derived from seaweed drying on the shore-line as the tide retreated. The island was taking on a different shape. Perhaps, he thought, he had misjudged Eric Branson. When they'd first met he'd thought him a rather ridiculous character, playing the lord of the manor from a bygone age. Maybe however he really did have the best interests of the island and its inhabitants in mind. He has certainly spoken with passion and Fin was sure he was sincere in his views.

Fin tapped on the door of the hide. 'Hello' he said quietly.

Lydia opened it up. 'Oh, hi Mr. Tulloch. What brings you down here?'

'Hello Lydia. Eric suggested I might be of some help with the bird watching. I'm not sure how however as my knowledge of bird life is negligible.'

She smiled. 'Oh, there's plenty I can find for you to do. Come on in. But first, we don't say 'bird watching'. We say 'birding'. I had to learn that when I first came over from Germany.'

'First things first, let's make some coffee or would you like tea' said Lydia and she busied with a small stove in the corner of the hide.

'Tea for me please.'

As Lydia busied herself trying to get the stove lit, Fin asked 'Which part of Germany are you from?' Lydia explained that her family used to live in what was former East Germany but both parents had died when she was young and that she was brought up by an aunt in Cologne where she was now studying nature conservation.

'You're English is really excellent' he said and she smiled, pleased with the compliment.

'Are all the volunteers taken from European universities?'

'They tend to be, although I think that there have also been a few Americans and some English. The problem is that there's only a small group of full time observatories across Europe and placements are very difficult to obtain. West Hunday's great. It's so well organised and is perfectly located as it stands right in the middle of the north/south migration route. It's also the first landfall before the main Orkney isles and as such it picks up lots of unusual strays as they're blown in from across the Atlantic or down from the Artic.'

'The Bransons must have made a big investment to get it established' said Fin.

'Huge, I imagine. It must have cost a fortune. They're very good to the volunteers too. We all get a generous living allowance, as well of course as our food and accommodation being covered. Of course, there's nothing to spend it on here, but it will be useful when I get back to university.'

Fin thought back to the squalor that Old Billy was living in.

'How long are you here for?' he asked.

'I came at the beginning of January and will return home at the end of June.'

'Gosh. That's a long time on a small island with no boys' joked Fin.

'That's the only down-side. The Bransons never take boys as volunteers. I guess they think they will be too much trouble.'

'Are there ever any Scottish volunteers?' he asked causally as he stirred his coffee.

'Yes, sometimes. We had a girl from Edinburgh but she left a few weeks ago.'

'Oh, didn't she like it here?'

'I think she had to go home to look after her mother when she became ill.'

'That's a pity' said Fin. 'Perhaps she will be back.'

'Yes, perhaps' said Lydia, drinking her coffee and starring out across the loch.

Lydia explained to Fin that they were to record the birds as they came in to roost in the loch as the evening arrived and the light failed. He gave Fin a section of the loch to monitor and a quick lesson in how to count the birds and as to what breeds to expect. It all went over Fin's head but he said he would do his best. In the event, he was surprised how much he enjoyed spending the afternoon watching the waterfowl on the loch and quietly chatting away.

Eventually the light began to fade and geese and other birds started to arrive for the night. He was surprised to see how quickly everything happened with the loch and its banks soon filled with noisy bird-life. Occasionally Lydia would point out to him an interesting arrival and by the time the hide was in semi-darkness, he was tired with the effort of concentration.

'Ok, she said. Now we can pack up and take our notes back to the observatory' she said. 'You'll be hungry after all your hard work. I hope Frigga and Fulla have something good in store for us.'

Going outside the hide, he was surprised at how dark it was. Lydia produced a powerful head torch from her back pack and slowly they made their way back up the path to the road. When they got to the top, two bikes rested against the stone wall. 'I see Eric left you some transport' said Lydia 'can you manage a bike with your leg.' Fin said he was game and carefully balancing his walking can across the handlebars, he mounted the first bike he had been on in probably the last forty years. He gently rolled down the road and over the causeway, free-wheeling almost all the way to the start of the track up to the observatory. Lydia said to leave the bikes there, and from that point they walked the final few hundred yards up to the lights showing through the sea mist.

'Thanks Lydia, he said when they finally arrived. 'I've really enjoyed that but now I think a beer is in order.'

***

As he walked in to the dining hall the first people Fin saw were Mr. and Mrs. Gillespie. 'Oh, I thought you were leaving on this evening's flight' said Fin. 'No such luck' said Mrs. Gillespie. 'It was cancelled due to the fog.' True enough, thinking back, Fin had not heard the plane overhead.

'Never mind' said Fin 'There could be worse places to be stranded.'

'Perhaps....' said Mrs. Gillespie, giving her husband a look that spoke to the contrary.

Becky was further down the table sitting with the volunteers. They were happily chatting away. Sir Rolf was still missing.

With no new guests to impress, Eric said a simple grace and Fulla and Frigga appeared with the evening's fare. As usual it was good heaty stuff and Fin filled his plate high. He was thinking back to Lydia's comments about how generous the Bransons were and how much the building of the observatory must have cost. Certainly, it was some achievement given that almost all of the materials must have been shipped over from the mainland. The luxury of the observatory, and the food served, contrasted oddly and not comfortably with the appalling living standards of the islanders. If Old Billy was typical, they were still caught in a cycle of poverty better associated with earlier times.

The chat across the table was about today's birding highlights and the weather. Fin was rather disturbed by tall tales of the island being fogged in for weeks at a time.

Just into their main course he heard what appeared to be a disturbance coming from the corridor outside the dining hall. Eric Branson said 'Frigga, can you please see what's up' but as she stood Old Billy came staggering in the room on uncertain legs He grabbed onto the edge of the table, his hands shaking. 'I need my backy. Have you got my backy?' he should down to Eric Branson.

'Now then Billy, you know it's not time for that' said Eric, rising out of his chair.

Frigga took Old Billy by the arm. 'Come on Mr. Tulloch, I'll see what I can find you in the kitchen.' With some persuasion, she managed to guide him out the room.

Mrs. Gillespie was looking aghast. Eric sat down again. 'Apologies for the entertainment. I'm afraid it looks like Bill may have had a wee bit too much of the drink.'

The voices outside died down but Frigga did not return for the remainder of dinner.

On retiring to the bar following dinner, Fin managed to corner Becky at the bar. 'Hello Becky, can I get you a drink'. She accepted and as they carried their drinks back over to a table he said under his breath. 'Let's catch up later and compare notes'.

'OK, shall be do the daily count?' said Eric Branson. As they ran through it Fin found himself paying attention, particularly to Lydia's report and took a small bit of pride from his small input.

Once the count was over, he took himself another beer as usual and settled back to listen to Mr. and Mrs. Gillespie bickering. The evening wore on and Fin felt himself starting to doze. 'You're looking tired' said Mrs. Gillespie. 'Yes, I might just get myself some fresh air and then turn in' he said. Outside in the night air, the temperature had dropped a few degrees and Fin felt himself shivering. He wandered a little way down the track from the observatory to where he could see the light from the end of Becky's cigarette. 'Let's walk on a bit' he said, adding in a whisper 'we may not be the only people out here at the moment.'

Once clear of the observatory and keeping his voice low he said. 'Let's go for a beach walk together to look at the seals after breakfast. It's too suspicious for us to spend time out here together at this time of night.' She gave a slight nod and they turned to back towards the building.

'That sounds really good' said Becky in a slightly raised voice 'glad to hear that you had such an interesting day.'

'See you tomorrow' said Fin as he turned towards the bunkhouse, leaving Becky to go back to the bar.

Wednesday 18 April

Fin was woken by the sounds of birds singing outside his window. Pulling back the curtain the day was dull but the haar was pretty much gone. He checked his watch – 7 a.m. If he hurried he could make the morning plane. So, pulling on his clothes, he made for outside, bumping into Becky on the way. 'I'm going to see if I can get over to Kirkwall this morning' he said, not stopping. The VW eventually kicked into action and he was off bumping down the path from the observatory.

When he arrived up at the airstrip, he found Mr. and Mrs. Gillespie and another couple of islanders already waiting in the tiny waiting room. Eric Branson was also there. 'Oh, morning Mr. Tulloch, are you hoping to catch a ride over to Kirkwall on this morning's flight?'. Fin confirmed he was. 'Let's see if they have any space available.'

Eric Branson picked up a radio phone, which crackled into life. 'West Hun to Kirkwall'. There was a muffled reply. 'Can you take another passenger on the 7.45 am flight to Kirkwall, no luggage, returning to West Hun...' he looked over to Fin, who mouthed *this evening* '... returning on the 18.05?' There was more cracking and then Eric again 'Name – Tulloch, initial F.'

'That's you booked.'

'No tickets?' asked Fin.

'No need for that. Just pay when you land at Kirkwall.'

Fin sat down next to Mr. and Mrs. Gillespie. 'Have you enjoyed your stay?'

'Super, said Mr. Gillespie. We'll be back here next year that's for sure.' Mrs. Gillespie rolled her eyes.

A few minutes later, the radio receiver crackled into life again. Eric lifted it up again 'West Hunday airfield'. After a pause '10 knots south westerly.'

'Ok' said Tom, that's the plane almost here. 'I'll call you through the gate when it's time to board.'

The five passengers tramped outside to stand by a farm gate blocking the way onto the grass airstrip. Old Billy, with Mitch by his side, was there, looking much more with it this morning. 'Morning Bill' said Fin, but Old Billy looked back as if not recognising him.

And then the wee plane was visible, coming in low over the fields. It's engine noise changed and it slowly bumped down towards them as if stalling in the sky. It looked as if it was off course and heading straight for them, but at the last minute it pulled round and landed softly onto the grass. The engine revved back and it taxied on a little before turning one hundred and eighty degrees and pulling up not more than ten yards from where they stood.

Quickly Eric Branson appeared pulling a small trolley. He opened up the rear door to the plane and out clambered a couple of passengers. Their luggage was pulled out of the hold and onto the trolley and they made their way over to the gate.

'Ok folk' called Eric and Old Billy opened up the gate to let them through.

The two islanders were obviously seasoned users of the inter-island plane service and climbed on board taking two seats at the back. Mr. and Mrs. Gillespie climbed on in front of them. 'If you could go around to the front' directed Eric. Fin followed him round to the door next to the pilot and opened it up. 'Morning, you're here next to me.' He climbed on board. He did not like flying at the best of times. He'd never been on such a small plane even in his army days and he'd certainly never had to sit next to the pilot. He tightened up his safety belt as hard as it would go. 'Here, put these on' said the pilot, handing him some head large phones. The pilot started up the propeller.

'Ok, everyone ready?' asked the pilot, looking back in the cabin. There were a couple of nods. 'OK, here we go.' And with that he opened up the throttle and within what seemed like only a few yards they were airborne and climbing out above the sea with a decided lean to the side.

'Are you staying at the observatory?' asked the pilot over the headphones.

'Yes' said Fin, looking down into the choppy water. 'How long is the flight?.'

'About thirty minutes should do it' said the pilot, flicking at a reading on the control panel he apparently did not like. 'I don't think I saw you coming over' he added.

'I caught the ferry' said Fin. 'I'm not so keen on flying.'

'Oh, don't worry. We've not lost a plane yet.' There was a bump of turbulence. Fin was glad he'd not had his breakfast.

Fin had once read that a plane landing was essentially a controlled crash and that certainly seemed to be the way with the Islander. As the sound leading into Kirkwall came into view, the small plane circled round to the airport and the pilot cut back on the throttle. The plane sank down through the air, taking a large dip to one side and then, as if out of the blue, it was brought under control and landed with only the slightest thump.

Fin was relieved to step down onto firm ground. He made his way through a surprisingly modern airport and out to a taxi rank. There were no taxis in sight. There was however a bus a little further forward and hurrying up to it he asked if it went into the town centre. The driver confirmed it did and he climbed on board as its only passenger.

'Where are you wanting to go' asked the driver.

'Somewhere near the Council's office'.

'No problem.'

***

Fin was pleased to find that the Council's headquarters were housed in a series of renovated buildings instead of the usual modern monstrosity so beloved of town planners. He asked for directions to the Planning Department.

'I'm interested in work currently being conducted on West Hunday' he explained to the young woman behind the desk.

'West Hunday you say, and what would you want to know about.'

'I was wondering if it was possible to search the records for planning applications' he said.

'You can do that through the planning portal'.

'Yes, but I am afraid I don't have access to a computer.'

'Oh dear. Well, if you tell me what you're looking for I'll see what I can do. There can't be many applications for over there.'

He explained he was interested in the lighthouse complex.

'It doesn't ring a bell but I if you want to pop back in a couple of hours I'll see what I can find out for you.'

He thanked her, and made his way back through the maze of corridors and onto the street outside.

His next port of call was St Magnus Cathedral. Its spire dominated the town centre. Stepping inside he took in the muted sandstone interior with tones of rose and yellow. There were some beautiful carvings but nothing on a par with the intricacies of the interior of the church on West Hunday. He picked up a guide and wandered down the central aisle. He was interested to read that until the fifteenth century the cathedral had been under the ecclesiastical control of a Norwegian archbishop based in modern day Trondheim. There were however no remaining Norse carvings or symbols he was able to identify. Perhaps any lingering pagan influences had been less strong here on the Mainland or perhaps the Presbyterians had cleaned out anything smacking of idolatry at the time of the Reformation.

'Beautiful, isn't it?'

He turned. A young man was standing next to him. 'Sorry.'

'The stained glass'. The young man looked up to the huge window in front of them.

Fin took in the window for the first time. 'Yes, it is. Do you work here?' he asked.

'I'm a guide so fire away if there anything you want to know.'

'I'm staying on West Hunday. Do you know it?'

'I'm afraid not, but I hear it's very interesting.'

'Yes, it is. I was hoping to learn some more about the church there. It is covered with old Norse carvings.'

'Sounds fascinating. I tell you what. One of our elders is in the cathedral today. I know he's got a keen interest in Orcadian history so he might be your best man.'

'If I could meet him, that would be great.'

'Well, there's a session meeting on at the moment but I think he should be free in about an hour. I could see if he has some spare time then.'

'Thanks'.

'Once you've finished looking around the cathedral why not go into the café and I'll send him over. Who should he ask for?'

'Fin Tulloch. What's his name?.'

The guide smiled. 'That will be easy for you to remember. He's called Findlay Tulloch.'

***

'Mr. Tulloch?' Fin looked up from his seat in the cathedral café. The man before him was not what he'd expected from a church elder. Instead he was faced with a young guy in jeans and a checked shirt, with long hair and an earring.

'Yes, you must be my namesake.'

Findlay sat down with a coffee. 'Can I tempt you with some carrot cake' asked Fin. 'It's very good.'

'I'd better not. I'm supposed to be on a diet. Now, I hear you're interested in the interior of the church over at West Hunday.'

'Yes, have you seen it?'

'I paid a visit about a year ago. From a theological perspective, it's absolutely amazing.'

'I was surprised that the church authorities would be comfortable with it.'

'Oh, the west Hunday church is non-denominational.'

Fin looked puzzled.

'I mean they're not linked to any established creed such as the Church of Scotland or the Catholic Church.'

'Are you sure I can't persuade you to share some cake with me? I'm going to take another slice.'

With a sigh Findlay agreed, and Fin brought back another mug of tea for himself and two pieces of the carrot cake. Taking a mouthful, he asked 'Is that why they've been able to preserve so many of the pagan carvings in the church.'

'I expect so' explained Findlay. 'Here in Kirkwall, a lot of paintings and drawings were white-washed over at the time of the Reformation. But before that I would suspect earlier non-Christian carvings and other symbols would have been removed as the Christian faith took a strong hold. Over on such a remote island as West Hunday, the former faiths and traditions would have retained a stronger presence, and somehow they've then been able to escape later destruction.'

'I believe that the carvings are all Norse in origin.'

'Yes, that fits well with the history of the islands. The old Norse faith shares a lot in common with the later beliefs of life, death and re-birth. It's all part of the same tradition.'

They chatted on for a while and Fin thanked Findlay for his time. It was early afternoon, and Fin wandered down the narrow cobbled high street to the harbour front where Findlay had told him there was an internet café. He went in and, finding himself the sole customer, bought himself a cup of tea and thirty minutes of internet access. From his lesson back in Edinburgh he was now a dab hand and he quickly accessed the Council's website, and from there into the planning portal. He searched for planning permissions affecting West Hunday. There were only a few entries. The earliest related to the construction of the observatory. There was another for the renovation of a farm house and a couple for the construction of domestic wind turbines. All were granted in favour of West Hunday Estate or in other words the Bransons. There was nothing showing for the lighthouse. He tried searching for planning applications but nothing current was revealed.

He tried searching against Sir Rolf Branson but only received an entry giving bare details. Against Eric Branson there were predictably a myriad of entries all to a quick glance irrelevant. Fairly quickly, he gave up.

Outside he sat down on a bench overlooking a small marina and called Mrs. Maclean to check on Sammy. She was pleased to tell him he was absolutely fine, although he had stolen an ice-cream from a man on the beach this morning. Would it be possible, he wandered, for her to hold onto him for another couple of days. 'Of course, he can stay as long as you need' he was relieved to hear. He then made a second call which lasted no more than a couple of minutes, and after that, walked back up through a narrow cobbled street towards the Council's offices on School Place. He passed a book shop and after hesitating went inside.

'I'm interested in lighthouses in the Orkneys' he explained to the assistant behind the counter.

'Oh, we have a good section on Orcadian history. Let's see what's in there.' She took him to a section at the back of the shop and after a few seconds pulled out a large book.

'Here one' she said, handing the book to him. Is this the sort of thing you're after?'

He took the book off her. 'Thanks, I have a look.'

Once she was away, he turned to the index and looked up West Hunday. Pointed to the right pages, he opened a whole chapter dealing with the construction of the lighthouse. What caught his eye were some old black and white aerial shots of the complex. They showed the tower itself and the keepers cottages. Also, however, visible was the path leading down from the complex to cliff edge. Looking closely, he could make out steps leading down to the foreshore below and a jetty pointing out into the sea.'

He put the book back onto the shelf.

'Was it not what you were looking for?' asked the assistant as he made his way past.

'It was exactly what I was after' he said.

She gave him a puzzled look.

He of course already knew that there was nothing to be reported but after the assistant in the Planning Department had made an effort for him, he felt he owed her his attention. He'd bought himself an ice lolly on the way and one for her as a thank you, but arriving at the office, he found she was not there.

'Can I help?' said a man in a suit standing in her place.

'I spoke to a young lady earlier and she kindly agreed to check out some planning history for me?'

'What did it relate to?'

'West Hunday.'

'I see. Well, we can't disclose that sort of information without a written application.'

'Oh' he paused.

'And sir, there's no food allowed in here'. The man in the suit pointed to the ice lolly.

A young woman interrupted. 'Mr. Tulloch, you're wanted in the back office.' The man in the suit gave him a curt nod and left.

Fin had the feeling that his request for information had been less than welcomed.

***

He was back at the airport in plenty of time for the flight back to the island. He checked in at the inter-island desk. The airport worker checked his name against a hand-written list in a large hard-backed diary by the desk and asked him to be back at the desk ten minutes before the flight was due to leave.

'I see you still use a manual diary' said Fin.

'Aye. It's more reliable than a computer.'

'Do you list everyone flying in and out?'

The woman gave him a slightly puzzled look. 'Yes, we don't issue tickets so we have to keep a note of who is booked on each flight.'

'That's a very neat system. I'll see you again just before six.'

He retreated to the airport café and bought himself a copy of the local paper and another cup of tea. From where he sat he had a clear view of the inter-island desk. There was very little activity. His plane was due at six and there was only his name and one other on the list. There was nothing scheduled before then. Half an hour passed and the woman at the inter-island desk, stood up and walked over past him and into the toilets. He casually made his way over to her desk. The black hard-back diary sat in a corner. He glanced around but no-one was paying him any attention. He took a deep breath, picked it up and flicked through until he reached the entry for 15 March. From what he understood from Becky, Offie had definitely still been on the island then. As quickly as possible, he ran his finger down the daily list of names. About a minute later, he'd reached 15 April and there was no sign of her name. He may have missed in in his rush but was pretty confident it was not there. Of course, she could have taken the ferry back but that seemed very unlikely when she didn't have a car to transport.

'Sorry, can I help you sir?'

He turned, startled. The woman from the inter-island desk was standing right behind him.

'Oh, sorry, I was wondering if I could check availability for another date.'

Giving him a skeptical look, she took hold of the diary. 'Yes?'.

'Sorry?'

'The date?'

'Oh. 30 May.'

She flicked through. 'Sorry, but the West Hunday plane is fully booked that date.'

'Never mind. Thanks for checking.'

He retreated again to his seat in the café area. She kept an eye on him until his flight was called.

He was only one of two passengers flying out, the other a birder from the States who looked decidedly fidgety when he saw the size of the plane. 'Don't worry' said Fin 'they haven't lost one yet.'

This time around he was able to enjoy the flight more and watched out as the plane skimmed low over the small islands, the houses, roads and occasional cows all clearly visible, until it turned west out over the ocean, before picking out West Hunday as a pinprick on the horizon. The plane circled over the village before turning in towards the airstrip and landing with a bump on the grass. It taxied up to the tiny terminal building and the pilot killed the engine. A moment or two later, his door opened and Eric Branson helped him down. 'Welcome back, Fin, if you wait by the gate I'll give you a lift back down to the observatory' and turning to the second passenger 'You must be Steve North. Welcome to West Hunday Mr.North. I'll sort your luggage and drive you down to the observatory.'

As Fin walked across the grass to the airstrip gate, he was met by Mr. and Mrs. Gillespie going the other way. They were bickering and he restricted himself to giving them a quick wave.'

***

'Can I buy you a drink?' Fin asked Becky. It was after dinner in the bar. They both sat with the new birder from the States. He'd introduced himself as Steve North.

'Did you have a good day?' asked Fin.

'Yes, said Becky, but perhaps tomorrow I'll try a walk up the shore-line. Would you like to join me?'

'If you don't think I'll slow you down, I'd love to. It's always nice to have company.'

Mr. North added in. 'Unless you think it would be rude perhaps I could join you. It would be good to get my bearings around the island, and I am only here for three nights.' Becky could not hide her disappointment but Fin said quickly. 'That would be super.'

They shared another couple of beers with Steve quizzing Fin about the island. Fin then made his excuses, leaving Becky to share a final drink with the American. Back in his room, Fin checked through his clothes for tomorrow. Everything was in its place but he was still fairly sure that someone had been through his belongings.

Just after mid-night there was a quiet tap on his door. He was ready this time as Becky came in. She sat down next to him on his bed. 'Well?'

'Offie did not fly off this island. Of course, she could have caught the ferry but why would she do that given the flight only takes half an hour and costs the same.'

'So, you're saying she's still on the island.'

'She must be.'

'In that case, we've got to confront Eric Branson about it.'

'We need something more to go on. It's got to have something to do with the lighthouse. I don't believe they're doing any works up there. There's something they're hiding.'

'So, let's drive up there first thing.'

'I've tried that and got no-where. We need a more subtle approach.'

'We don't have time for subtlety'. Her voice was slightly raised.

'Shuh.. we can't just go barging in. It might panic them. Trust me.'

'OK' she 'whispered. We'll give it one more day, but after that I'm going to start taking this island apart.'

Thursday 19 April

Fin strolled steadily down the track from the observatory, his cane clicking against the ground in time to his steps. Behind him trailed Becky chatting to Steve North. Steve was a big guy, about 40 and well over six foot. Over breakfast he'd let them know he was from California originally although he'd lived in London for the last five years.

Fin had said that he was keen to walk up the east side of the island as he'd read that there were a couple of interesting archaeological ruins up there. Becky and Steve had seemed quite happy with this suggestion. After the good weather from yesterday another haar had covered the island this morning, although not quite as bad as before, and Steve had said that he did not think it would be a great day for bird spotting. Frigga had kindly made them up a pack lunch for each of them so they were well provisioned for the day ahead.

'Let's walk up the road to the airstrip and then cut down to the shore from there' said Fin. 'I'm sure I saw a path from the plane.' The other two nodded in agreement and together they wandered up the single track road towards the ruined castle on top of the rise. Steve stopped to take some photos of the castle, leaving Becky to catch up with Fin.

'What did you make of Old Billy the other night' asked Fin as she reached him.

'Poor old man' said Becky. 'Must have been a bit pished. How do you think he made it all the way down to the observatory.'

'I'm not sure he was drunk. I'm seen a lot of drunks in my day and he didn't look like one.'

'What do you think was wrong with him?'

'I'm not sure, but if I didn't know better I'd have said he was behaving like a junkie in need of a fix.'

Becky was silent for a moment and then asked 'so how do you know that Offie did not fly off the island.'

Fin explained about his searching through the flight diary at the airport.

'It doesn't say much for their security' said Becky. 'Why do you think it's all tied to whatever is going on at the lighthouse.'

'Call it a gut instinct.'

There was a footstep behind them. They both turned at the same time. Steve North stood immediately behind. For a large man he'd been very quiet.

It was clear that he had been listening to their conversation. 'I don't want to be rude but it sounds as if you two guys are here for more than the birds.'

Fin considered his options and then said 'Sorry Steve, I don't want to spoil your day. Just ignore us rambling on'.

'Hey, don't worry about me man. With this fog, I don't give us much chance of bird watching today so anything else to pass the time would be good.'

'We call it a *haar*' said Becky. 'I mean instead of fog. It refers to a sea mist coming in over the land off the cold sea. You tend to get it at this time of the year when the sea water is still cold from the winter.'

Steve ignored the weather lecture. 'So, do you guys know one another? Only, it didn't seem that way last night at dinner.'

'That's how we'd like to keep it' replied Becky with a thin smile.

They walked on for a few minutes, occasionally coming upon a seal pulled up onto the rocks. Steve remained silent.

Eventually Fin said 'Let's have a brew up here'. Seeing Steve look vague he added 'I mean a cup of tea.'

They settled down against a stone dyke and Fin poured out cups of tea for him and Becky. Steve poured himself a cup of coffee.

'So Steve, what's brought you up to West Hunday?' asked Fin, trying to break the ice, as they settled down with their drinks.

'Since I moved to London from the US, I've never been to Scotland so I thought I should see what I've been missing. I've a keen bird watcher so I thought this would make a good stopping off point on my way up to Shetland. It's just a pity the weather had turned against us.'

'Yeah' said Becky 'that's a shame. Hopefully it will get better. Mind you I've never met a birder who didn't bring a pair of binoculars with him.'

'I left them by mistake in Kirkwall.' It was a quick response. Too quick for Fin. He took a sip of his tea. Steve did likewise with his coffee.

Steve broke the impasse. 'So, what's the score with you guys?'

Fin thought for a moment, trying to weigh up how much he could trust this newcomer. 'One of Becky's friends who used to work up here has gone missing and we've come up to see if we can get to the bottom of it.'

Steve considered this. 'Any joy?'

'Nothing so far, but we think it may have something to do with the lighthouse, hence our walk up here today.'

'You won't mention anything to the folk at the observatory?' said Becky.

'No' said Steve 'you can trust me'. He looked her straight in the eye. She was not convinced.

They packed up their things and started again up the coast, allowing Steve this time to take the lead.

'So, said Steve after a few minutes, why do you think your friend's disappearance is suspicious?'

'Nothing specific but something here does not add up' said Fin.

Steve looked disappointed by his answer, but did not say anything more. Fin wandered what he was thinking, walking up a deserted coast of a remote island with two people he didn't know who appeared to be completely nuts.

They walked a bit and then Becky said 'Fin, I really don't like this island. There's something about it I can't put my finger on but it creeps me out.'

He tried to change the subject. 'Did you learn anything useful yesterday from Yulia and Anya?'

'Not really. Almost all their chat was moaning about the lack of any boys on the island, although that hasn't stopped Fulla from becoming pregnant. There's much speculation as to who the father is as there's never been a boyfriend over to see her.'

'Who's the chief suspect?'

She giggled 'Eric Branson of course!'

Fin almost choked. 'You're kidding.'

'Well, there's not much competition that I've seen.' She laughed again, and he was pleased to see her happy for a fleeting moment.

***

The walk along the shore was tough going and Fin's leg was aching. It did not have shingle like the beach at the village but was made up of larger rocks interspersed with areas of sand.

'Where have you covered on the island?' asked Becky as they walked.

'I've been though the village. There a church over there full of tombs of the Branson family. Boy, those people must have had a lot of money.'

'They still must' said Becky. 'Anya said they give each volunteer £500 pocket money a week. They even cover the cost of the girls' flights.'

'Very generous' said Fin. 'Mind up anyone who could afford a fancy bird observatory like that can't be poor. It's a pity they don't keep the islanders better off.'

They walked on further, the haar off the sea creating an errie atmosphere.

'How long has your friend been missing?' asked Steve.

'About a month' explained Becky.

'And what is it about the light house makes you think it may be connected?'

'I was up there the day before yesterday and was turned away in no uncertain circumstances. There's a big fence all around it. Why would you need that on a wee island like this? Eric Branson told me they were doing renovation works but I couldn't see any evidence of any works going on and there no evidence of consent to works being issued by the Council.'

He added 'something smells fishy on his island and it's not just the seaweed. The observatory must have cost a fortune. Where would the Bransons get the funds to build it.'

They were now scrambling over rocks as the going got tougher still, frightening birds into the air as they went. Finally, they reached a large mound of stones sat back slightly from the shore. 'Do you know what that is' Fin asked Steve.

'No idea. Looks like a pile of rocks to me.'

'How observant. I guess that's one way to look at it. Another is that is a three thousand year old 'broch''. Fin led him round to the far side of the broch and pointed out an entrance low at the foot of the mound.

'Was it a house?' Steve asked.

'No-one really knows. It might have been a house, or perhaps a burial chamber. What it does mean is that there were people living here a thousand years before Christ. Does that not amaze you, that you are walking in the foot-steps of those people.'

'Where did they come from?'

'Again, no-one really knows for certain but there were probably Norse. They seem to have populated the islands one by one. Legend has it that two brothers, both giants, first landed on West Hunday. The older borther took the north island for his own and the younger one took the south island. At first they lived happily side by side. Then the older brother grew jealous of the other because the fishing from the south island was so much better than his own. So, he formed a pack with a selkie woman, that a woman half human and half seal, and persuaded her to trick his younger brother to join her in the sea. She sang to the younger brother and he joined her on the rocks. Then she led him into the sea. Once in the water, she led him down to the bottom of the sea and then drowned him. He then turned into a seal. The older brother then took control of his brother's island. But when he went fishing, he found that there were no fish. The seals, his brother included, had eaten them all, and explains today the poor fishing at West Hunday. Just crabs and scallops.'

'Is that true or did you just make it up?' Becky asked.

'I read it in a tourist brochure back when I was over in Kirkwall yesterday' he confessed 'mind you it's a good yarn. Did you really learn nothing new from the volunteers yesterday?'

'Not much really, although I did find out that Anya only joined as a volunteer about a month ago. That's just before Offie disappeared. And I'll tell you something. The universities in Poland must be crap as her knowledge of birding is about as bad as mine.'

'Nothing else odd?'

'Nothing really, although all three of us had something in common'.

'Oh, aye?'

'Yeah, we're all orphans. What's the chance of that?'

'No idea' said Fin.

'Shall we press on up the coast. I've not been up the top of the island yet and I'd like to see what's up there.'

They wandered on across the rocks. The island was still shrouded in mist and it showed no sign of lifting. The occasional call of gulls accompanied them. What breeze there had been had completely dropped away and there was hardly a wave lapping against the shore-line. You'd really need to be born and bred to live here, thought Fin. Their tramp over the couple of miles up to the top of the island took them a good hour, the going hard over wet rocks. Becky seemed to be in her own world and they spoke very little as they went.

Fin needed a rest. His leg was troubling him and he was not as fit as he used to be. He was relieved when they finally reached some more open ground with moss covered grass leading down to the shore. He pulled off his rucksack and flopped down against a low stone dyke. Even on this gloomy day a myriad of wild flowers across the grass lifted his spirits somewhat. 'Let's have another brew here' he said, pulling out his packed lunch and taking a bite out of a sandwich. Becky dumped herself down beside him. Steve went off to relieve himself behind a dyke.

'What do you make of Steve?' asked Fin.

'Well he's certainly not a birder. He couldn't tell you the difference between a bonxie and a puffin and no birder's ever going to forget his binoculars.'

'We're not getting anywhere are we?' she said 'As soon as the mist clears, I'm catching the first plane out to Kirkwall and reporting this to the Police.'

'Aye, maybe that's for the best' he said 'although we still don't have any evidence that anything untoward has happened to Ophelia, so I'm still not convinced they'll do anything.'

'They'll have to. There's no way Offie has just vanished off the face of the earth and has not been in touch. She's on this island. I just know she is.'

Fin wanted to say she was exaggerating, but in his gut he was not sure. He poured out two cups of tea and offered her one with a sandwich.

'Perhaps we should confront Eric Branson and see what he has to say for himself' she said.

'Any what exactly shall we say? That we're concerned he's done away with one of the volunteers. We can't make an allegation like that.'

'Oh, I don't know' she said 'but we've got to do something and soon. Its over three weeks since I last heard from Offie. There's no way she wouldn't have been in contact by now.'

'Maybe she has and she just can't get hold of you because of the lack of a bloody signal on this island.'

'No – I left my phone with Magnus. I've just borrowed his. If she'd phoned he would have got in contact with me somehow.'

Steve returned. 'I think you should both get off the island as soon as you can and report your friend, Offie did you say, to the authorities.'

Again, Fin wondered if he'd been listening. 'Yeah, I think you're probably right' he said.

It was starting to drizzle and Fin suggested they walk on. They kept to the grass and, although they were now going uphill as the cliffs began to form along the shore-line, the going was easier than over the rocks.

Eventually looming out of the mist they sighted the bulk of the lighthouse tower, the top lost from sight. They were approaching it from the rear and he saw that the complex of the keepers' cottages and outbuildings was larger than he'd realised from his first visit. A couple of lights were burning in the cottage windows and he saw two SUVs parked together by the side of the cottages, one presumably Eric Branson's and the other the car he'd been given a lift in the other day.

The fog had without warning grown thicker and they almost bumped into the chain link fence. 'What the fuck' exclaimed Becky. 'Aye, there's a fence around the whole of the lighthouse' Fin explained 'this is as close as we can get.'

'You're kidding me' she said 'we've walked all this way and we can't even get in – and why would anyone want to put up a fence in the first place. Who are they trying to keep out – the locals or the bird watchers.'

'Eric said that they had been undertaking renovation works and were not allowing folk in for their own safety.'

'Aye, and I'm the Easter bunny' she said. 'Come one, let's jump the fence and do some poking around.'

'I'm not sure I can get over it' said Fin

Steve added 'Given how quickly you were picked up on your first visit I'd be fairly sure its wired. As soon as you touch it they'll know you're here and you'll have some explaining to do. One visit you can put down to error. A second and you'll have some serious explaining to do.'

'What would be your suggestion?' said Becky, both impressed and irritated at the same time.

'You need to look for a better approach. There a high tide now but by this evening it should be well out. We should be able to skirt round the fence on the shore and then have a peek around and see what we can find.'

'Heh guy, you're only here for the ride. There's no 'we'.' Becky sounded angry and frustrated.

'Well, I just probably saved your ass, so perhaps I might be worth dragging along.'

'Oh, and how are we going to be able to get away from the bird observatory unobserved?' she asked sarcastically.

'Don't worry, I've got a solution there' said Fin.

***

They followed the fence as it curved round the complex but there was no gap that would allow them in. Fin suggested that they should make their way back along the island road, so they made a bee-line for it across a couple of fields south of the lighthouse, being careful to skirt around one with a bull in it. They'd made their way about a mile down the road, when an ancient tractor with no lights on came trundling towards them. They stepped onto the verge to let it past but it pulled up next to them. 'Good afternoon Mr. Tulloch. Would you like a lift?' It was Old Billy. Becky looked a bit wary but Fin and Steve threw their bags into the tractor's trailer. With a sigh, Becky helped Fin in and then scrambled in after him. Old Billy's dog, Mitch, was in the far corner of the trailer growling in a low pitch. The three of them took up position in the opposite corner.

'Never mind the dog. He'll do you no harm.'

Old Billy started down the road, chatting away, but with the noise of the engine, they could not make out a word. A few minutes later they pulled up near the war memorial. 'This is as far as I can take you I'm afraid'

'That's very good of Billy' said Fin 'by the way, are there any boats on the island? I was wondering about going fishing if the weather improves.'

'Fishing is it? I'm not sure about that. There's no boats here other than the two lobster skiffs you'll have seen down at the village and I don't think either of those do fishing trips. It's a pity you know. At one time, there were perhaps a dozen or more boats based here.'

He paused and then added 'that's of course if you ignore yon big rib that the young laird uses.'

'Oh, where does he keep that' asked Fin, suddenly interested.

'In the boat-shed doon at the pier.'

'Well, thanks for the lift Billy. Really appreciated. Perhaps we can catch up before I need to leave.'

'Aye, you do that Mr Tulloch. I've always time for a good blether.'

***

By the time they reached the turning up to the observatory, Fin was keen for a hot shower and a fresh cup of tea, but Becky insisted on them walking the few hundred yards down to the pier head. They left Steve to walk up to the observatory and said they'd catch up after dinner. 'Mind you don't mention anything to anyone' said Fin.

'I don't trust him' said Becky as soon as Steve was out of hearing.

'If he'd being going to say anything, he'd have done so last night. He obviously had us sussed by then.'

'What do you mean. He said he hadn't realised anything until this morning.'

'Bullshit. He cottoned on straightaway. That's why he was so keen to tag along with us today.'

'Perhaps. All the more reason not to trust him. If he's not a birder, just what is he doing up here.'

'I hear all that Becky, but he's probably already saved our necks by warning us about the fence being wired.'

'Who's to say he didn't already know?'

Fin pondered for a moment. 'OK, I'll tell you what. Let's agree not to trust him. But let's also agree to keep him close. Agreed?'

She paused. 'Agreed' she finally conceded.

They'd reached the pier. It was disserted with just a single light glowing in the dusk at the far end. To one side of the path up from the pier he driven up when he'd first arrived on the island there was a low rise stone building he'd not paid any attention to. It was well maintained with large doors both at the front and the side. The front doors were secured with a heavy padlock. The side doors were however open. Inside sat a number of containers marked 'West Hunday', together with the names of the various island families printed around the walls. He had read that the locals were able to order their food and other supplies from the local shops in Kirkwall which were then be carted down to the harbour and put in containers on the weekly boat out to the island. When the boat then arrived, the containers were lifted by a fork-lift up to the boat-shed and divvied up amongst the islanders. There were about thirty names listed on the walls all by reference to their croft or home. The observatory was the first name and took up twice as much space, presumably due to the amount of provisions it needed to service its guests. There was Old Billy's croft Halfway listed and the manse. However, what caught Fin's eye was the final name listed. It looked like a relatively new entry and simply read '*Lighthouse*'. 'That's interesting' Fin said quietly to himself 'and I thought nobody lived there.'

'What?' said Becky.

'Look' said Fin, pointing to the entry for the lighthouse. 'It might be interesting to be here on Friday to see exactly what type of supplies they receive.'

Becky said 'Why do you think Eric Branson feels the need to lock up his boat? It's not as if any of the locals are likely to pinch it.'

'I don't know' said Fin 'but I do know that I am dying for another cuppa. Let's get back up to our rooms and get out of these damp clothes. We can see what Frigga or Fulla can rustle up for us.'

***

After dinner Fin sidled up to Steve North. 'Can I buy you a beer Steve?'

''That would be great Fin. What would you recommend.'

'Oh, it's got to be one of the local Orkney beers.'

'Two Scapa Specials please'. Frigga behind the bar handed two bottles to him and he took them across to a table at the far side of the lounge.

'I'm glad to see it's cold' said Steve, pouring himself a glass.

'I need to know why you're here' said Fin taking a seat opposite Steve.

Steve lowered his voice. 'I've already told you Fin. I'm on holiday and touring the islands.'

Fin leaned in and without raising his voice said 'Now Steve, we both know that's crap. I used to be a police officer and before that I was regular in the army so I can smell another uniform from a mile. So why don't you tell me what's going on before I mention this to Mr. Branson over there.'

Steve took a long drink from his beer. Fin waited, allowing Steve to break the silence. Eventually, he said 'I can't tell you what I am doing on the island. The governmental department I work for does however have a current investigation on-going and I'm here in connection with that.'

'Are you investigating Ophelia's disappearance.'

'No.'

'I need more than that Steve.'

'Well, I am afraid that is all you're going to get.'

'If this connected to the Red Flag.'

'The what?'

Fin slowly finished his beer. As he got up, he said. 'Be outside the bunkhouse at midnight.' Steve nodded.

***

Fin knocked quietly on Becky's door. She was ready and already dressed in dark leggings and a waterproof jacket. 'OK, what's the plan?' she whispered. He beckoned her to follow him outside. Steve was already there standing in the shadows. He was in a camouflage jacket matching Fin's army surplus job.

Fin whispered 'I thought the VW might be a little visible but I've come up with a Plan B.' He took them over to the bikes lying by the bunkhouse and said 'Pick your stead.'

'You've got to be kidding' said Steve. Fin made it clear he wasn't.

They pushed the bikes quietly down the track to the road, Fin balancing his walking cane across the handlebars. With some difficulty, he managed to get on board and the three of them began to cycle slowly up to the causeway. In the moonlight, Fin felt very exposed as they made their way across it but they reached the far side after only a couple of minutes. The going then got slightly harder as they cycled up the rise to the ruined castle, rolling down the far side. There was a slight tail wind and the going from there was easy. There was no-one around and the few cottages they passed were in darkness. The road up to the lighthouse was straight and before long they were at the turning up to it. Fin stopped near the cattle grid and lifted his bike into a hollow in the verge. Becky and Steve followed suit.

The light from the tower revolved around in a slow circle lighting up where they stood. They crouched down behind a stone dyke. Once the light passed all was dark around them for a minute or so.

'Ok, Fin whispered. 'We'll wait until the light does its next turn and as soon as it's past cut across the grass down to the shore-line. Keep close to me and as quiet as possible.'

They waited a until the light was about to turn past them. Fin held up his hand and just as they stream of light moved past sending them into semi-darkness he dropped his hand and moved out as quickly as he was able, with Becky and Steve following on this tail. He was aware that he was not as fast as either of the other two and was putting both at risk. He pressed on as quick as possible, feeling the pain from his bad leg shooting up. The grass was soft and spongey and it was like running on treacle. It became clear very quickly that they would not make it all the way to the rocks before they were again illuminated by the lighthouse. As the light slowly turned towards them, he ducked and pulled Becky down next to him 'Stay still' he whispered. He could feel her breathing heavily.

'Come on' he called. The night returned again to darkness and he was off again propelling himself forward with his cane. His trousers were already soaking wet from the grass. There was a call from a nesting bird disturbed as they approached. It seemed incredibly loud in the stillness of the night and he sensed Becky flinching. Steve grabbed her hand and he pulled her on. The light seemed to be coming around again more quickly. Just as they were lit up again, they reached the rocks on the store and dived down low behind a huge slab of stone. Through the half-light they could see that the sea was far out. The tide looked already to be at its lowest point.

Fin pointed along the beach. 'Over there.. you see the fence going down to the shore. We'll go around it and then track back up along the foot of the cliffs.' They moved on along the beach keeping below the rock line. Reaching the fence, it was clear that it led further out into the beach than was apparent from a distance. However, at its far end there was still a split of dry sand just visible. Fin took the lead and led them out, again illuminated by the lighthouse. The sand was soft and their footsteps showed a clear line.

At its end where the fence would have fallen under the sea at high tide it was covered in seaweed with barnacles growing along it. A heavy line of concrete posts held it in place. They pressed on around in and made their way along its inside edge up to the beach and then the rocks. Crouching down Fin whispered 'follow me. There are steps up from the base of the cliff.'

The moved along the bottom of the cliff it growing higher the further they went. Eventually, after about eight hundred yards, they came upon the stone jetty that serviced the lighthouse. A series of steps with a chain link fence had been cut into the cliff face. 'This way' pointed Fin.

The steps up the cliff were worn and broken and the fence loose in places, but they made it up to the top. Risking a look out over the edge, Fin saw that they were only about a hundred yards from the base of the tower. Steve peered over to check the position. He whispered to Fin. 'Right, you stay here. Signal if you see anything. If we're not back in ten minutes get out of here. Becky, as soon as its dark again, we'll run up to the tower. Wait this side. Understood?' She nodded.

Fin wanted to object but he knew he was slower than the other two.

Steve was up and off as soon as the darkness hit with Becky close behind. Every minute or so Fin watched as they were caught in the light, panic rising within him at the risk of them being noticed. But the lighthouse cottages remained in darkness and there was no sign of anyone.

Becky reached the base of the lighthouse just a second or so after Steve, leaning down on her knees next to him. She could hear him panting as he recovered his breath. Slowly they crept around the circular base of the tower until they were just out of line with the two cottages. He pulled a torch out of his jacket and handed it to Becky. 'OK, Becky you keep watch here. If you hear or see anything flash a couple of times and then make your back your way back to Fin as quick as you can.'

'You've got to be kidding. I'm not staying here alone'. She sounded scared. He knew he was. 'Ok, then, but keep as quiet as you can and no talking from now on.'

Keeping low to the ground they half-crawled around to the front of the tower. It was now starting to drizzle with a light rain. He pulled her arm and they started in a half jog/half crawl across the cobbled courtyard towards the first cottage. They'd taken perhaps only half a dozen steps when the yard was suddenly flooded with light as a series of flood lights switched on. A dog started barking. 'Come on, quick' he urged Becky and they up and running over to a bin store next to the first cottage. Steve pulled Becky down next to him, pressing themselves in the side of the store.

As they stood frozen, there was the sound of the door to one of the cottages being unbolted and the door opening. Steve held his finger up to his mouth. There was a long pause and then a male voice inside the cottage called. 'What is it?'

A reply came from the doorway 'Err...nothing. Probably just another stupid seagull.'

'Shall I send Mitch out' asked the voice from inside.

'Shit no, he'll just be tearing around all night. We'll never get the bugger back in.'

They waited for a time frozen in position and finally heard the door closing and the bolt being slid back into place. They waited another couple of minutes and the floodlights went off. Steve sighed with relief. He carefully peeked around the corner from their hiding place. The cottages were back in darkness. Then a curtain was pulled back. He was not sure but he thought he saw Eric Branson's face looking out. He quickly pulled back into the darkness of the bin store.

'Let's see what's round back' whispered Steve.

Keeping pressed up to the wall to avoid the flood lights being triggered they inched their way around to the rear. In the darkness they could make out a walled garden laid to grass and the remnants of an old wind turbine. There were no lights showing in the rear windows of the cottages. Steve crept ahead, signally Becky to stay put. He reached the first window. It was barred and shuttered. The same for the second. Both looked new. Moving on to the second cottage, the two windows were again bolted and shuttered. He noted however a narrow bathroom window which was just glazed and perhaps could be used for access if the person was small enough to squeeze through the opening. He thought of Becky, but that would have to be for another time. They'd been here long enough.

Back with Becky Steve whispered 'The lights will go on again and this time they'll send the dog out. We need a diversion. I'm going to make for the fence at the rear. I'll then make it down the east coast. When the trip wire on the fence triggers, they're bound to set off after me. As soon as they're away from the cottage, you run as fast as you can back down to Fin. We'll rendezvous back at the observatory.'

'Ok' she said in a low voice, shaking with fright.

He touched her on the shoulder and was off into the dark. She was alone, terrified.

Becky crouched in the dark. It seems to be for an eternity. Suddenly there was a piercing alarm, followed a few seconds later by Eric Branson appearing from the cottage together with another well-built man she did not recognise. The flood lights switched on. Mitch followed barking loudly. The dog made straight for her, but Eric Branson shouted. 'Here Mitch'. The dog hesitated. 'Now' screamed Eric. The dog turned back. Eric was by one of the SUVs. He called Mitch again and the dog jumped in. The car sped away across the grass towards the eastern boundary.

She waited a couple of seconds and was then out sprinting in the glaring light. She ran over towards the lighthouse tower and then fell helter-skelter down the grass bank and onto the links. On she ran into the night. She listened for someone following her, but heard nothing. Reaching the top of the steps she almost threw herself into Fin's arms.

'Come on'. She started pulling him down the steps.

'Where Steve?'

'He's made for the east coast. Says he'll meet up at the observatory.'

She was still breathing heavily. 'We saw Eric Branson.'

'Let's speak when we get back.'

'Ok'.

At the bottom of the steps they scrambled along the base of the until they reached the chain link fence. They started out along it but almost immediately they found that the tide had already started to come in. Only half way out to the end of the fence there was already perhaps a foot of water and it was rising fast.

'Come on Becky, we'll need to get wet' said Fin. 'Stay by my side.'

The sea water felt freezing cold. They pushed on, finding it hard to work against the rising tide. By the time they reached the end of the fence, it was well above their knees. Fin had never felt as relieved when he was able to turn landward again. Now they had the benefit of the tide working with them but the wind which had helped them earlier on their bikes was now blowing stiffly into their faces.

'I'm not sure I can do this' said Becky 'it's so cold'.

'Yes, you can' he said and he pulled her along. Juggling both the girl and his walking cane, he pressed on. It seemed to take an age but eventually they reached dry land again. Becky lay down on the sand.

He forced her onto her feet.

Supporting her, they trudged slowly up the beach and then across the links. The light from the tower still lit them up as it turned but they were too cold and exhausted to care. Finally they were back to where they'd left the bikes. Thankfully they were still there.

'Right' now back to the observatory. If you see anyone, get down into the ditch as quickly as possible.'

They set off into the head wind, the adrenalin pushing them along. It seemed to take twice as long to make it home and Fin was grateful for the small slope down from the castle to the causeway. He pulled in waiting for Becky to catch up.

'Why are we stopping?'.

'I thought I saw lights at the observatory.'

Sure enough, in the distance a pair of headlights were coming down the track from the observatory.

'Down here' said Fin and he pushed his bike off the roadway and down the side of the causeway. Becky did the same and they both scrambled down the side of the road to hide behind the boulders protecting the causeway.

'Stay down' whispered Fin pulling Becky in beside him.

They could hear the car approaching. It came speeding towards them. Surely, they had been spotted. He took a deep breath and it sped by.

'Wait' he whispered.

He watched as the car went over the brow of the hill by the castle. He counted to twenty and then stood.

He lifted the two bikes back onto the roadway and they both climbed on board and cycled up to the turning to the observatory. With heavy legs they pushed their bikes back up the bunkhouse. Thankfully, the observatory sat in darkness. Fin checked his watch. It was 4 am and would be dawn in only an hour or so.

He helped Becky into her room, keeping as quiet as possible. She was shaking and looked as white as a ghost. 'It's too late to speak now' he whispered. 'Get some sleep and we can catch up after breakfast.'

He lent over and gave her a kiss on her forehead. 'Good night. You did good.'

Leaving Becky, he checked Steve's room but it was empty. He went into his own, pulled off his wet clothes, leaving them on the floor, climbed into bed and was asleep within a few seconds.

Friday 20 April

Fin was late for breakfast and Frigga was busy tidying the dishes away. 'M..mm..morning Mr. Tulloch. I thought you were sk…sk…skipping breakfast this morning.'

'Must have slept in what with all the fresh West Hunday air' said Fin.

'Dinnie w..w..worry. I'll bring you some tea and get some toast on. There some por…porr..ridge left if you'd like some.'

'That would be great thanks' he said. 'Has everyone else already gone out for the day?'

'Aye, with the first flight running, those two chaps from London and yon Ms. McPhail are away so you and Mr. North the only guests left at the moment.'

'Sorry, did you say that Becky, I mean Ms. McPhail, caught the morning flight?'

'Yes, she didn't even appear for breakfast. Would you like a packed lunch today?'.

'But she can't be gone. I was out with her yesterday and she said she was staying on for a few days.'

'She must have changed her m….mm....mind then.'

Fin did not enjoy his porridge. I had an odd taste to it as did the explanation about Becky. Why would she up-sticks without speaking to him. Perhaps, the night before spent out in the cold had taken its toll. She'd been shivering when they'd returned and he'd put it down to the cold, but maybe it was more than that. She was tough but it was too much to ask a young woman like her to be involved.

Frigga brought him some more tea. 'Was your p… p.. porridge not good?' she asked eyeing the half-full bowl.

'I just seem to have lost my appetite this morning. Did Mr. North say where he was going?'

'I think he said something about taking a walk along the bay.'

'I'll take that packed lunch if it's still on offer' he said.

He went back to the bunkhouse, passing Becky's room on the way. Quietly he opened the door. The room had already been cleaned and tidied ready for the next guest. The bed was neatly made up. He looked in the wardrobe but it was empty. There was nothing in the desk drawers other than a Gideon bible. He had a quick look under the bed. The bathroom was also clear. Suddenly he heard a noise in the corridor. He stood still. The footsteps outside approached closer. His heart was racing. They were right outside the door. He could hear himself breathing. Then the handle turned. He took half a step back and the door was pulled open. Fulla stood there with a handful of towels. She jumped back 'Oh, Mr. Tulloch, you surprised me.'

'Sorry Fulla, I was just looking for Becky,… Ms. McPhail.'

'Oh, she's gone this morning. Did you not know? I'm just making up the room.' They did a little dance and she squeezed by him into the bathroom.

'Never mind, then, I'll just have to entertain myself then' he said.

'Errr… yes, I guess so. See you later.' She stood embarrassed in front of him.

'Yes, see you later Fulla.'

He left Becky's room quietly closing the door behind him. He walked the few steps further on into his own room, standing behind the door. He opened up his fist. In his palm he held the pendant with the Orcadian symbol on which he'd complimented Becky when they'd first met in the Swedish bakery. It was not something she would leave behind. He put it into his pocket.

Returning to the kitchen for his packed lunch he disturbed Frigga and Fulla speaking together. They stopped as soon as he approached, Fulla looked down to the floor. 'Here you are' said Frigga, passing him his lunch. 'Thanks, see you later for dinner' he said. 'Enjoy day and be careful o' the selkies' she replied.

***

He saw Steve in the distance down on the beach. He appeared to be holding something up to his ear but as Fin approached, he put whatever it was in his jacket pocket.

'I thought there was no telephone signal' said Fin.

'I thought I would give it a go but no joy' said Steve.

'Did you know that Becky had left?'

'What do you mean 'left'?'

'Frigga tells me she caught the morning flight to Kirkwall. Did she say anything to you last night about doing that?'

'No.' Steve paused 'She was scarred last night Fin. Maybe she just needed to go home.'

'I don't think so.' Fin let his comment rest in the air.

They walked on a bit, a seal watching them from the water.

'Did you discover anything last night?'

'Not much' said Steve, 'except that the fence is definitely alarmed and the windows to both cottages are secured at the rear. I would be amazed if they were not alarmed as well.'

'Who did you see?'

'There were two but I didn't recognise them.' He made no mention of Eric Branson.

'That's not much to go on.'

'No, it isn't.'

'How did you make it back in one piece?'

'I climbed the fence and then made it trekked back along the coast the way we'd come the day before.'

'And you managed that despite the dog after you.'

'I dealt with the dog.'

Fin's trust in Steve North was beginning to evaporate. Becky had warned him not to trust him and now she'd disappeared like Offie.

'So, what's the plan now Steve?'

'I'm going to catch the ferry back to Kirkwall. I'd suggest you do the same.'

'Sorry. I'm not leaving here without Becky.'

'What makes you think she's still on the island.'

Fin could feel the pendant in his pocket but he just said 'Call it intuition.'

'It's your call' said Steve. 'I'm sure however she's okay.'

Fin remembered saying much the same to Becky about Ophelia. 'Can you do me a favour Steve.. When you get back to Kirkwall can you check the flight log for his morning's flight and see if Becky was on it.'

'Sure. Be careful Fin.' It was the same message as Frigga had given him.

***

Fin watched from the boatshed as the ferry arrived. The sea was much calmer today and the boat did not have any problem tying up alongside the pier. Very quickly the little crane was in action lifting off all manner of freight. Eric Branson was acting as chief stevedore directing the two islanders maneuvering the rope netting as the cargo was pulled down onto the pier. One of the locals plied up and down with a forklift moving the island's weekly supplies into the shed. There were perhaps a dozen folk at the shed all eager to get their hands on their groceries. He watched as the crates were distributed around the various crofts but nothing was left for the lighthouse.

As soon as the cargo had been unloaded, the crane started in reverse to lift on board items going back to the mainland. There was a float full of sheep, presumably for the auction mart and a tractor presumably for repair. There was no sign of the SUV or Laurel and Hardy. They were clearly not departing today.

Finally strolling down the pier with a large rucksack walked Steve North. He turned and waved to Fin who acknowledged him with a raised hand. It was some distance down to the ferry, but as Steve made to climb onto the boat, Eric Branson came over to him and appeared to say something as he leaned in to shake his hand.

***

Fin drove the VW back up to the village and parked next to the two small wooden boats pulled up onto the shore. Both had flaking paint hanging off and barnacles along their bottom. A heap of lobster creels lay next to them. They did not look fit to go out to sea. He was glad he was not a fisherman.

He sat in the van looking out to the horizon. The sky today seemed huge and he squinted against the glare from the sun now .emerging from the clouds. Looking up and down the shale beach he could see no-one. Putting his backpack on, he started to walk north from the village towards the rough track beyond the school house. He reached the church. He stepped up the path towards the churchyard. He cast his eye over the head stones. A faded inscription on one read 'John William Tulloch – 1824-1830'. An ancestor perhaps he thought. A tough life for sure. Moving on, a more substantial stone with inter-linked triangular carvings announced 'Erik Sigurd Branson – 1920 - 1965'. He wondered if this was perhaps a brother of Sir Rolf and what he had done not to justify being buried in the family crypt. A voice disturbed him and looked around to find an elderly woman dressed all in black with a head scarf covering her white hair. She could not have been more than five feet tall taking into account a decided stoop. She grinned up at him exposing two rotten teeth. 'Not a bad place to spend eternity' she said, pointing to the view of the sea.'
'Not bad indeed' he replied. 'Apologies if I am disturbing you'.

'Not at all, not at all' she chuckled 'I'm just sorting the flowers for Sunday's service. Just some daffs you know, but it helps cheer it up inside'

'I hadn't thought there was a minister on the island' he said, remembering back to what he'd been told on his visit to St Magnus Cathedral.

'Oh no' she said 'there's no minister here. There was a priest in days gone by but there's no been one here for many a year' she added by way of explanation

'Is someone coming over then from Kirkwall to conduct the service?' he asked.

'Bless you no. The young laird acts as our pastor and leads us in worship.'

'Oh yes, I remember now he was just back from the church the day I arrived.'

'Aye, he leads us both as laird and in matters of the spirit.'

Fin was not sure what to say. 'I'm afraid I am not a religious man myself. Is it a special service on Sunday?'.

'It is indeed. We're having a wedding. The whole island will be here.'

'Sorry, what did you say' he said, thinking he had misunderstood her accent.

'A wedding dear. We're having a wedding' she chuckled.

'And Eric, I mean Mr. Branson, can conduct a marriage?'

'He can in our eyes. We don't need any outsiders telling us how to do such things.'

'Who's getting married?'

'Why the young laird himself of course.'

'Sorry, I know he is conducting the service. I meant who are the lucky couple who are tying the knot?'

'The young laird and a lassie from the mainland.'

'You mean Eric is conducting his own marriage service.'

She looked at him as if he were daft. 'Yes, that's what I've been saying, isn't it.'

It seemed a rum arrangement. 'Well, let's hope they have a great day' was all he could think to say.

He smiled and started to walk away, but she said 'Do you want to see the grave?'

'Sorry.. the what?'

'The grave dear'. She tootled on towards the rear of the churchyard. He hesitated and then followed her. There, sitting against the back wall to the church was a freshly dug grave.

She smiled and said 'All ready and waiting.'

'I am sorry. I didn't know someone had died.' he said.

'Sir Rolf dear. He passed last night. They found him in his bed this morning.'

'Oh, I'm sorry. No one said.'

'Don't be sorry dear. He'll have travelled to the other side and will soon be re-born amongst us.'

He didn't know what to say. She started to decorate the grave with her flowers.

'I'm intruding.' He started to step away.

'There to be a party up at the laird's house tomorrow night to see Sir Rolf on his way. Everyone is sure to be there. It's bound to be quite a party. You'll be more than welcome.' She smiled at him.

'Where is the laird's house?'

'Why up at the top of the hill of course' she said, pointing south. He realised she meant the ruined castle where the volunteers netted the birds.

'Very nice to meet you' he said.

'See you on tomorrow night' she called after him as he walked back around to the front of the church.

He tried the church door and stepped in to the cool interior. The first thing he saw was a wicker coffin set out at the front of the nave. Embarrassed, he closed the door and walked quickly down the path to the roadway.

Keen to be away he fairly much marched up the road out of the village. He'd seen on his map of the island an old boat house marked north of the village and was keen to check it out. He couldn't however take his mind off the revelations about Eric's father and his impending marriage.

***

As he walked on past the school, the children were in the yard playing. He waved to them and they came running down to the gate by the road waving sticks at him.

'Kill the selkie! kill the selkie!' they chanted at him, prodding their sticks through the gate.

'Freya, Thelma, Eric! Come here this minute.'

A woman dressed in a black skirt and white blouse appeared at the doorway to the school hall. Her hair was pulled back into a bun and she had small pinched mouth.

'This minute!' she shouted. The children turned and ran back to her. She scowled at Fin and hurried the children indoors.

'A better day today' he called but she shut the door firmly without replying.

Fin wandered on, thinking of Becky. There was no way she would have left without her pendant. He was sure she would not have forgot it. It was like a talisman and had been round her neck every time he had seen her. If she had left the island then she had not gone voluntarily. If she was still on it then he had to find her.

As he walked the early morning clouds disappeared and he found himself starting to sweat in the midday heat. A swarm of flies started to bother him and he stepped down from the path onto the beach to get away from them. Across the bay lay the lighthouse sitting on its hillside. For all their effort last night, they were no further forward. Perhaps that was why Becky had called it a day. He sat down on the sand by a rock pool. Flicking his hand across the water, he disturbed a small crab which scurried away under a ledge. He mind wandered back to Sir Rolf's death. Although he was very old and it could not have been unexpected any loss would be another body blow to the island. But the old woman at the church had not seemed at all upset. It was all very odd. He wandered on along the shore line dawdling as he went.

Eventually, and after walking and scrambling much further than he'd anticipated, he reached the old boat shed. Its roof was caved in with only a few wooden beams turned white by the salt from the sea still showing. He looked inside but apart from the skeleton of what looked to be a long dead cat it was abandoned to the elements, light showing through rotten roof beams. The hulk of a wooden boat half eaten away stood outside pulled up onto a ruined jetty. It was still moored by a sea bleached rope to a rusted metal ring. It was as if one day the fisherman had returned from the sea, tied up his boat and then simply decided not to take it out again. Perhaps he had died or perhaps he had been not longer physically able to man the boat.

Fin had heard Old Billy's dog 'Mitch' being called last night and wondered what the old man had been doing so late in the night up at the lighthouse.

He decided to cut across the island to the hide by Hoy loch to see if one of the volunteers was on duty. He could also call in at the airfield and see if he could find out who exactly was on this morning's flight.

When he got to the hide it was empty but he saw two figures across the far side of the loch among the reed beds. As he walked over he saw that it was Yulia and Anya 'Hello ladies. How are things going today' he asked with fake bonhomie.

'Hi there Mr. Tulloch' said Yulia, looking pleased to see him. 'Are you going to join Anya and me in the hide this afternoon?'.

'Perhaps not, but I'll join you for a cup of tea if there's one on offer.'

'Sure' she said. 'We've lost track of the warbler we've been chasing round the reeds, so a coffee break is just what we need.'

He wandered back to the hide with the two girls. 'What have you been up to today?' asked Yulia.

'I've just been meandering around. I was hoping to do a shore crawl with Becky but she caught this morning's plane.'

'Oh, I didn't know that. Never mind, you can join us if you like' she said.

'Wasn't she at breakfast with you?' asked Fin.

'Yes' said Yulia, 'but she never mentioned catching the flight. It must have been a spur of the moment thing.' He thought back to Frigga saying that Becky had skipped breakfast. Why would she lie?

'Is it tea or coffee for you?' asked Anya, busy with the kettle. 'Always tea for me thanks' he replied.

Anya brewed up a strong cuppa and they shared a cheese sandwich in the sun sitting on the wooden step into the hide. The girls chattered on about an exciting new sighting they'd seen, saying it was likely to bring some twitchers in as soon as it appeared on the observatory's blog. 'We're hoping for some hunky young guys' joked Yulia 'but it will probably be the usual old men' adding 'no offence Mr. Tulloch.' She was obviously warming to him.

'None taken Yulia' laughed Fin. 'Do you know when this afternoon's plane is due in?'

'It's usually about 5 o'clock' said Yulia.

'You're from Russia, Yulia?' he said. 'It must be very different here.'

'Yes, not so cold.'

'What do you want to do when you finish university?'

'I'm hoping to get a job in nature conservation, although perhaps somewhere with less rain.'

'Any what about you Anya, what are your plans?'

'Oh, I've already graduated. I work as a secretary in a law firm, but I'm taking a break and hoping to take a new course in zoology.'

'That sounds like a big change. I hope it works out for you.'

After trying and failing to locate the missing warbler, Fin asked 'Would you mind if I borrowed one of your bikes?' I've left my camper at the village and don't have the energy to walk back to pick it up. I can put the bike in the back and drop it back to you.'

'Sure, just take it. It's by the wall up at the top of the track.'

***

There were already four cars parked up at the airfield when Fin arrived. He parked up next to them. Two men were leaning on a gate into the field. One was Old Billy. There was no sign of Mitch. He nodded to Fin. 'Afternoon Mr. Tulloch, are you taking the plane over to Kirkwall again?'.

'No, I just thought I would watch it arriving'.

'Aye, said the second man. That's bout as exciting as West Hunday gets.'

Eric Branson appeared from the terminal building. He gave Fin a smile.

'Good afternoon Fin. You here to see '*Heathrow*' in action?.'

He went on through the gate clipping it closed behind him. He then jumped into an old Landrover with its hazard lights flashing and sped off down the runway. 'That's him scarring the birds away' Old Billy explained as a flock of geese rose into the sky ahead of the car, circling round and then landing again a little bit further down the runway.

'Mind you', laughed Billy, 'feck all use it is.' The second man laughed at the joke. Fin's only thought was that he was glad he would be catching the ferry the next time he left.

'Here's the plane' said Billy's companion, pointing up to the horizon. Fin looked up west towards the setting sun and picked out a small plan banking round in a tight circle at a height of perhaps a couple of hundred feet. It skimmed over the fields towards the airfield. Fin could hear a change in the note of its engine and it seemed to stall in the air. It was approaching directly towards the gate where he stood and for a moment he felt indecision as to whether to make a run for it. Then, at the last minute, the pilot pulled the nose round and the plane bounced down onto the runway and taxied along. It stopped in a few hundred yards, turned and then accelerated back up to the shed with its engine revving. The engine died and the propellers slowly came to a halt. Eric Branson then appeared pulling the luggage trolley. He opened up the passenger door and a single man stepped out. He had the look of a birder. The boot of the plane was then opened and the man's rucksack pulled out. There was a quick chat then between Eric and the pilot through the pilot's window. The window closed up, propellers kicked back on and the plane taxied away and was up in the air again after a few seconds. All in all, the landing and take-off had last no more than five minutes tops. 'Beat that Heathrow' said Eric Branson as he trundled the luggage trolley past.

'Aye well' said 'Old Billy' that's the excitement over for today.

'You've not got your dog with you today?' asked Fin.

Billy gave him a hard stare. 'Found him dead at the cliffs this morning.'

'Oh, I'm sorry to hear that. Were you here for this morning's flight?'

'Aye.'

'My friend Becky was on it. A young girl about twenty.'

'I dare say.'

'Did you see her?'

But before he could reply Eric Branson appeared with the passenger from the plane. 'Fin' he asked 'are you by any chance going back down to the observatory. If so, could I trouble you to give Mr. Macpherson here a lift down. I need to tidy up here.'

'Sure. No problem' said Fin. 'You really are a jack of all trades.'

'Aye, that's me, ground crew, stevedore and anything else needed. You need to multi-task on a wee island like this.'

'I was sorry to hear about your father.'

Eric's smile vanished. 'He was a great man, Fin. I have a lot to live up to as the new laird.'

'I'm sure you'll do absolutely fine. On a happier note I understand that you're getting married.'

'Who told you that?'. His tone had hardened.

'Oh, sorry if I have got it wrong. I bumped into an old woman doing the flowers up at the church.'

'What, you mean Mary. Don't pay any attention to her. She's away with the fairies.'

The new arrival was standing impatient with his bags. He handed the larger one to Fin.

'Mr. Macpherson is it?' said Fin. 'Welcome to West Hunday.'

He threw the bags into the boot of the VW and they then made their way down to the observatory, the newcomer pressing Fin for news of the most recent sightings on the island. He seemed impressed when Fin was able to relay the news of the warbler spotted earlier in the day by Anya and Yulia.

***

Fin spent the evening in the bar contemplating what was for the best. Becky had said that the island gave her the creeps and he was starting to feel the same. As he sat nursing a Corncrake he remained disturbed by Becky's sudden departure and his inability to find any clue as to why she or Ophelia should have disappeared. All his amateur pottering had simply led to dead ends and he decided he needed to front it up. Despite his father's death Eric Branson had attended dinner and had seemed to be in fine form. He was now tidying away the paperwork from the evening's bird count. Fin knew it was not a good time but he couldn't put if off. Taking a deep breath, he walked over and asked if he could have a word.

'Sure Fin, come have a seat. Can I get you a new beer?'

Fin took another deep breath and said 'As I said earlier I was very sorry to hear about your father. I appreciate you must have other stuff on your mind but I need to raise this with you.'

Eric smiled. 'How can I help?'

'Look Eric, I don't think Becky left this island of her own accord.'

After the briefest hesitation Eric said 'What, Miss. MacPhail. Whatever makes you think that?'

'I found this in her room' said Fin, holding out Becky's pendant.

Another fleeting hesitation. 'Sorry but I don't understand. What on earth were you doing in her room?'

'I was worried about her' said Fin, feeling slightly foolish.

'How do you know it belongs to her?'

'I saw her wearing it the other day.'

'Are you sure?'

Fin did not reply but instead took a swig of his beer and looked straight at Eric.

Eric's wiped his hand across this face. 'Well there's nothing to be worried about, I can assure you. I gave her a lift up to the airfield and saw her on the morning plane myself. She's no doubt back home by now. If you give me the jewelry I'll make sure it is posted on to her.' He held out his hand but Fin said 'That OK, I have her address and can hand it in to her when I am back in Edinburgh.'

They sat in silence for a few moments, and then Eric said. 'Don't take this the wrong way Fin but I think you've been letting your imagination run away with itself. Small islands can have that effect. Why not just take it easy tomorrow. Perhaps you can show Mr. Macpherson over there around the island. It does not do one any good to spend too much time by themselves.'

Fin took another swig from his drink. 'Err.. yes, perhaps. I'm just being daft that's all. I sorry to have bothered you at such a difficult time.'

Eric seemed satisfied with that answer. 'Now' he said, smiling 'what about that other beer?'

Fin had felt foolish speaking to Eric, but he knew one thing from his years in the police force. Eric Branson was lying. His speech pattern and body language had been telegraphing his deceit to Fin.

Fin did not bother going outside to try to call Mrs. Maclean. He knew there would be no signal. He finished Eric's beer and then went out to make his way over to the bunkhouse. The night was cold and clear with the sky covered in stars. It was like nothing he was used to in Edinburgh with the sky crowded in by the narrow streets and tall tenements. As he looked up in awe at the enormity of it, flashes of coloured lights, greens, blues and reds, started to light up the night sky. He watched in amazement. He was aware of others joining him and gasping up at the light show. Eric Branson was by his side. 'That's the Northern Dancers' he said 'absolutely magical isn't it.'

'Amazing' was as best as Fin could do by way of a reply.

The light show continued for several minutes before dying away.

'You're very lucky, said Eric. 'We've had visitors coming up here for years who have never experienced the Aurora Borealis. You know the ancients used to think it was a message from the Gods. We think we know better now, but we shouldn't ignore our forebears. They were more connected to the spirits than us and they felt the force of nature.'

'What's the message?' asked Fin.

'I'm not sure' said Eric. 'But it will reveal itself.'

Fin stood watching the light show until eventually the sky returned to darkness.

He was exhausted when he returned to his bunk room. Lying down on his bed, his clothes and boots still on, he took out Becky's pendant and closed his fist around it.

Saturday 21 April

Frigga and Fulla were quieter than usual at breakfast. Perhaps, thought, Fin, they were upset at Sir Rolf's passing.

Fin was seated next to the new arrival, Mr. Macpherson.

'I understand that you are going to be my guide today. I hope you're as excited as I am.'

'Yeah, my excitement is bubbling over.'

Please call me 'Harry' he had said. It transpired that Eric Branson had spoken to him the previous evening and Fin had been sold to him as someone who knew the whole island. He produced an island map showing the various bird hides he wanted to visit highlighted. 'Eric told me' he said, 'that a big Atlantic storm is due to blow in this evening so I am hoping to tick off some rarities before I go back south after the weekend.'

'Well, let's see what we can do' said Fin, trying to smile and indicate a modicum of enthusiasm but thinking privately what a bunch of arse holes some of these birders were.

Harry, when he appeared around the front of the observatory after breakfast, was kitted up for a serious tramp. He wore the latest waterproofs and was carrying over his shoulder the largest pair of binoculars Fin ever had seen. It didn't improve Fin's opinion of him.

'Shall we try the loch first', he said, 'pointing to Hoy Loch' on the map. 'That sounds ideal' replied Fin. He had decided over breakfast that there was nothing fruitful he could do on the island. He was resigned to having a quiet day, packing up and then catching a flight in the morning to the mainland. He'd need to ask Eric to arrange for his VW to be loaded onto the following week's ferry.

Tramping down to the hide, Fin saw two men cutting reeds by the loch side. They were throwing them onto a large pile already cut. 'What do they use them for?' asked Harry.

Fin thought back to the wicker coffin in the church but said 'I'm afraid I don't know. Perhaps they use them to make furniture.'

'That must be furniture for a giant given the amount they've already cut.'

Fin gave the thinnest of smiles.

When they arrived at the hide it was empty. Harry spent an age setting up his binoculars whilst Fin passed the time making up a brew. Together they watched out over the loch from the narrow window in the side of the hide, Fin enjoying the silence. He sipped his tea. He still did not believe that Becky would have got on the plane under her own free-will without letting him know. As soon as he got to Kirkwall he'd catch the first flight down to Edinburgh to find out what had happened. He found himself dosing in the morning air and was not sure if he had drifted off to sleep when the hide door opened. He was pleased to see Anya standing there.

'Hi there, Mr. Tulloch. We don't seem to be able to keep you away. We'll make a birder out of you yet.'

'Shuhh' whispered Harry.

Ignoring him Fin said 'you'll have your work cut out. This is Harry by the way. He arrived last night. He's the real McCoy birder-wise. Harry, meet Anya. She knows all you'll ever need to know about ornithology.' Anya blushed at the compliment.

Harry said hello and asked Anya if there had been any sight of the warbler this morning. He looked disappointed when she said no.

Anya joined them in a cup of tea, or in her case, coffee. She'd brought some chocolate biscuits and Harry and Fin were happy to share them. 'Harry was wondering what the men over there will be using the reeds for' said Fin.

'I'm sorry but I've not seen anyone cutting the reeds before. I think they used to use them to make Orkney chairs and other bits of furniture. Perhaps that is it.'

They watched the men working on methodically with two large scythes collecting together a huge bundle which they loaded onto the back of a tractor trailer.

'They must be building a mighty big chair' said Harry, cracking the same joke as before. Anya just looked puzzled. It obviously did not translate well into Polish.

The morning passed on slowly with Harry jotting down various sightings in his notebook as Fin gazed out across the loch. He seemed frustrated at Anya's inability to identify a few of the species and tutted loudly.

Ignoring him Anya said to Fin with a concerned voice 'You seem very quiet today.'

'Oh, don't worry about me' he replied quietly 'I was just thinking about Becky. It wouldn't be like her to go off without telling me first.'

'I thought you'd just met her' whispered Anya, trying not to interrupt Harry's concentration on the birds.

'Aye, but we'd planned to do some further walking together' he said trying to correct himself.

'Oh, you know young people are like' said Anya quietly. 'She probably just had a change of plan. I'm sure she'll be OK'. He could sense however some doubt in her voice.

'I wish I could be so confident' he said. He lowered his voice 'That's two girls if you include Ophelia McLeod who've apparently just abandoned ship without telling anyone. Tell me about her.'

Anya thought for a moment and then picked up the tea and coffee mugs to clean them outside out of Harry's earshot. Fin followed her over.

'I didn't know her long but she seemed a nice girl, Fin. Perhaps, as you say, a bit rough around the edges, but with a good heart. I understand she'd had a tough upbringing and was an orphan, just like me and Yulia. She was very easy going but behind that she was really focused and hard working. He kept a really detailed record of her sightings.'

She rinsed out the mugs and went on 'Her birding knowledge was immense and she seemed determined to get as much out of her placement as possible. It meant such a lot to her and I know she was really chuffed to be selected. That's why it was a shock to the three of us when she just up and left without any notice. It just wasn't like her. Eric said it sometimes happens and some volunteers just can't hack it, what with the isolation and all, but Ophelia wasn't like that. She also left some of her sketches and drawings behind and there's no way she'd do that. To tell you the truth Mr. Tulloch the longer it's been since she left the more worried I've become.'

'Perhaps you can show me some of her drawings' he said.

'Yes' she said distracted. 'The thing is… we expected her back within a day or so. The longer she'd been away, the more you start to think something must have happened to her. Yulia and Lydia are even talking about cutting their placements short. We don't like the atmosphere here. Those two girls in the kitchen are so odd and half the islanders seem to be in a daze. We can't even talk to our friends back home with the phones being down.'

'I wouldn't worry' he said without conviction. 'I am sure Becky and Ophelia are both well and will turn up soon.'

'You won't say anything, will you. I wouldn't like Mr. Branson to think I was unhappy. I was so lucky to get this placement'

'Don't worry. I won't mention it to anyone.'

But although he said this what Anya had said caused him to worry even more. Not for the first time, he thought about the fact he was on a remote island with no police presence and with no way of contacting the outside world.

Harry interrupted. He'd seen enough here and asked if it would be possible to pay a visit up to the hide by the lighthouse complex. 'Sure' said Fin but allowing Harry to set off up the path ahead of him, he held back for a moment and said to Anya 'I'm sure everything will be OK and there is nothing to worry about. Let's me buy you and the other girls a drink this evening as a thank-you and I'd love to see those drawings.'

'Is Anya an artist?' asked Harry as they got in the VW. He must have overheard.

'No, but a good friend is' said Fin.

***

They parked up at the spot where they had left their bikes for their night-time sortie up to the lighthouse. Fin saw that Steve's still lay in the ditch where it had been abandoned. The wind was picking up but the sky was still clear with only a few distant clouds against the horizon. The flowers on the links were in full bloom and Harry stopped to take some photos.

'That is a very impressive structure' said Harry, snapping away at the lighthouse. 'Ships must be able to see its light for miles. It's a shame it's closed to the public.' Fin looked up towards it. He said 'You could try asking Eric Branson to organize a tour around it but I'm not sure you'll have much joy. I certainly didn't.'

They wandered down the embankment from the road onto the grass, Fin bracing himself with his cane. 'Is it arthritis you have?' asked Harry. 'No, I used to be in the police force and unfortunately I suffered an injury on duty' said Fin.

'I'm sorry to hear that' said Harry. 'Your family must be proud of you though.'

Fin didn't answer. He perhaps had a granddaughter he didn't know but how could she be proud of him. He'd done nothing to help her and hadn't even met her.

Reaching the hide, he called out a hello and Yulia opened up the door. 'Do you mind if we join you? Harry here is keen to see if there is anything interesting.' 'Good timing' she said, 'there's been a Great Northern Diver circling. If we're lucky it will still be around.' Harry looked as if his Christmas had come early as he set up his equipment.

They spent the next couple of hours watching the Diver and Harry providing a running commentary about it. Fin passed his time by keeping them fortified with tea and coffee. Mid-afternoon Fin said that he was going for a stroll and he started out in the direction of the lighthouse away from the shoreline on which the Diver was performing. It was a gentle climb up the hill and soon enough he was up to the line of the fence being careful not to touch it. Peering through it up to the lighthouse complex he caught a glance of a man walking across the courtyard. He was a good distance off but he was sure it was Stan Laurel from the ferry. Whoever it was wearing what appeared to be a white lab coat. The figure in the distance disappeared behind the side of the far lighthouse cottage just as a SUV with Eric Branson and Oliver Hardy in the front seats came rattling down the track from the complex. It pulled up at the gate. He saw Oliver Hardy jump out of the passenger side, open up the gate and wave Eric through. He then looped a large padlock across the gate and having checked it was closed by giving it a firm tug, got back into the car. It zoomed off scattering gravel and chasing a few grazing sheep onto the surrounding grass. Neither man in the car noticed or paid any attention to him.

He spent some time watching the lighthouse but the man in the white coat failed to re-appear. There was no other sign of life. He was wasting his time. Wandering slowly back to the hide, he was met by Harry who was disappointed to tell him that the Diver had disappeared. 'Tell you what, said Fin, 'I know where they're a really big bird due to come into land soon. In this wind, it should be an interesting sight. Would you like to join me?' Harry looked at him as if he were daft but said he would, the other option being a long walk back to the observatory and after saying thanks to Yulia, they set off for the campervan.

After a few yards Harry said 'Now Yulia. She's a real expert. Far more knowledgeable than Anya.'

What an arse hole thought Fin.

'Maybe' he said 'mind you Anya makes a better cup of tea.'

***

The usual twosome of Old Billy and his friend were leaning against the gate into the airfield when they arrived. Eric Branson was already out in the Land Rover ineffectually trying to chase away the gulls.

'Is it on time?' asked Fin.

'We'll know when it arrives' said Billy. They stood looking to the south and after a few minutes a small dot appeared in the late afternoon sky. It quickly grew larger and they could hear the noise of the small plane working hard into the head wind. Its tone changed as it turned to approach the runway. Wavering right and left it descended like a drunk man making his way down a set of stairs, bumping down in starts. Harry looked apprehensive as it came towards them but Fin was now an old pro and took it in his stride as the Islander pulled round at the last moment to land with a bump, the pilot throttling back with all his might. The plane then swirled around and taxied up to its usual spot.

Harry looked a little peaky, no doubt thinking that he would need to be boarding the same plane in couple of days' time. 'Don't worry' said Fin 'I don't think they've lost one yet.' That didn't help the green look on Harry's face. Arse hole thought Fin.

Eric Branson appeared with his luggage trolley and opened up the passenger door to the plane. It was busy and a group of three got out, no doubt islanders home for the weekend. Then another squeezed out, much taller, with a dark beard and wearing a cycle cap. It was Becky's Magnus. He waved over and Fin held up his hand in acknowledgement. Magnus slung a canvas travel bag over his shoulder and came over.

'Hello there Fin. I was not expecting a welcome committee.'

'What, you didn't think I'd be here to meet my grand-son.' He said it loud enough for the two old men at the airfield gate to hear. 'This is Harry' he added. 'I've have been showing him the highlights of West Hunday.' Harry said hello.

'Where's Becky' asked Magnus.

Fin was conscious that the islanders, including Eric Branson, were watching them.

'Let's put your stuff in the van and I'll run you down to the observatory. I assume you're saying there? We can talk better down there'.

They dropped off Harry Macpherson by the start of the trail up to the observatory, leaving him to lug his huge binoculars up the track, and then drove down to the pier-head and parked up looking out to sea.'

'So, what's going on?' asked Magnus.

'I really don't know' said Fin. As economically as possible he briefed Magnus on the events of the week including Becky's disappearance and his discovery of her pendant.

'There no way she'd leave that. Offie gave it to her when she was eighteen. It meant a lot to her that necklace. I told her not to come up here and just go straight to the police but she wouldn't listen. Now look at the mess we're in.'

'You need to see if you can catch the first flight back in the morning' said Fin. 'I'll write a report tonight that you can hand over to the polis.'

'Bullshit! I'm not leaving here without Becky. She must still be on this fecking island somewhere. I'll find her if I need to turn over every stone to do so.'

'Listen Magnus, we can't simply go crashing about. That's not going to do Becky or Ophelia any good, even if they are still on West Hunday. We need to think this through and work out a plan of action.'

'And do you have a plan Fin?'.

'Oh yes. Now you're here I do indeed.'

'Are you going to share it.'

'Later, but first of all, when I called you from Kirkwall I asked you to see what background you could find out on the Branson family?' asked Fin.

'It wasn't hard. Just some Googling needed. They've been around forever. Did favours for the English in both Jabobite risings, and after the second got a good chunk of the Orkneys as a thank you. Spent the next hundred years or so clearing the crofters off the land and introducing sheep instead. Seem then to have made a string of bad investments and they've ended up only with his God forsaken spot.'

'And what about Sir Rolf and Eric Branson?'

'Both born up here. Sir Rolf was educated at Fettes and Oxford and later was a director in a small Edinburgh bank which failed in the 1980s. Eric fared not much better. He worked for a hedge fund for a while in London, but it all ended badly. There was court case started over alleged embezzlement of clients' money but it all seems to have been swept under the carpet.'

'And where does the cash come from to maintain his place?'

'I've no idea. There's an article from the 1970s which says West Hunday was one of the poorest places in Scotland with the residents trapped in a feudal time warp, so how they've turned it all around I've no idea.'

'They haven't. The crofters are still living in poverty. But from somewhere they've secured the cash to build the poshest bird observatory you're ever likely to see and to turn the lighthouse into a fortress.'

The sun was starting to fall into the sea and Fin realised the time.

'We'd better get you up to the observatory. Dinner's due bang on seven so we'd better not be late. Eat well. We're going to be busy tonight.'

***

Magnus had been given Becky's old room. Arriving down for dinner he was the centre of attention. 'So, you're Fin's grandson then?' said Eric Branson.

'That's right' said Magnus. 'I had some holiday due so I said I would come and then we could share the long drive back to Edinburgh.'

'Have you been to the northern isles before?'

'No, it's a first for me. I'm hoping to see if I can check out a few of them whilst I'm here.'

It seemed a tall tale but Eric Branson seemed to buy it.

'Are you a birder?'

'No' said Magnus 'but my girlfriend is quite knowledgeable. Hopefully she's passed on a little to me.'

Fin had noticed the eyes of the three volunteers on Magnus, but on mention of a girlfriend he sensed a slightly disappointed atmosphre. He thought back to Becky emphasising to him that Magnus was only a flatmate. Obviously Magnus had a different take on their relationship.

'So, what's your plan for the week ahead' Eric asked Fin.

'I thought I would show Magnus the highlights of West Hunday tomorrow and flights permitting we'd then go over to Kirkwall and check out Skara Brae and perhaps some of the other Orkney isles. I understand that there's a bird observatory on North Ronaldsay and I'd like to visit it.'

'Two observatories in one visit! We'll make a birder of you yet' exclaimed Eric.

There was a good smell from the kitchen tonight and when the food arrived, they sat down to a hearty meal of haggis, neeps and tatties followed by cranachan. Both Magnus and Fin ate well, with Fin making his excuses after dinner while Magnus took in a couple of beers with the volunteers. Fin casually slipped a note under Magnus's door in the bunkhouse as he walked past it to his own.

***

Just after midnight Fin tapped quietly on Magnus's bunkroom door. The door opened an inch, the light already off inside. 'You ready?' he whispered. 'Aye' came the reply. Outside it was raining and the wind had risen sharply. Tightening up their coats they hurried over to the VW camper van. No messing with bicycles tonight. Fin started up the engine. It sprang into life on the second attempt. He left the lights off and started quickly down the track to the road, the old camper bumping from side to side through the pot-holes. Reaching the road he pressed full on the accelerator, crunching through the gears and they sped up the road and across the causeway. He flicked on the side lights.

'What's the score?' Magnus asked.

'It got to be the lighthouse. Something's not right up there and we're going to find out what.'
|
'OK, step on the gas and let's see how fast we can get there.'

They sped up to the top of the hill, bouncing over the rise. At the turning marked with the war memorial, Fin stepped on the brakes and they took a sharp right.

'I thought it was straight ahead' said Magnus.

'It is, but first we need to check out something else.'

They rushed down the single track road and within a minute had reached the village. They sped through it and Fin pulled up with a jolt by the path up to the church.

'What are we doing here?' asked Magnus.

'Follow me' said Fin.

He led Magnus up the path to the church. He tried the door and it opened. He took out a torch and shined it around the empty interior. Faces from the carvings starred back.

'Some place' said Magnus, looking around the elaborate decoration.

Fin shone the torch around towards the alter. Lying before it was the reed coffin.

'Shit Fin' whispered Magnus. 'What are you doing?'

'I need to see who it is' said Fin.

He walked down the aisle. The coffin lid was now decorated with flowers.

'Hold this'. He handed the torch to Magnus.

He could hear Magnus's breathing. Taking a gulp of air he lent down and prized the coffin lid off, pulling it to one side. He forced himself to look down. There in the coffin lay the alabaster face of Sir Rolf. He pushed the lid back into place.

'I had to be sure' he said, quickly marching back up the aisle.

'You didn't think it might be one of the girls.'

'I just had to be sure.'

As they got outside, they heard a dog barking in the distance. In silence they climbed back into the VW. Fin reversed up and they started back through the village. Lights had come on in a couple of cottages but Fin ignored them and began to accelerate back up to the turning to the lighthouse.

The road was clear and they sped forward. Up at the top of the island he swerved around the corner leading up to the lighthouse, the old van lifting onto two wheels. The complex ahead was lit up by the light from the top of the tower circling round in the night sky. He accelerated on up the track towards the gate.

'I thought you said it was locked' said Magnus.

'Knock, knock' said Fin and he rammed the VW straight through the padlocked gate. It burst open, one half shooting into the air and landing yards down the drive.

'Bloody hell Fin' shouted Magnus, hanging on to his seat.

Fin sped up the drive and screeched to a halt by the lighthouse tower. 'Right let's see who's at home.' He was out of the van and marching over the courtyard. Magnus trailed behind a couple of steps still in shock from their violent entry.

A light had come on in one of the cottages. 'Come on Magnus' said Fin. He was almost at the door when it opened and the man he'd nick-named Stan Laurel stepped out in shorts and a t-shirt. He starred at Fin and then down the track to where the gate lay in bits.

'You'll pay for that gate old man. Now get the fuck away!' He spat the words out menacingly. He pushed Fin who stumbled back losing his balance. Magnus stepped in 'Hey there wee man, get your hands off him.'

'And who the fuck are you big boy?'

'I'm Becky's boyfriend and I'm here to take her home'.

'Listen I don't know no Becky or what you are talking about but I want you away from here now.'

Stan Laurel took a step towards Magnus but Magnus was a big guy and he stood his ground. He held up a finger and said in a low voice 'Now just you step aside and I'll not need to deck you.' He pushed past the man with Fin following and they stepped into the cottage. There was a door to the right and one to the left. Trying the one to the right, Fin found himself in the kitchen. Whatever Laurel and Hardy were, they were not house proud. Dirty dishes filled the sink and covered the counter-tops. Turning to the room on the left, he found an equally messy living room.

'You need to get out of here' called the man, but Fin paid no attention. He walked down the corridor to the rear. The first door led into a bedroom. Piles of clothes lay on the floor. The second was into a dirty bathroom and the third was locked.

'Open it up' said Fin.

'You're going to regret this' said Stan Laurel.

'Magnus, see if you can get this door opened' said Fin.

Magnus stepped forward and tried to shoulder barge the door. 'Oomph..' he cried. The door creaked but remained in place. He lifted his leg and crashed into the door with his boot. It shuddered but held firm. He took a step back and smashed his boot again in it. The door splintered open, the lock breaking loose. Magnus rubbed his leg. Fin stepped forward and flicked on the light switch. It was a store room but in contrast to the remainder of the cottage it was immaculately clean. A row of metal shelves stood on one wall and a metal table stood in the middle. There was a weighing machine on the table. White coats hung on pegs by the door. A couple of brown packages sat on the shelf.

'What is it?' said Magnus.

'Drugs' said Fin. 'This must be where they cut it up. Get that guy back in here.'

Magnus stepped into the corridor. Stan Laurel was just standing there looking worried. He dragged him back into the store room by his neck.

'You're so dead man'.

'Listen, I don't care about whatever you have going on here. We just want Becky and Ophelia. Now start talking or we're going to start breaking some bones.'

'I've already hold you. I don't know what you're talking about. If you fucking touch me, you'll both be dead.' The man was shaking. Magnus gave him a stiff kick and he slumped to the ground.

'We need to check the other cottage' said Fin. 'You' he said, pointing to the man. 'Get up. You're coming with us.'

Pushing the man forward with them, they started across the courtyard to the second cottage. It was locked.

'Keys' demanded Magnus.

'I don't have them' said Stan Laurel.

Magnus thumped him in the solar plexus. He doubled over in pain.

'You'll need to do better than that' snarled Magnus.

He pulled Stan Laurel back upright and thumped him again. Again, he doubled over.

'Look!' called Fin. A set of headlights appeared around the corner up to the lighthouse. They were moving fast.

'What now?' asked Magnus.

Fin grabbed Stan Laurel and pulled his arm up his back. He let out a cry.

'Now, no messing wee man or you're going to get hurt.'

The SUV was now at the entrance to the courtyard. It pulled to a halt, its headlights lighting up Fin and Magnus.

Out stepped Oliver Hardy and Eric Branson. They casually wandered over. Eric smiled at them. 'Fin, what brings you out so late, and with young Magnus I see.'

Eric glanced into the open door to the first cottage.

'Oh, I assume you've discovered our little operation' he said. 'That's a pity, a real pity.'

Oliver Hardy took a couple of steps towards them.

'Hold it there, and I won't have to harm your wee pal here' shouted Magnus. He pulled up Stan Laurel's arm and he let out another yelp.

'I'm afraid we can't simply let matters be' said Eric.

'Listen Eric' said Fin 'we're not interested in whatever you have going on here. We just want Becky and Ophelia back.'

Eric Branson looked puzzled. 'Becky and Ophelia. But I've already told you. They've both gone. Now it's late and I don't have time for all this silliness'

He walked over to Oliver Hardy and said 'I'll get the goods. You deal with them.'

Hardy nodded. Calmly, he reached into his inside jacket pocket and pulled out a semi-automatic. It was large and glinted black. He pointed it at Fin. 'Right' he said, 'enough fucking around, you two are going on a fishing trip.'

Despite his army training and police service Fin did not know much about modern guns but knew he was on the wrong side of this one.

Magnus waited a couple of seconds and then released his hold on Stan Laurel who stumbled away holding his stomach.

Oliver Hardy waved the semi-automatic towards the lighthouse. 'OK, you two.' Pulling out a set of keys he threw them to Stan Laurel who opened up the heavy door. Flicking the gun, he indicated to them to step forward. 'Get inside' he said. Magnus half moved towards him but Oliver Hardy simply growled 'Don't be a numptie'. He waved the semi-automatic in the direction of the tower door and Magnus and Fin stepped into the dark interior. The door immediately clanged shut behind them and they heard the lock turning. They were in almost total darkness.

They would hear Oliver Hardy speaking to Stan Laurel. 'Okay, me and Eric will tidy up here. You radio the boat and organise the pick-up. We can dispose of the waste at the same time.'

A moment later they heard the car pulling away. Magnus and Fin stood in silence. Slowly growing accustomed to the gloom they looked around their make-shift prison cell. It was the ground floor of the lighthouse, with circular steps leading up to the floors above. It was wood lined but, apart from a narrow skylight above the door letting in a crack of light, windowless. 'Let's try upstairs' said Fin and slowly the climbed to the floor above. They found that level empty but with a small barred window looking down onto the courtyard. They could see Eric Branson below. They watched as he locked up the first cottage and then walked over to the second, took out a key and opened it up. A moment later he re-appeared holding Becky's hand. She was dressed in a white frock and stumbled slowly forward looking down to the ground as if in a trance.

Magnus called out her name, but she showed no sign of recognition. He called again and Eric Branson glanced up, smiling. He was speaking to Becky but they could not hear. He guided her with his arm over to his SUV and helped her into the front seat. He then got in the driver's seat and they departed down through the broken gates towards the road.

'Oh my God' said Magnus. 'What do you think they've done to her.'

'She looked completely out of it' said Fin. 'Drugged up the eyeballs.'

'We've got to get out of here' said Magnus. He started up the spiral stairs from the current level. They led in loops all the way to the top deck of the lighthouse. Fin was out of breath by the time he reached the top deck. There, a huge multi-faceted light was rotating slowly on its axis. Tracking round it shone a beam for miles in every direction. Fin looked down. It seemed very high. 'It's automatic' said Magnus. 'It must work off a timer. We could try turning it off. That might alert someone.'

They looked around the deck for a control switch but couldn't find anything. Frustrated, Magnus gave the light a kick but it simply juddered and then kept rotating. He kicked it again and this time it gradually ground to a halt. 'What now?' he asked.

'We need to get out of here' said Fin. 'We must be over a hundred feet up. We'll kill ourselves if we jump. Let's see if we can force the door down on the ground.'

But when they climbed back down they found the door to the lighthouse much more robust than the bedroom door in the cottage. Magnus exhausted himself trying but it showed absolutely no sign of movement. He thumped it with his fist in frustration and then collapsed down onto the cold stone floor.

'Well, I've really fucked this up' said Fin.

'Nonsense' said Magnus 'we had to do something. At least we know Becky is alive. I take it that was a drug laboratory in the cottage.'

'Aye', said Fin. 'It's the perfect base when you think about it. A small island with no police presence and completely under the control of the laird. I suspect they pick the supply in bulk from passing fishing boats, cut it down to street size packages in the lab and then import it on the mainland along with the other island produce. A very neat solution when you think about it.'

Magnus said 'it explains how the Bransons could afford to build the bird observatory and all the other investment into the island.'

'Yes' said Fin 'those SUVs they're driving around in don't come cheap either.'

'Do you think that Ophelia and then Becky somehow found out about it?' asked Magnus.

'Perhaps' said Fin. He left it hanging in the air. It did not want to think about what might have happened if the girls had somehow stumbled on the goings-on at the lighthouse.

Sunday 22 April

Fin told Magnus to try to get some sleep and they made themselves as comfortable as they could on the cold stone floor. For ages they lay in silence staring into the darkness but eventually Fin heard Magnus's breathing change as sleep came to him. But he had too much on his mind to sleep himself. He felt responsible for Ophelia and Becky and he had let them down. The same now applied to Magnus. He was seriously out of his depth but, somehow or other, he had to find the girls and get then off the island. He tried to think of a way through but nothing would come to him. His mind wandered to Old BIlly with his stories of the family history of the island, perhaps even his own family; then to the strange old woman at the church and her happiness in the thought of an eternity spent in a graveyard looking over the bay to the lighthouse. He must have drifted off because with a start he suddenly woke to find that dawn was breaking. Slowly the light in their prison cell grew slightly brighter. He let Magnus sleep on. They would need all the energy they could get. He stood up and stepped over to the door to examine it in more detail. It was solid with an old fashioned and sturdy mortice lock. He looked down through the key hole but only had sight of an empty courtyard. He sat back down thinking of options. Perhaps they could rush the guys when they came for them. He looked around for a weapon. The ground floor was completely empty. He set off back up the stairs. Up in the light room, he found a wooden tool box. Opening it up he picked out a spanner about eighteen inches long, presumably used for adjusting the light mechanism. He picked it up. It was nice and heavy.

'What are you doing?'

He turned to the steps. Magnus stood there.

'We need to be tooled up for when they come back.' He showed Magnus the spanner.

'Are you kidding? That guy has a gun. We'll have no chance.'

'Well, we certainly have no chance unless we do something. There's no way they're going to let us off the island now we've found their drug lab.'

Magnus did not say anything. Instead, he climbed up into the light room and started to rummage in the tool box for something for himself. He pulled out a long screwdriver.

They made their way back to the ground floor. Fin stood to one side of the door. He opened up his jacket and tore a hole in the lining. He checked to make sure the spanner fitted.

'Okay, when he opens the door, we step out nice and calm. We'll only have one chance. Best option is when they put in in the car.'

'What if they decide to top us here?' asked Magnus.

'If they were going to do that, they'd have done so last night.'

Fin sat down with his back to the wall. Magnus did likewise.

They must have waited a good couple of hours, Fin was dozing. He was startled by the sound of a car approaching. He was up in a flash his adrenaline pumping. Then there were steps of two men on the courtyard cobbles. Quickly they each put their weapons in the inside pockets of their jackets.

A key rattled in the door, unlocking it. 'Come on out' shouted Eric Branson.

Fin opened the door and stepped into the day light. Magnus was right behind him. Eric Branson and Oliver Hardy stood about ten feet away. Both were dressed in yellow oilskins. Hardy was pointing his semi-automatic directly at Fin's head.

'Now behave boys' said Oliver Hardy smiling 'or I'll have to pop the old guy here and now.'

'I hope you had a good sleep' said Eric with faux politeness. 'Now, I need you please to follow me and my friend here. I am sure you will behave, yes? My friend has a very twitchy trigger finger and won't hesitate to demonstrate if necessary.' He beckoned them towards his SUV.

'Now I need you two please in the front. Magnus here will drive. Don't be silly please Magnus, or we'll have no option but to blow Fin's brains all over the dashboard which would be an awful nuisance to clean up.'

Magus followed by Fin eased themselves on board. Oliver Hardy then slipped in the back, keeping the semi-automatic pointing at Fin's head. Finally, Eric got on board. He threw the car key over into Fin's floor well.

'Now, nice and easy Fin, hand the keys to Magnus'

Slowly Fin stopped down and found the keys. He handed them over to Magnus.

'Where to?' asked Magnus

'Down to the pier' said Oliver Hardy. 'Nice and slow.'

Magnus started to pull his seat belt on.

'No seat belts' said Oliver Hardy I don't want you accidentally driving into a wall.

Magnus drove as instructed, passing the airstrip just as the morning flight arrived. As they drove past the track up to the observatory, Fulla and Frigga were walking by. They waved a morning greeting as if everything was normal.

'Carry on' said Oliver Hardy, poking Magnus in the neck with his gun.

Magnus rumbled on over the cattle grid and up to the shed by the pier. The double doors were open and a large inflatable rib sat in the water roped up on the jetty. 'Pull up here'. Magnus did as he was told.

'Okay, let's do it all in reverse' said Eric.

Fin and Magnus sat still.

'Keys' shouted Oliver Hardy.

Magnus pulled them out and handed them to Fin. Fin then threw them back towards Eric. The keys landed in the rear floor well. Eric started to bend down to retrieve them but Oliver Hardy said 'Leave them'

Oliver Hardy opened his door and eased out keeping his gun trained on Fin. Eric then stepped out the other side.

'Right, old man, you first' shouted Hardy.

Eric eased himself out, leaning on his walking cane. Magnus then opened his door and started to step out. As he did so, Fin pulled out his spanner and back handed it into Eric's face, catching him a fleeting blow. Eric instinctively put his hand up as protection. Fin lashed down at it with his cane.

At the same time, Magnus was trying to pull the screwdriver out of his pocket. He had it free, but just as he lifted it up there was a deafening roar as Oliver Hardy let out a single shot, shattering the rear window of the SUV.

Fin froze. Magnus was in shock.

'No more messing, mother fuckers!' screamed Oliver Hardy.

Fin dropped the spanner. A second later Magnus followed suit with the screwdriver.

'Get on the floor!' screamed Hardy. 'Now!'.

Fin slowly lowered himself down onto the ground. Oliver Hardy stepped over and gave him an almighty kick in the side. Fin couldn't breathe. He was sure his ribs were broken.

'Okay, no more fucking about. If either of you twitch I'll burn you right here.'

'Check their pockets' Hardy ordered Eric.

Eric Branson lent down and went through first Fin's coat pockets and then Magnus's.

'Nothing on them' he said.

'Okay, on your feet mother fuckers.'

Fin pulled himself up, holding on to his cane to balance. His side was hurting like hell.

Eric Branson was holding his face. He smiled at Fin and then struck him with the back of his fist across the face. Magnus tightened but stood his ground, Oliver Hardy ointing his semi-automatic straight at his head.

'I hope you both have your sea legs' sneered Eric. He pointed to the rib on the jetty.

Fin and Eric looked down at the inflatable.

'Get on board' shouted Oliver Hardy. 'Now!'. He kicked Fin down towards the rib. Fin lost balance and lay sprawled on the ground his cane falling out of his hand.

Magnus bent down to help Fin onto his feet, but was waved away by Oliver Hardy. 'Get on board' he ordered 'young Eric here will give a hand to the old man.'

Well, thought Fin through blooded teeth, now at least we know who the boss is.

They were made to sit down at the bow end. Firing up a huge Evinrude outboard, the rib powered away from the jetty, lifting up out of the water and bouncing over the waves. It was not a comfortable nor dry ride for Fin and Magnus as they were bundled about at the front of the inflatable.

The boat roared over the sea, spray blasting into the faces of the two captives. Without the benefit of oilskins, both were soon wet and freezing cold despite some morning warmth from the Spring sun. They turned north up to the coastline quickly passing the village and then the skerries off the north of the island. They carried on at speed into the open sea bouncing over the increasingly large waves. Eventually, after a pummeling ride, the sound of the outboard eased and they could feel the boat slowing. A large rusted bute and white trawler sat in front of them. The name 'Adonis' was painted on its side.With practised skill, Eric pulled up along side it and threw out a rope caught by a crew member on the trawler. A second rope secured the rib to the side of the trawler and it drifted up and down with the larger boat. Eric killed the engine.

Almost immediately large brown packages started to be thrown down from the trawler and Oliver Hardy began to store these down the centre of the rib. Once they were all on-board, a rope ladder was swung over. 'Go on then' Hardy shouted to Fin 'up you go.'

Fin, with help of an arm from Magnus, made it to the foot of the rope ladder. He struggled to take a grip with his hands so cold. 'He can't do this' shouted Magnus above the sound of the waves. 'Then he can go to the bottom here' said Hardy. He raised his semi-automatic up and pointed it at Fin. But Eric Branson stepped forward and pushed Fin up with an arm around his waist, manhandling him up and into the trawler. Magnus followed suit and then Eric Branson jumped back down into the rib. The ropes were eased off, the outboard kicked into action and the rib pulled away. Neither Eric or Oliver Hardy looked back.

Fin and Magnus lay exhausted on the wet deck of the trawler. A figure stood over them. He spoke with a foreign accent. 'OK, you two, inside.' He pointed to a cabin door and with the boat rocking with the sea swell Magnus helped Fin inside. 'This way' the crew member said and he led them down a flight of stairs and along to a cabin at the stern. They stepped inside and the door slammed shut behind them. Taking in their surroundings, they appeared to be in some crew quarters. There were two bunk beds against one wall and a table and bench against the other. At least it was dry. Both were shivering from the cold. 'We need to get out of these clothes' said Magnus. Pulling off their coats, they wrapped blankets from the bunks around themselves and slowly they felt their circulation coming back.

'What do you think they have in for us?' asked Magnus, his teeth still chattering from the cold.

'Well, I don't think they'll be giving us a lift to the mainland. My best guess would be that they're going to take us further out into the ocean and away from the island and then dump us over-board.'

The cabin door opened and a tray was shoved along the floor. The door slammed shut. 'Our last supper?' said Magnus. 'Not if I have my way' said Fin 'How many of them are there?'

'There were two crew hurling down the boxes onto the inflatable. If you add a skipper in the wheelhouse, perhaps three or maybe four max?' suggested Magnus.

'Ok then. We'll need to get them separated. Have you seen any guns?' said Fin.

'No' said Magnus 'but I would put money on them being armed to the teeth if they're drug running.'

'We need to act quickly' said Fin. He looked around the cabin checking the shelves above the bunks. There was nothing they could use as a weapon.

An idea came to Fin. 'Get up' he said to Magnus. Magnus looked puzzled but stood. Fin turned the bench he'd been sitting on upside down and smashed off one of its legs. The noise of breaking wood seemed very loud in the confined space. They waited for a crew member to appear to see what was happening but heard no-one.

'Right' said Fin 'when the guy comes in for the tray I'll hit him with this and you then drag him in. We'll take the others the best we can.'

They sat waiting but there was still no sign of the crewman. Slowly they realised he would not be appearing until the denouement of their trip. Magnus got up and started banging on the cabin door and calling out for the crewman. Eventually a voice called 'Keep it down in there.' 'You'd better get down here now. I've got an old man down here needs the toilet' yelled Magnus.

'Well he'd better just take a piss in the corner' called the voice.

'Your choice but you'll have shit all over the floor to clear up' called back Magnus.

There was a second or two's pause and then 'Ok, Ok, I'm coming in. Get back against the far wall.'

The door opened a fraction and Magnus immediately kicked as hard as he could back against it. It burst back, hitting something soft. Magnus pushed open the door. The crew member lay dazed on the other side. Magnus kicked him in the side of the head and then pulled him into the cabin. He went quickly through his pockets and pulled out a knife. Fin stood watching, impressed. Magnus manhandled him out of the cabin and closed up the latch. They stood listening for a moment sure that the noise would have alerted the crew but no-one appeared.

Magnus pointed forward and Fin nodded. The crept forward along a tight corridor. There was a light on ahead and they heard loud pop music playing. The door into the aft cabin was open. A man with his back to them sat drinking beer from a can. Magnus inched forward. He was at the doorway to the cabin when the man turned around, sensing his presence. He leapt forward reaching for a revolver on the table in front of him but Magnus was already on top of him. They struggled on the floor for a moment but then the man went limp. Fin was standing over them holding the full can of beer with which he'd hit the man over the hand.

'Cheers' he said.

'Come on' said Magnus, picking up the crewman's revolver. 'They may have heard us.'

The man was large and in the small cabin he struggled to turn him onto his stomach. However, eventually he managed. He sat on top of the man and pulled back his arms. Looking around the cabin he wrenched the cord from the kettle and used it to tie the man's arms together. He was still out cold. They left him where he lay.

Fin followed Magnus up a set of rusty steps which led them onto the open deck and into the weather. The wind was howling.They were directly behind the wheelhouse. Keeping themselves flat against the side of the wheelhouse they inched around until they were standing by its closed door. Fin pressed his cane against the side railing, struggling to stay upright as the boat rolled about. Magnus's hand was on the handle to the door. He looked Fin in the eye and nodded. He pulled open the door and rushed in. The skipper was resting in a chair studying some charts. He looked up at Magnus, then focused on the revolver, but did not say anything. 'Is there anyone else on board' asked Magnus. The skipper remained silent just starring at the revolver. Magnus took a step forward and held the revolver direct to the man's temple. He said slowly. 'I won't ask again. Is there anyone else on board.'

The skipper shook his head. 'No'.

Keeping the revolver pointing at the man, Magnus said 'Right, we need....' but suddenly the man leapt at him, knocking back his chair and scattering the papers around him. The revolver was knocked from Magnus's hand and the man made a dive for it. He reached it just before Magnus was able to re-balance himself. Magnus watched in horror as it was raised in his direction. But then the revolver was falling to the floor. The skipper had dropped it with a cry, his other hand reaching up to his arm. Blood was spurting from it. Fin stood over him, an open sword from tinged red resting by his side. He wiped it on his leg and then threaded it back into this cane.

Magnus pulled himself off the floor. 'That's some weapon Fin. Now I know why you're so attached to your cane'

'I bought it in an antique shop in Edinburgh. Useful on a dark winter's night in the Old Town' said Fin. He picked up the revolver and handed it to Magnus.

'Sit back down' Fin shouted at the skipper. The man recoiled. 'Sit!' He pointed at the chair. The skipper did as ordered, holding his arm down by his side.

'Do you have a first aid box on board' asked Magnus.

'Down in the gallery' murmured the skipper. Again, he had a foreign accent.

Magnus said to Fin 'I'll get it. If you move an inch you'll get it like your two friends down below. Understood?'

There was no reply.

'Understood!' he shouted.

The skipper nodded.

'Fin, if he as much as coughs, plug him full of holes' and with that Magnus was gone.

Fin starred at the skipper, blood dripping from his arm. He did not look like causing trouble.

'Where are you from?'.

'Sorry?'

'Which country are you from?'

'Latvia.'

'That's a long way. Well, if you behave exactly as you're told, you might just make it home.'

Magnus was back up in a couple of minutes. 'The one in the aft cabin is dead' he said to Fin. The skipper's eyes followed him. Fin looked aghast.

'Let's see if we can get this one patched up' said Magnus. The materials in the first aid box were old and dirty. Magnus tore off a length of bandage. He then ripped off the man's shirt. He was bleeding badly. He quickly wrapped the bandage around the man's arm and pulled it as tight as possible creating a makeshift tourniquet. 'That will need to do for now' he said.

'What do you want?' asked the skipper.

'I want you to turn this crate around' said Magnus 'and take us straight back to West Hunday.'

'No way' said the skipper. 'I can drop you on Shetland maybe but I am not going back to West Hunday.'

'You can take us back or you can go over the side right here' said Magnus.

'Listen, I'm just a messenger boy. I deliver packages, that's all. I don't want any trouble. If I take you back, they'll kill me.'

'Your choice' said Magnus, pulling the man to his feet and pushing him towards the door.

'Ok, Ok' said the man. He slumped back into the chair. 'You'll need to take the wheel. We need to turn around. Pull it down hard to the right.'

Magnus pulled down on the wheel and the boat lurched violently to starboard. He and Fin were knocked off their feet. The skipper made a grasp for the revolver, but Magnus was too quick and smacked him across the face with it.

He fired a warning shot into the ceiling. The noise was shattering. 'Right. No more fucking around' he shouted.

The boat was still rocking around violently in the swell. The skipper said. 'Bring it round to the left... gently.' Magnus did as told and this time the boat eased back round.

'Keep it there' the skipper ordered. Slowly the crate turned around.

'How long will it take us?' asked Fin.

'Perhaps three or four hours' said the skipper. It depends on the weather.

'Fin, why don't you go down below and see if there's anything to eat on board. We need to get something into us' said Magnus. 'I'll keep an eye on the captain.'

Fin was reluctant to leave Magnus alone but did what he was told. They hadn't eaten since the evening before and would need all their strength for what looked like being a long day. He clambered back down the steps and then along to the galley. There was an empty space where he had expected to find the body of the second crew member. For an instant he thought that Magnus must have thrown him overboard, but then he remembered his size and heard a muffled voice behind him. Turning around, he found the crew member trussed up in the corner like a turkey. There was a large swelling on his forehead. Clearly, the can of beer has not done as much harm as he'd feared. He was staring at Fin with fear in his eyes.

'Now you sit there quietly while I rustle up some grub.'

He found the galley well stocked and soon had a big fry-up of bacon, sausage and eggs on the go. Popping a piping hot sausage in the crew member's mouth, he precariously carried a pot piled high back up to the wheel house. 'Here you go'. He passed the pot to Magnus, taking hold of the revolver in return. 'Dig in Magnus. There may not be much more of this for a while.'

Fin turned to the skipper. 'Where are the other guns?'

'What guns?'

'Don't bullshit me.'

'There are no other guns.'

Fin cocked the trigger and placed the revolver onto the skipper's temple. It felt heavy in his hand.

'Last chance, fatso.'

The skipper's eyes widened. 'I'm telling you. There are no guns.'

Fin stepped back lowered the revolver slightly, but keeping it trained on the skipper.

'If I find you've been lying, you'll go the same way as your compatriot downstairs.'

The skipper did not respond. He had very reason to believe Fin was serious.

They made slow but steady progress. If anything the trawler was even less stable than the rib Fin soon started to regret the fry-up as the boat rocked from side to side. He was relieved finally to see the familiar lighthouse coming into view. 'Keep well off shore' he ordered. 'I don't want anyone on the island identifying the boat.'

'Don't worry' replied the skipper 'neither do I.'

They passed along the east coast of the island and then turned into the bay by the pier and observatory. The skipper slowed the boat to a crawl and moored up along-side a set of steps leading down from the pier. There was no one in sight.

Fin and Magnus had commandeered some thick wool jumpers from the crew and were looking, and smelling, the part of two fishermen. 'Get over there' Magnus ordered the skipper, pointing to the far side of the cabin. The man cowered, fearing his time had come, but Magnus grabbed him and pushed him across onto the floor. Then, using the butt of the revolver, he began to smash the boat's radio equipment. 'I don't want you announcing our arrival'.

Keeping his revolver trained on the skipper Magnus positioned himself by the door to the bridge. 'OK, Fin, we'll need to make a jump for it. Are you up for it?'

'Just you watch me' said Fin and he climbed down the steps from the wheelhouse onto the deck, holding on to his cane. The boat was bobbing up and down against the steps. The next he knew Magnus had jumped down next to him and was taking him by the arm. Together they leapt from the deck onto the steps first making it to dry land. 'Come on' called Magnus and he dragged Fin up the steps two at a time. Behind them they heard the trawler's engines revving up as it reversed away from the pier. The skipper clearly had no intention of remaining around to explain what had happened.

'Hurry!' said Magnus. 'We're too exposed out here.' They made their way up the pier as quickly as Fin could manage and then up the path leading to the boat shed. It was open and they stood catching their breaths pressed up to its flank wall. Slowly Magnus peered around the bottom corner of the door, holding his revolver down by his side. The shed stood empty where the rib was normally housed. Fin appeared at Magnus's shoulder. Magnus said 'They must have dropped the drugs up at the jetty by the lighthouse. They'll want to get the rib back in the shed before dark but should give us a good couple of hours to check out the observatory.'

Looking up the road towards the causeway to the north part of the island, there was no-one visible. The whole island seems dead.

'Let's cut across the fields' said Magnus. 'I don't want anyone coming down from the north and spotting us on the open road.'

Magnus helped Fin over the nearest stone dyke and they followed it up towards the observatory. Again, from their position, there was no sign of life at the observatory and the only vehicle parked outside it was Fin's VW. Suddenly there was a cacophony of sound to their left. They both dived down on the grass. Fifty yards to their left a dozen or so grey-leg geese were taking to the sky and making a tremendous din.

Slowly they stood up, soaked from the wet grass.

'I'm starting to hate birds' said Fin. Magnus managed a thin smile.

They made the final hundred or so yards to the observatory without stirring up any more wildlife. The first port of call was to their rooms in the bunkhouse for a change of clothes, but they found that both had been emptied of their possessions.

'It's as if we were never on the island' said Magnus.

'Yes, just the same as the two girls. What do you think they'll do to the VW?'

'Push it off the pier probably.'

Fin did not like the thought of that.

They walked over to the main building. There was no sign of the volunteers. They went quietly through to the back towards the staff accommodation. They could hear voices coming from the kitchen. Getting closer, they could make out Frigga and Fulla chatting. They were talking about the wedding.

'Do you think she's be happy?' said a voice Fin recognised as Fulla.

'Of course, who wouldn't. She'll be the laird's wide.' It was Frigga.

'Only if she produces a son' cautioned Fulla.

Fin smacked open the kitchen door. 'Hello girls.'

'Oh…h…h..hello Mr. Tulloch' said Frigga. 'I thought you were gone.' She was obviously shocked to see them and blushed scarlet. Fulla just stood there with her mouth open. He was staring at the revolver in Magnus's hand.

'No, still present and correct Frigga. You can set another two for dinner.'

She smiled but remain agitated, rubbing her hands together. 'I'd better get on with my w..w..work' she said and turned back to the sink.

The moved on down the corridor towards the staff accommodation. 'You ca..ca..cannot go in there' she said.

'Don't worry Frigga. I'm sure Eric won't mind' and he opened the door marked *Staff Only*. Magnus joined him, giving a small wave to Frigga as he passed.

Off the corridor ahead of them were a number of rooms, the doors all closed. Fin opened the first door. It was a bedroom with two single beds, both unmade. It was a mess with clothes and bird watching equipment scattered around the floor. A typical student room. There were some photos pinned to a wall. There was a copy of the photograph of the volunteers he'd first seen on Ophelia's Facebook page. There was also a picture of Yulia and a young man. It was obviously her room. He did not know with which of the other volunteers she shared.

The second room was similar. Also, a mess of clothes and birding gear. This must belong to the third volunteer.

Magnus called him. He was in the next room. It was also a bedroom but this one was immaculately tidy.

'This was Offie's room.'

'How do you know?'

'That's her teddy.' He pointed to an old teddy bear lying on the bed.

Magnus pulled open the wardrobe. It was full of clothes. 'These are all Offie's.' He traced his finger lightly along the rail of clothes.

There was a desk by the window. Fin opened up the drawer. He rummaged amongst it.

'Did she keep a diary?'

'I don't know' said Magnus.

Her boyfriend would have known, thought Fin.

He had a quick look through the draw but couldn't see anything that might help.

He looked into the bathroom. It was empty.

'What sort of girl leaves all her clothes but takes all her toiletries?'

'It doesn't make any sense' agreed Magnus.

The last two rooms were a bedroom for presumably Frigga and Fulla and a small living room with a surprisingly expensive looking stereo unit in the corner and a large library of birding books.

'Where do the Bransons live?' asked Magnus.

'I'm not sure' said Fin. Eric had mentioned that his father was up at the lodge but I am not sure where it is.'

'Let's ask the lovely Frigga' said Magnus. 'Perhaps they can also caste some light on the whereabouts of Offie and Becky.'

But when they went back to the kitchen there was no sign of either girl.

'They must have legged it up the road' said Fin.

They walked outside. In the far distant they could make out two figures walking quickly across the causeway.

'There must be something on the island you've missed' said Magnus. 'Are there any parts you've not searched.'

'I don't think so, but let's get a map out and we can have a look.'

They went through to the dining hall, taking a beer each from the bar as they passed. They found one of the island maps and sat down to work through it. Checking north to south Fin went through each birding area. He got as far down as the village and then remembered the tractor he'd passed on the first day on the island working in one of the fields leading up to the village. He seemed to recall a farm track off to the right a little beyond the field. Looking at the map, there was a rock formation marked 'The Selkies' but no sign of a farm.

'I'm sure I saw a building up there sitting back from the shore when we came in on the trawler' he said. 'That must be it. I've covered every other square inch of this bloody island.'

'Ok' said Magnus 'Let's get going.'

Outside, Fin said 'Hold on a minute.' He went over to the VW. It was too good to be true. There was no key in the ignition.

'Can you start a car without a key' he asked.

'Sorry, no' said Magnus.

'Me neither. We'll need to use Shanks' pony, but we can't risk getting caught on the road. As soon as we're over the causeway, we should scout around the coast and coming up that way once it gets dark.'

'Agreed, but we'd better start now' said Magnus 'I am starting to feel like a sitting duck the longer we stay here.'

They made their way on foot down the track from the observatory and then started across the causeway. Fin knew that they were very exposed on the open road and he pressed on as quickly as possible. They had just reached the far end of the causeway when Fin called 'Look!'.

A car was coming towards them at speed from over the hill by the ruined castle.

'Down here' said Magnus. He pulled Fin off the road and down the grass embankment.

Stay still' he whispered.

Fin watched as the car, one of the SUVs, sped down the road towards them. Fin felt his heart beating fast. Had they been seen? They must have. The car was almost upon them. It braked hard, but then sped on across the causeway.

The lay where they were until they saw the car turn right up the track to the observatory. It bounced up the track and out of view.

Magnus said 'come on, we need to get away before they decide to have a look down here.'

They claimed over a gate and started off along the line of the stone dyke keeping to the sea side. Fin looked back every few minutes but no one was no sign of the car or anyone following them.

The sun lowered in the sky as they walked along, dodging the rabbit burrows. A strong wind was still blowing which would shelter the sound of their approach and there was no rain for which both men were grateful. A pair of seals followed their progress from just off-shore as they made their way on. When Fin had first watched the seals, he had been entranced by them. Now, all he could think was that they could be giving their position away.

The walk was much harder than expected, with the grass at parts turning to shingle. It was like treading through treacle and Fin's feet ached. Reaching the spit at the south westernmost corner of the island the wind picked up even more and turning north it was into their faces, exacerbating their hardship. The ploughed on through the gloaming. The lighthouse was just visible although there was no light shining from it tonight. It was dark by the time they saw in the distance lights from the village.

'Let's rest here' said Fin and they hunched down in a dip in the ground, sheltering as best they could from the wind.

They waited for about an hour. There were no stars showing tonight through the clouds. Magnus was restless and twitching to get started. They made their way slowly forward until they saw the roof of a building sitting back from the shore line. They crawled forward and the lodge came into view. It was a large modern single-story building built of stone like the observatory. They crawled on further until they were only about a hundred yards from it, ducking down behind a low stone wall. A few sheep in the field beyond broke at their approach, bleating into the night. They waited a few seconds and the silence of the night returned only broken by the wind from the north.

'OK, you stay here' said Magnus. 'I'll scout around and see what the lie of the land is. I'll be back in ten minutes max. If I am not, get out of here pronto.'

'No way. I'm coming too' said Fin.

'No, we need to find out what we're up against. We can then decide how best to launch a raid.'

Fin thought back to the night with Steve and Becky at the lighthouse. Steve had said much the same thing then. He wanted to argue but knew that Magnus was right. He was too old and slow.

'Here' said Magnus, handing Fin the revolver. 'If you see any dogs, deal with them for me. Yeah?'

'OK' said Fin.

Magnus was out of sight almost immediately hidden by the darkness of the night. Fin looked at this watch. 10.15 it read. The minutes ticked by slowly. He pulled up his hood and slid further down to shelter from the wind. Time crept on. Ten minutes had passed with no sign of Magnus. He waited another five and then started to slowly make his way forward. He came to an outbuilding and skirted around it. Silence rung out across the night and he tried to move as carefully as possible. Creeping round to the front he came into an open courtyard. A single lamp set high on a wall caste a small amount of light over it, allowing him to see the lodge in front. It sat in darkness. There was a single front door which appeared to be open a crack. Trying to keep in the shadows he eased around the edge of the courtyard and crept up to the door. Sure enough, it was open an inch or two. He stood for a few seconds. There was no noise from inside. Gently, he took hold of the door handle pushed in inward. With the smallest of sounds it yielded. The inside was in darkness. He stepped inside and was conscious of a whizzing sound and his lights went out.

***

Fin came to with a start. Another slap across his face and he was fully awake. He tried to get up but found his hands were tied behind his back. He felt a small trickle of blood slowly dripping down from his mouth. He tried to get his bearings but his head was swirling.

'Mr. Tulloch, what an awful inconvenience you are proving.'

He looked up through a swollen eye. Coming into focus was Eric Branson.

'I'm sorry for the mess I made of your face, but, frankly, what can you expect, breaking into someone's home.'

'Where's Magnus' asked Fin.

'Mr. Macpherson, if that's really his name, is fine. Just resting until we can arrange another fishing trip. In the meantime, both of you will be my guests. I'm sorry if the accommodation is not quite of the same standard as at the observatory but I'm afraid your behaviour has necessitated some precautions.'

'What I can't understand' went on Eric Branson 'is why you have gone to all this trouble for these two girls. Waifs and strays they are. Surely you know that. What are they to you? Now young Mr. Macpherson, I can understand his infatuation with Rebecca, but what about you? Surely you're too old for all that.'

'And what about you. Are you too old…'

Eric Branson smashed his fist into Fin's face.

Fin could feel his lights going out again, but then recovered.

'Have some respect when speaking to the laird' he spat out.

He was breathing heavily and trying get himself back under control. He smiled. It was as if a switch has been pressed. He was back to his controlled self.

'I'd assumed you were a Customs and Excise agent, but even they couldn't be as cumbersome as you. No, I think you are just a sad old man who's got out of his depth. Well, your return is a blessing. You will have a purpose. Isn't that great.' He was grinning widely.

He's absolutely mad, thought Fin.

'Why can't you just let them go? Surely you cannot want the murder of two young girls on your conscience just to cover up a smuggling racket' said Fin.

Eric laughed. 'Smuggling racket. You think this is to cover up our little operation up at the lighthouse. You couldn't be more wrong.'

'Well, what is it about then?' asked Fin, but Eric Branson was pulling him to his feet. He pulled out a large knife and held it up to Fin's face. 'Now, I need you to promise to be good, eh Fin'. Fin nodded. Eric swirled him round, cut through the ropes binding his arms and pushed him down head first onto a bed

He shut the door as he left and Fin heard a large bolt being slid across.

Left alone Fin checked out his room. It was fitted out with a single iron bed with a thin mattress and a desk and chair. That was it. Off it, there was a shower room with toilet. There was no door to the shower room. The outside door was heavy duty and there was no possibility of Fin forcing it. There was no window. He lay down on the bed and spotted a camera fixed to the corner of the ceiling above the door. His head was throbbing and he suddenly felt very tired. He struggled for a few minutes to stay awake but quickly drifted off into a deep sleep.

Fin was with Becky. They were walking down a beach with Sammy. He was barking and Becky seemed upset. They were now in the sea. Sammy was swimming. Becky was gesturing to Fin. She was diving down and then up and out of the water. She had transformed into a selkie. She took Fin by the hand and swam down with him. Down and down they went and darker and darker the water became. He was struggling to breath but she was pulling him down. He was starting to choke but she was smiling. He was panicking. He was drowning.

He woke with a start, his heart racing and sweat on his brow. There was a knocking on the door. The bolt slid back and it opened up to show Frigga. 'Mm..mm.morning Mr. Tulloch, I've brought you some breakfast.' She came in with a tray which she placed on the table. There was bowl of porridge, a pot of tea and some toast. 'Thanks Frigga'.

She backed out and the bolt slid back. He was sure that a second person had been standing outside the door.

As soon as he'd finished the food, Frigga returned to clear away the tray. They must have been watching on the camera. 'I've brought you a change of clothes.' She handed him a set of freshly laundered clothes.

'Where's Magnus?' he asked. She smiled but said nothing. She left again and the bolt clanged over again.

He took a shower, washing the sea salt off his skin. He knew that he must have smelled awful and he luxuriated in the hot water, taking his time. Once cleaned he put on the fresh clothes. He was dressed like one of the men on the island, dark trousers, white collarless shirt and a waistcoat. He didn't bother with the jacket provided.

He checked the pockets in his clothes but Becky's pendant was gone. There was also no sign of his cane. He threw the dirty clothes into a pile in the corner, lay down again on the bed and starred at the camera.

He had lost sense of time and did not know if it was now night or day. He dozed off and on but could not sleep due to the light in the room. He looked for a switch but there was none. He lay a towel over his eyes, giving him some privacy from the camera starring at this face.

There were steps outside. He heard muffled voices but could not make out what they were saying. The bolt on the door rattled but no-one came in. The foot-steps died away and he was left alone again with his thoughts. Fin had always prided himself on his disciplined mind and ability to keep under control but he was slowly losing it. He had a growing sense of panic. There was no way out of here. He was going to die here like the two girls and no-one would know. He felt himself perspiring. He went over to the corner under the remote camera and crawled up in a ball to keep out of the sight. He felt tears coming to his eyes. '*Keep yourself together man, keep yourself together man*' he recited to himself under his breath.

Why they were waiting. Why not simply kill him now and bury him somewhere on the island. Nothing made sense.

More steps outside again stopping by the door to his room. He stood up and retreated across the room to the far wall. A pause and then the bolt went back and the door opened. Oliver Hardy stood in the doorway. 'OK, old man, it's time for your guest performance. You'd better smarten up your face. He threw a small canvas bag onto the bed. You've got fifteen minutes so be quick.' He pulled the door shut.

Fin opened up the bag. It contained a shaving kit. He took it into the bathroom and looked in the mirror. Looking back at him was a bedraggled old man with at least two days of stubble. He set to work with the shaving soap. The razor was blunt but it did the job. He splashed cold water on his face. If he was not feeling any better at least he no longer looked as bad. Back in the bedroom, he lay back down on the bed. From a microphone on the camera a voice said 'Stand up and face the far wall.' He sighed and stood up facing the wall. The disposable blade from the razor lay hidden in the palm of his hand.

'Come on then' said Oliver Hardy pulling the door open. He pulled Fin out into the corridor. He pushed him forward. Fin stumbled onto his knees. 'I need my cane' he said. 'No chance big man'. Hardy bent down to pull Fin onto his feet. Fin grabbed Hardy's arm as if to help himself up and as he got to his feet, slashed the man as hard as he could across his face with the blade. Hardy yelled out in pain instinctively raising his hand to his bloodied face and Fin kicked him with all his might between his legs. There was an 'ouff' sound as the man hit the ground. Turning on his heels, Fin half hobbled, half ran down the corridor. It opened out into a hallway and standing there dumbstruck was Frigga. He pushed by her to the front door. His cane stood in an umbrella stand.

Outside stood a SUV. 'Where's the keys?' she shouted at Frigga but she just looked blank. He ran out to the car. A key was in the ignition. He jumped in and, struggling to find a gear, sped off down the farm track. At the bottom he slammed on the brakes and did a sharp left turn back up to the main road. Shooting across that he made for the airfield. He stopped immediately in front and jumped out, rushing into the building and the making for the radio. He stood looking at the wall. There was a gap here the radio had stood. He looked around but there was nothing there. He gave out a cry.

He trudged back outside to consider his next move. He lent on the gate looking out over the airstrip. For the first time, he realised his heart was beating ten to the dozen. He watched as a flock of birds settled on the runway. He needed to get off the island. There was Eric's rib but that was bound to be locked away. The only other boats he'd seen were the two crabbers pulled up onto the shore at the village. Perhaps he could persuade one of the fishermen to take him over to another island.

He took the key out of the SUV and threw it as far as he could. He left the SUV where it was and made inland on foot across the fields, keeping out of sight along the stone dykes. His boots and the bottom half of his trousers were soaking by the time he reached the back of the village and he must have looked an incongruous sight. He cut down into the village by the school. There was no one to be seen outside but he spotted smoke rising from a cottage chimney. He tried the door. After a minute it was opened by an old woman he'd not previously seen. 'Oh, hello Mr. Tulloch. I see you're all ready for the party.' She was quietly giggling.

He hesitated. 'I was wondering if you could let me know who owns the crabbing boat over there.'

'Why, that's Halvar's boat. Would you like to come in for a cup of tea?'

'Err.no thanks. Where does Halvar live?'

'Oh, that's his hoose over there. The one with the red door.' She pointed down the road to a modest cottage with a sea bleached door. If it has been painted red, it must have been many years ago.

'Thank you Mrs.....' he trailed off. 'Helga will do dear. You'd better hurry if you want to catch him as all the men will be needed up at the castle soon.'

Fin made his way down to Halvar's cottage. He knocked on the front door but there was no reply. He went around the back to try the door there but again there was no reply. A voice called 'hello' and turning around he saw a large man of about sixty approaching. 'Halvar?' he asked. 'Aye that's me'.

'You have one of the boats pulled up on the shore?' asked Fin.

'Aye, the Hefring'.

'I was wondering if you could do something for me. I need to get across to Kirkwall today and was wondering if you could possibly take me over there.'

'To Kirkwall. That's some distance. No, I'm afraid I cannie do that that for you today.'

'I can pay you' said Fin. 'I really need to get there.'

'Well, it would take at least four hours there and four back, so that's a lot of fuel.'

'Would five hundred pounds cover it?'

'The man's eyes opened wider. 'Aye, that would cover the fuel and perhaps the same for my time.'

'OK, agreed. Can we leave now.'

'What? Right now? No, I've got something I need to do first. But I can take you after that. You can stay here in the cottage if you want to wait. Will it just be yourself?'

'Yes' said Fin 'Just me.'

'Come inside' said Halvar. He showed Fin into the kitchen. 'I'll be back in about an hour.'

Fin sat down to wait for the fisherman. He didn't have any money to pay the man but he could address that when they arrived in Kirkwall. He had nothing he could do but wait for Halvar to return. He looked around the kitchen for something to eat and found a loaf of stale bread, cutting off a thick slice and spreading some jam over it. He sat down at the kitchen table to count off the time.

Halvar was back in less than twenty minutes. He came bursting through the back door. 'OK, we can leave now.' Fin followed him out the cottage and down the path to the front. Sitting outside was Eric Branson's SUV with Eric standing by the driver's door. Fin turned back but Halvar was right behind him. Oliver Hardy also stood there scowling with a large plaster over this cheek. His semi-automatic was in his hand.

'Be sensible now' said Eric. He opened the rear door. But Fin was bored of being sensible. He drew out the blade from his cane and waved it above his head shouting 'Stand back!'. Eric and Halvar ducked away but Oliver Hardy stood his ground. He let off a burst from his semi-automatic and then calmly pointed it at Fin.

'Put it down wee man.'

Fin hesitated, considering his options, and then dropped the cane onto the ground. Oliver Hardy kicked it away. He then stepped forward and gave Fin a thump in the solar plexus. Fin dropped down to the floor. Oliver Hardy and Halvar then together bundled him into the back seat of the SUV. Oliver Hardy got in beside him any pushed his head roughly down to the floor. 'Careful now' said Eric Branson 'I need him to look presentable for this evening.'

Arriving back up at the farmhouse, Fin was bundled back down the corridor, passing Frigga on the way, and down the stairs into his cell, the door slamming shut behind him.

'Get some rest' said a voice from the microphone. The light in the room went off. Fin lay on the bed nursing his stomach.

Monday 23 April

The light clicked back on, dazzling his eyes. He had no idea how long he'd been back in the room, but he knew he was hungry and he knew he was angry.

The door opened and Eric Branson stood there. The know he'd christened Stan Laurel stood behind him. 'Now, are you going to behave?'

Fin nodded.

'What did you say?' asked Eric.

Quietly Fin replied 'Yes'.

'Well, I'd like to think that was so, but I'm not sure.'

'I'll behave' snarled Fin.

'Yes, I think you will' said Eric and he made way into the room. Fin stepped back, but Eric twisted him round and pushed him down onto the bed. He sat on top of him and pulled his arms up his back.

Stan Laurel then came in. He was holding a needle and syringe. He roughly pulled down the sleeve of Fin's shirt. He pulled his arm straight. Fin tried to move but Eric twisted his other arm tight up his back. He cried out with the pain sure it was going to break.

With a thin smile Stan Laurel njected the needle into his arm and pressed down on the syringe. Fin almost immediately felt himself floating away.

'A side benefit of our little import business up at the lighthouse' said Eric. 'Along with the heroin and coke, we get all sorts of other goodies. My friend here, amongst his other gifts, is a qualified chemist and had made up this little cocktail to keep you feeling nice and mellow for this evening. We can't have you misbehaving again, can we'

Fin was aware of being pulled onto his feet and taken through to the bathroom where water was splashed on this face. His jacket was put back on and he was taken out of the room and back up to the hallway.

'Now this is a very special day for the island' said Eric. 'I am taking my new bride this afternoon and then we'll have a celebration' He paused 'But before then a toast is in order.' Fin was led through to a sitting room and pushed down onto a sofa. He felt half in the room and half floating above it.

Eric took a decanter from a side table and poor out a large measure of whisky. He handed it to Fin, pushing his fingers around the glass.

'This is a great island' said Eric, sitting down opposite Fin. 'The Bransons have been its guardians for over two centuries. We have a duty to the islanders. There was a time when there were well over three hundred folk living happily here. Now we're down to under fifty and do you know what their average age is?' He thumped his glass back down on the table. 'Over sixty. That's what. We need new blood on this island Fin. And what does the Government do to help us. Nothing, that's what. There's been no investment here for years. They're even now talking of closing the school. Well, I'm not willing to let that continue. Is that such a bad thing Fin?'

'Here's to the island. Slainte!' Eric held up his glass and took a drink.

Fin tried to focus on Eric Branson but his head was spinning.

Eric rambled on. 'The current islanders do what they can, but its new blood we need. That's the key. New children and new families. Do you understand, Fin?'

'We need to get going father. The service is due to start at four o'clock. We can't keep the island waiting.' The voice came from a chair to Fin's side.

Fin was suddenly aware of another person in the room. He was struggling to concentrate and his vision was blurred. Something in the voice was still familiar.

'Yes, of course' said Eric and turning again to Fin. 'You've already met my son of course. A true islander. Just like his father and his father before him. The same Norse blood runs through him as it has ran for thousands of years through our forebears. He laughed. I really thought you would have picked up the likeness. But I'm droning on. I can't be late for my own wedding can I.' He downed the remainder of his Scotch in one gulp.

'Son, can you give Mr. Tulloch a hand.' Fin looked into the smiling face bending down to lift him up. It didn't register. It couldn't be. The face looking down at him was Magnus's.

'Hello Fin'.

Fin found himself in the SUV and the next he knew they were pulling up outside the church. Oliver Hardy helped him out of the car, handed him his walking cane and taking a firm grip on his arm, assisted him up the path into the church. A fiddle was playing. The small church was already crowded inside. All of the islanders were there, dressed in their Sunday finest. Fin spotted Frigga and Fulla sitting in the Branson family box. Magnus sat next to them. He was assisted by the elbow down towards the aisle and pushed into a vacant pew. Oliver Hardy squeezed in next to him. Fin tried to take it all in but he was struggling against the effects of the drug he had been given.

The music faded away and Eric Branson appeared from a side door and stepped up to the pulpit. He wore a long black gown, the same one when Fin was originally met him at the observatory. He held up his hands and his congregation fell silent.

'Welcome my family!' he called.

'Brothers and sisters of Hunday, we are gathered here today before Frigg and Freyja to celebrate a holy union. We pray to Odin that that this will result in a new start for our island and that we will again be able to grow our community. We pray for the gods to bless us with new sons and daughters as we pray for the new season to bless us with a bountiful harvest. We must put the past behind us and look forward with joy to the future.'

'We have at times not been loyal to our true Norse heritage. We have worshipped the Christian god and forsaken Odin and the rightful Norse gods. We must make amends for our failings and go back to our Viking ways. We need to make amends. Odin has punished us for our failings. We need to regain his love. We will therefore offer up one of our daughters as thanks the gift of a new bride.'

There was a hushed murmur among the crowd.

'First, let us give our thanks through song'.

The fiddle music started up again and Fin felt himself helped up onto his feet. He head was swimming around. He heard singing but did not recognise any of the words.

The music died away and he was conscious of a breeze of cold air. Turning to his side he saw through his blurred vision the church door standing open. People were coming in but he could not make them out above the heads of the congregation.

And then he saw her alongside his pew. It was Becky. She wore a white frock and had a garland of flowers in her hair. She looked ahead with dead eyes. By her side and holding her arm stood Frigga.

Behind Becky stood Fulla and by her side another young woman also dressed in white. Through the fog of his drugs Fin recognized her as Ophelia. She stood quietly, staring blankly ahead.

Eric Branson had come down from the pulpit and stood by the altar.

'Bring the chosen one forward' he commanded. Frigga led Becky to him. Fin tried to call out but no voice came.

Taking Becky's hand Eric said 'Please join me, Thor in taking as my wife Sif, daughter of our land. May the ancient gods bless our union with many children.' He lent in to kiss her on the mouth against cheering and applause from the congregation.

'Now join me in taking our holy communion.'

Stan Laurel appeared and placed on top of the altar a silver tray holding a small mound of wafers. One by one the congregation came up. Eric kissed each on the forehead and handed them a wafer. 'Bless you' he said to each. Magnus leaned in and whispered to Fin 'no need for any more for you.'

Eric held up his hand and again a hush fell over the congregation. 'We have come here in joy today, but there is also sadness. Just as the Lord Odin sacrificed his only child, so we must give to Odin one of our own. Only by so doing will the island be re-born and blossom again.' There was a dark murmur of approval from the islanders.

Magnus pulled up Fin and they shuffled out of the pew, following the other islanders out to the graveyard at the back of the church. The walls of the church were floating in and out and he struggled to focus. It was drizzling outside and the wind had dropped away. The crowd parted to let Magnus and Fin through. Eric Branson took his hand but he recoiled away. He knew he was crying and his tears mixed with the rain. Before him lay the wicker coffin covered with wild flowers taken from the links. Next to it stood the open grave.

'Come forward Fin. You have sought to betray our hospitality and trust, but now is the moment of your redemption.'

Eric held up his hand and Magnus pushed Fin forward. Frigga stepped forward and placed a garland of flowers on his head. Eric gently took Fin's cane from him and pulled out the blade, the steel glimmering in the late afternoon light. He took a firm hold of his hand and wrapped it around the handle of the blade. He forced his arm up until the sword stood pointed down over the coffin. Fin struggled but his strength was gone. 'Forgive him Odin' shouted Eric and he thrusted down Fin's hand. The blade split through the top of the wicker lid. Fin felt tears streaming down his face. He fell down onto the soft ground.

Old Magnus and three other of the island men came forward, each taking a cord of rope beneath the coffin. Eric helped Fin gently to his feet. He forced a rope necklace of seaweed and shells into this hand. 'This is for the journey to the other side.' He pulled back the wicker lid of the coffin. Fin tried to look away, shielding his eyes, but unidentified hands from the crowd around him pushed him back. 'No, no' he repeated in a murmur. But Eric guided him forward to the grave side.

Fin slowly forced himself to look down into the coffin. He starred down, trembling. In it lay a seal pup in a bed of seaweed. A weeping red spot marked his stab wound. He dropped the shell necklace and fell down. Down and down into the grave, the earth opening up to embrace him. The seal was beside him and then they were swimming together through the dark cold sea. He held Ophelia by his hand and on they swam.

***

Fin woke to the sound of fiddle music and laughter. He made to sit up but found his hands and legs tied. He tried to focus but his head hurt like hell. He lay on his side trying to make sense of what had happened. He thought he'd been in the church and had fleeting memories of seeing Becky and Ophelia. He also remembered his sword. Oh my God, had he killed them?

The music was gaining pace and the noise and laughter was growing.

He struggled onto his feet. His head hit of the roof above him. Crouching down he made his way forward towards the light. His feet hit against a stone step and he stumbled forward. Pulling himself up, he started to climb up the steps. The noise was getting louder.

Again, he hit his head. This time it was against metal. Looking up there was a metal railing above him. He tried pushing it open but it held firm.

'So, you're awake!'.

He turned up towards the voice. Above him stood Magnus. He was dressed in a long sheep-skin cloak.

'If I'd had my way this is where we would have kept you.'

Magnus lent down and undid the bolt on the railing. He pulled it up.

'Come up' he ordered.

Fin started up the steps. As he reached the top Magnus shoved his boot into his face. He stumbled back a couple of steps.

'That's to remind you to behave.'

Fin collapsed down onto the steps. Magnus lent in and pulled him up by the hair, forcing him to his feet. He pulled him up the steps and then threw him onto the ground.

Fin looked around. He was in the ruined castle.

'For God's sake, what's happening Magnus?'.

'For the gods' sake, indeed.' Magnus pulled him up onto his feet.

'Come join the celebration Fin.'

Magnus kicked Fin forward. Losing balance, he fell face first onto the ground smashing his face off a rock. Magnus hoisted him up and kicked him forward again. Again, he fell. He was manhandled once again onto his feet. Magnus wrapped a rope around his hands and then dragged him forward. He was led out of the castle and into the opening where they conducted the bird netting.

Ahead of him, there was a bonfire with flames rising up into the sky and around it he made out people dancing. He was thrust forward towards the flames. Falling to the ground, he felt the thud of boots landing on him. He tried to cover this head. A chant started up 'Kill the dog, kill the dog, kill the dog.' Still the music played on. He tried to look up, but the faces were all painted and unrecognizable.

And then the music died and there was silence apart from the sound of sparks from the fire.

'See the dog on the ground' shouted a voice. 'See how he cowers in shame.' And before him stood Eric in a long white robe.

'Finbarr Tulloch' you lied to us. You pretended to be a Hunday man, but you are an outsider. You have killed a dog and now you must die like a dog.'

The chant started up again 'Kill the dog, kill the dog, kill the dog.'

'Not so fast my family. First, Finbarr must atone for his sins. Our dear father has passed and we will in the morn sacrifice this miserable sinner so that he may be re-born. But tonight we celebrate my joining with my new bride. Frigg and Freyja, bring forward your new sister and lead her to our marriage bed so we may consecrate our union.'

Fin was lifted onto his feet. The crowd parted and Frigga appeared with Becky. He was dressed in a white shift with a garland of wild flowers around her head. Her eyes were dull and she stumbled forward. Frigga cried out. 'Fer....fer....follow us friends. Let the ger....ger... Gods bless this union with a child as they have bl...bl...blessed Freyja and me.'

Old Billy took Eric's hand and he and Frigga led Eric and Becky down the beach. The islanders followed with Fin being dragged along at the end of the procession. They stopped by a raft of wicker reeds topped with animal furs. Old Billy pulled off Eric's robe, his white torso clear in light from the fire and he climbed onto the furs. Frigga then took Becky forward. 'Odin' she cried 'bless my sister Sif with a child tonight' and she pulled Becky's robe over this head. She stood naked in the light of the bonfire. She was pushed onto the bed. New fiddle music started and the crowd of islanders surrounded the bed, chanting to a crescendo 'Bless them, bless them, bless them.'

Fin cried at his helplessness.

'Come on Fin', said Magnus. 'You need to rest for tomorrow.' He was pushed to the ground and Magnus forced something into his mouth. He forced open his mouth and poured a tumbler of water down. Fin started gagging and was thrown to one side. He lay on the muddy ground weeping. Quickly, he found himself drifting off into sleep.

***

Opening his eyes he was in semi-darkness but he was familiar with the circular walls and knew he was back in the lighthouse. His head was throbbing like hell and his throat dry as sandpaper. He lay on the floor looking at the heavy door. He tried to ease himself up but found his arms bounded behind his back. Eventually he made it to a seated position. He was dressed in a long white shroud and his feet were bare. The half-recollected horror of the night before came back to him and he shuddered.

There was the sound of voices outside and lights flickering in above the door. He tried to pull himself together and make sense of things. He was half aware that he had been drugged. He had flashes of clarity, of Becky in the church and the coffin in the grave yard, but then felt himself beginning to hallucinate, transposing Becky's face for that of the seal, and feeling himself falling back down into the grave. He tried to control his consciousness, concentrating on the floor in front of him, but felt himself slipping away again to the grave side, floating now above the grave and watching Becky fall down into the empty hole as he thrust his sword into her repeatedly. He realised suddenly that he was crying and slumped back down onto the stone floor, pressing his face against the cold stone.

When he came too again, he had crawled into a ball. He was very cold. His head still hurt but was becoming clearer. He was conscious of footsteps outside. He heard the bolt on the door sliding back. It opened into the half-light of pre-dawn and he was manhandled out into the courtyard. In front of him were Eric and Magnus Branson and four other men. All were dressed in dark green robes and carried burning torches.

'Judas, you took the life of the child of a selkie. Now her kin are calling for you to join her. Prepare to give yourself up to the sea and allow our blessed father to be re-born in her form.' A rope was looped around his neck and he was pulled forward as in a line led by Eric Branson they made their way down the embankment and across the links to the steps down the cliff.

'This is crazy' he cried.

'Silence Judas!'. Magnus slapped him hard across the face.

He stumbled down the steps slippy in the morning air. Magnus pulled his up roughly bythe hair.

They arrived at the foot of the steps and started along the broken jetty. Fin stumbled on, kicked forward by Magnus. There was a breeze of sea air and the smell of seaweed. Beyond the jetty endless sand led out to the horizon with the tide lying at its lowest point.

Reaching the end of the jetty, Eric lifted up his torch and the procession stopped.

'Lord Odin, we have come here with an offering for you. Take him and released our blessed father back into life.'

Fin was cold and scared. He desperately looked around for a way out. There was nothing.

He saw a series of torches coming down the cliff steps. They gradually got closer and he saw that it was a group of women in green robes like the men. They were led by the old woman Fin had met at the church. Behind her, with a rope around her waist, was a girl dressed in white. It was Ophelia. She wore the same glazed look as in the church and traipsed aimlessly along at the end of the line.

'Mother Earth' intoned Eric Branson, 'what offering have you brought for the Gods.'

The old woman called out 'Thor, we have brought a pure young girl as a present for Aegir. May she bless us in return with a child from your union with Sif. What offering have you brought, my Lord, for the Gods.'

'We have brought an evil man as a penance for the death of a selkie child.'

The old woman dragged forward Ophelia. Her eyes were fixed and starring but her face was wet with tears. It was clear that she was petrified.

Eric yanked the rope around Fin's neck and pulled him forward to the end of the jetty. There were some broken steps leading down to the sea bed. He pulled Fin down. Magnus was right behind. At the bottom of the steps, Eric jumped down onto the sand below with Fin following. He pushed Fin back onto the stone wall of the jetty. Two heavy rusty iron rings were set into the stone. Magnus pushed Fin's head forward and then wrapped the rope from his neck around his arms. He then tied Fin to the ring, pulling the rope tight.

Opheila was then led down the steps and tied to the iron ring next to Fin.

Eric held his hands up to heaven and called out 'Aegir, accept these offerings we beseech you.' He took up a handful of water from a pool by the jetty and sprinkled it over Fin and the girl.

'For God sake' shouted Fin, full lucidity starting to return. 'You can't do this to us'.

Eric smiled at Fin and said 'Don't fear Fin. Let the sea take you. You will soon be re-born', and with that he and the others started to climb back up the steps to the jetty.

Left along Fin struggled against his ties but he was fixed firm. He shouted 'Eric, Eric…' there was no response.

Fin turned his head to the girl. 'Ophelia?' he said. She said nothing for a few minutes and then whispered her name as if remembering it for the first time. Fin said 'Don't be afraid Ophelia. We'll be OK.' He tried to touch her hand but could not reach.

Fin was now very much back in the present. He had told Ophelia they would be alright but inside he had given up hope. He had been through a nightmare and his only salvation now would be to die on this wind-swept beach. The tide had already started to turn and the white horses on the breakers could now be clearly seen. The light was becoming stronger as the dawn arrived and Fin had to squint against the rising sun to make out the beach ahead of him. The wind was slowly rising and birds were circling above. He could hear Ophelia softly weeping next to him. 'I don't want to die' she whispered.

Fin focused on the area of sand in front of him and he watched a small crab scurrying across it and digging a hole. The crab hurried down the hole just as water started to lap forward, touching Fin's bare feet.

Within a few minutes, the water was an inch deep, the coldness eating into him with each lap of the incoming tide. Slowly it rose up his leg towards his knees.

'Stay with it' he said to Ophelia. She had stopped weeping but her could feel her shivering.

'Please help me' she whispered.

***

The waves were now larger, breaking into him and pushing him back against the side of the jetty. The water had risen to his waist. Ophelia was silent.

He heard the noise of the morning plane arriving over the island and getting louder as it turned in to land. Except that it didn't. The plane wasn't landing but carrying on up the island. It was now very loud. It wasn't a plane. Instead, he made out the wop, wop, wop of helicopter rotor blades cutting through the sky. He turned his head up to the right and, suddenly, a huge black helicopter appeared low in the sky making a deafening noise as it passed overhead, wind rushing down into his face. It pulled past them along the line of the cliffs and then turned out to the sea. He watched as it wheeled around and then returned back over their heads towards the lighthouse. The engine noise then started to die down to a throb.

Suddenly, there was a series of loud bangs and flashes of light followed after a few seconds by the crack of three gun shots in rapid succession. He heard shouts and dogs barking.

He called out 'Help' but there was no reply. 'Over here' he yelled, but still no response. The sea was now lapping around his chest. His teeth were chattering. 'Over here' he shouted but his voice carried away on the breeze.

He was starting to drift off into unconsciousness. He could see Sammy. He was walking him along the links but he wouldn't come back when he was called. He called his name but he dog kept on running. He started running after him and on and on they ran across the grass.

With a start he was brought back to the present by the roar of a large outboard. The engine pulled back and the boat pulled up only a couple of feet away from him, spraying water over his face. It was Eric's rib. And then he felt strong arms clinging around him, cutting his ropes and hoisting him up and onto the floor of the boat. Ophelia was pulled in beside him. A masked man looked down. 'Police. You're safe.'

The boat's outboard started into life and it lurch forward onto the jetty ramp. He saw Ophelia lifted out and carried away up the cliff steps.

He was helped out. 'Are you able to climb up the steps?'.

'Yes, I think so.'

He started up the steps, supported by a police officer in anti-terrorist fatigues. He was shivering like hell. Back up at the top, another officer wrapped an emergency blanket around his shoulders. He watched as an officer lent over Ophelia, giving her CPR. He worked hard, calling out a rhythm. On and on he went, eventually sitting back on his heels. He shook his head at the officer next to him. Ophelia's face was ashen white.

***

'Come on, we need to get you out of those clothes.' It was the officer who'd helped him up the steps.

'What about Ophelia?'

'Let the medics deal with her. They're going to lift her over to Kirkwall.'

Fin found himself guided across the links grass towards the lighthouse. Somehow energy was coming back to him. Another officer walked over to him. 'Are you Fin Tulloch?' he asked. Fin nodded.

'We need to ask you some questions but before that we need to get you into some warm clothes.' He held out his hand but Fin shook it off.

The walk back up to the lighthouse seemed to take an age but eventually he made it up the slope. He turned back to look down towards the sea. A stretcher was being loaded into the helicopter sitting on the grass. Its rotors started up and it quickly lifted up into the air and wheeled away over the sea.

Entering the lighthouse courtyard, the first thing he saw was a body lying prostate on the ground. It was the one he'd nick-named Stan Laurel, his arm stretched out ahead of him. A gun lay a few feet away. Half his face had been blown away. The second thing he saw was Steve North coming towards him, dressed in black like the police officers.

'Fin, I'm sorry. I didn't think it would turn as bad as this.' Fin could do nothing other than nod.

Steve helped Fin over to the keeper's cottage. He handed him a bundle of dry clothes. 'Here, put these on'. He directed him to one of the bedrooms. The dry clothes felt good. Coming back out he was handed a mug of hot sweet tea.

'I remembered you were a tea man' said Steve. Fin held it in his hands which he found were shaking.

'Don't worry' said Steve 'it's the shock.' They went into the kitchen, where another three men, each armed with semi-automatics, were crowded around a map of the island.

'How's Ophelia' asked Fin.

'She's on her way Kirkwall' said Steve, not looking Fin in the eye.

'Why did you come back?'

'Becky wasn't on that flight. We've been monitoring the island for months, but when Becky disappeared we knew we had to take immediate action.'

'So you knew about the drug smuggling operation?'.

'We suspected it but had not evidence.'

'And you did nothing about Ophelia?'. Fin's voice was raising.

'The first we'd heard about her was when you mentioned it to me.'

'And you thought it was just the ramblings of an weird old guy.'

'I did until Becky went missing.'

'She's still missing.'

'I know and we need your help to find her.'

One of the police officer's made space for Fin and he sat down at the table.

'Fin' said Steve 'we need to find Becky. Do you have any idea where she might be held.'

'I think so' he said, pointing to where the lodge was located. 'That's the Bransons' home. There's some cells in the basement.'

'OK, John here will look after you.' Steve indicated the armed officer next to him. 'You're safe now.'

'No way' said Fin 'I'm coming with you.'

'Sorry, but that's just not on. John, you stay here with Mr. Tulloch. Radio if anyone approaches.'

'You left me behind once Steve. I'm not doing it twice.'

Steve considered it for a moment, and then said 'OK, but stick close to me. These guys are almost certainly armed.'

'I can confirm that' said Fin. 'There's at least one semi-automatic.'

***

Back down the cliff steps to the jetty, Fin climbed onto the rib. He was joined by Steve and another three officers all heavily armed. Steve fired up the outboard and they sped off along the coast. Pulling south they made for the village. Each officer was checking his weapon.

Approaching the village, there was no sign of life. Steve pulled the rib up onto the beach and they jumped out rushing up the shingle and taking up position by the crabbing boats. They looked up and down the road but there was no one in sight.

'OK, in twos' ordered Steve, and they broke cover. Steve and Fin started up the road, with the remaining officers following at twenty yard intervals.

They walked up through the village, watching for curtains twitching, but all was dead. The villagers had obviously heard the helicopter and were keeping low.

'How far is it?' asked Steve.

'About…' He was stopped by the crack of a gun. They dived down for cover.

Another bang. Steve pointed over to one of the cottages. An officer darted down its side.

There was another bang, this time dust blowing up from the road by Fin's side. Then, a burst of automatic fire.

'Clear' shouted the officer.

Slowly, they rose to their feet. The officer had appeared by the edge of the cottage. Fin and Steve walked over. On the ground lay Old Billy a shotgun by his side along with a couple of spent cartridges.

'How far did you say we were?' asked Steve.

'It's along a track over the rise there' said Fin, pointing along the road. 'No more than half a mile. It's a large modern single storey complex.'

'Okay, you two take up over the fields to the west. Radio when you have eye contact with the building. Mike and me will go in from the track. Fin, you come with us.'

The two officers climbed over a stone dyke and started up the fields. Meanwhile, the other three walked quickly along the road until they reached the track up to the lodge.

'Ok, we'll go over along the coast.'

They climbed over a gate and made their way over a field until they reach a dyke by the edge of the shore. Easing themselves over, they walked forward until the roof of the lodge was in sight. Ducking down they crawled another fifty yards along the line of the dyke. Steve peered over using the sights of his rifle as a scope.

'What can you see?' asked Fin

'There's two SUVs in the yard but otherwise nothing.'

'Where's the main entrance' the second officer asked Fin. Fin pointed to where he had entered the lodge.

'Is there another entry point?'.

'Sorry, no idea.'

Steve opened up a walkie-talkie. 'Red to Blue. Where are you?'

'We're in position. One hundred yards to target. There's a rear door but no sign of life.'

'Ok, you take the rear. We're going in the front. Five minutes to impact.'

'Roger that Red.'

Then to Fin. 'OK, let's work our way around to the side of the courtyard'.

The crawled forward through an opening in the dyke until they reached an outbuilding. From there they had a clear line of sight to the front of the lodge. The two SUVs stood in the yard, each with WHBO on the side. The front door was closed. There was no still sign of life.

Steve pulled out a handgun and gave it to Fin. 'I assume you know how to use this.'

'Aye.' He clicked the safety catch off.

He took out his walkie-talkie again. 'Red to Blue. Are you in place?' he whispered

'Confirmed.'

'Commencing in sixty.'

'Roger that.'

'Fin' you stay here. Mike and I will go in. If anyone comes out and it's not Becky shoot them. Got it?'

'Got it.'

Fin felt his heart racing as they counted down the seconds. Bang on sixty, the officer named Mike stepped around the corner and fired a stun grenade through the front window of the lodge. There was a huge explosion of light and noise followed almost immediately by the same to the rear. Then both Mike and Steve were sprinting off across the courtyard to the side of the front door.

Fin saw Mike open the front door and Steve rush in. There was shouting and then gun fire, three rapid shots in succession. Then silence. Fin waited but nothing. Able to stand it no longer, he moved across the courtyard and peered into the hallway. There was shattered glass everywhere.

He crept inside, holding his gun in front of him, inching down the hallway to the stairs to the basement. Taking each step slowly he made his way down. His breathing was heavy and he could feel his hand shaking. At the bottom of the steps he turned infinitely slowly round the edge of the corner into the corridor. An automatic weapon was pointing direct at his head. He twitched and then lowered his gun. Steve stood in front of him. By his feet lay Oliver Hardy with what remained of his face. Steve raised his fore finger to his mouth to signal silence and then started along the corridor. There were three doors.

Steve inched up to the first door and very slowly tried the handle. It opened an inch. He kicked it fully open and it sprang back. The room inside was empty.

They moved on to the second. Fin was sweating. The same routine. Steve inched the door open and then kicked it back, springing in. Again, it was empty. On to the final door. This time the door would not open. Steve indicated to Fin to step to one side. He stood on the other and shouted out 'Stand back'. He opened up his semi-automatic at the lock. The noise inside the tight corridor was shattering. Steve kicked at the door and it sprang back. He very slowly looked inside. Fin recognised the room as the one in which he had been imprisoned. He followed Steve in. For a minute he thought the room was empty, then he heard a sobbing from the bathroom. He pushed past Steve. There, hunched on the floor of the shower was Becky.

He dropped his gun and stepped forward to take her in his arms. She clung to him. All he could think to say was 'you're safe now Becky.'

***

Ten minutes has passed. They'd brought Becky up to the lounge. One of the police officers had given her a blanket and was trying to comfort her. Steve had called for an air ambulance and one was on the way from Kirkwall.

Fin was back in the courtyard, talking in a low voice to Steve. 'What the ETA for the plane?'

'About twenty minutes tops. I want to see you on it' said Steve.

'I'm not leaving before we have Eric Branson.'

'Becky needs you Fin.'

'I know but I owe it to her.'

There was a shout from the lodge. 'In here' called one of the police officers. They each ran inside. The call was from the basement. They rushed downstairs to the first room they had cleared. The bed stood pulled to one side and under it a trap door was open. Looking down it a flight of steps led into a tunnel. 'Into the corridor' ordered Steve. Fin and the other officer retreated outside. Steve took out a stun grenade and threw it down the hole, dashing out into the corridor and pulling the door shut. A second or so later there was a blinding flash of light and a deafening bang. Dust squirted out from around the edges of the door. Fin struggled to get his senses to work.

Steve counted to ten and then pushed the door open. The room was full of dust. A flood light was produced and Steve dropped down the hatch. 'It's an escape tunnel' he called, adding 'empty.' As he spoke there was the sound of gun-shots from outside. Rushing back up the stairs Fin was in time to see a SUV accelerating away down the track from the lodge. A police officer lay outside, a colleague already tendering to him.

Steve was outside only a few seconds later. 'Shit'.

'Come on' said Fin. He pointed to the second SUV. He was already opening up the driver's door.

'Secure this area' shouted Steve and he jumped in next to Fin. Fin powered away down the track.

'Where's he going?'.

'Only one place.'

***

Fin sped up the road towards the lighthouse. Turning up towards it and past the broken gate Fin had burst open with the VW, they could see Eric's SUV parked up ahead by the first cottage.

'He's after the drugs' shouted Steve.

Fin bounced up the track and stepped on the brakes slamming into the other SUV. They both leapt out and threw themselves behind the SUV.

'Cover me' cried Fin and Steve opened up with his automatic at the cottage. Fin rushed over to the door into the cottage. He let off a series of shots as he burst inside. Steve followed, spraying shots into each room. They cleared them one by one. Empty. Shit, shit, shit! Where was the bastard?

'What now?' asked Fin.

'The second cottage' said Steve. The ran back out to the courtyard.

A single shot rang out. Instinctively Fin ducked down. Steve doubled-down next to him, falling over. He reached for this shoulder a red mark already showing through his hand. Another shot rang out. Fin dragged Steve inside the cottage, pulling his semi-automatic after him. He turned Steve onto his back and ripped opened up the top of his tunic. It was clear his shoulder was a mess of shotgun pellets. He crawled through to the kitchen keeping low and pulled a tea towel off the table. Returning to the corridor he pressed it against the Steve's shoulder. 'Hold it here' he said taking the man's hand and pressing it to the wound. Steve was breathing heavily but his eyes were alert. Fin saw that his radio had fallen on the ground where he'd been hit. He tried to reach out to grab it but another shot rang out ricocheting against the door frame. Shit, they were pinned down.

'He's in the lighthouse' said Fin. He risked a glimpse up to the top of the tower and caught the flash of a movement. Then a series of flashes of light. He held up his hand against the sun. In the distance he made out a trawler sitting in the bay. At its stern an inflatable was being lowered into the water.

'He must have radioed for help' said Fin. 'I can see a boat in the bay with men about to come on-shore.'

'I think you can get out back' said Steve.

'Can you cover me when I shout.'

Fin pulled Steve up to a sitting position. He cried out with pain. Fin handed him his weapon and he tried holding it up to his good shoulder. Wincing he said 'I think so'.

Fin went through to the back of the cottage. There were bars across the bedroom window. The same with the bathroom. He tried the lab. A hold-all full of brown packages lay on the floor. Shit! That was what Eric had come back to the lighthouse for. He looked to the window. Barred like the rest. There was no way out. Desperately he looked for alternatives. Then, he noticed a cover into the attic. He pulled over a chair, climbed on top of it and thumped open the ceiling cover. He tried to pull himself up into the ceiling void but was too weak. He dragged across a sideboard to give himself some greater height. He tried again, but still did not have the strength. 'Come on you old bastard' he shouted and with one more effort he managed to scramble up. It was dark inside but as his eyes adjusted he saw that the ceiling void ran the length of the cottages. He dragged himself across, hitting his head against a wooden joist, until he reached the ceiling hatch into the next door cottage. Opening it up he eased himself down until he from hanging from the opening by his shoulders. Then he let go and crashed down to the floor. He yelled out in pain. His bad leg felt like it was broken but he managed to hobble to his feet.

The second cottage was empty of furniture. It could not have been lived in for years. He went to the back. In the first bedroom a dirty mattress lay on the floor with empty syringes by its side. This was where they must have held Becky. The window was barred. He tried the second. The same. Then the bathroom. It had a small window to the rear. There were no bars. He stood on the side of the bath and tried the window catch. It was rotted with the sea air and gave almost immediately. He pushed it open. The opening was small but he managed to squeeze through head-first. He dangled for a minute and then fell with a thump onto the ground outside. He let out another muffled yell.

As he picked himself up, another shot rang out. A familiar voice shouted out 'Fin. Come on out. It's your time. You cannot fight your destiny. You have taken the life of a selkie child and now you must repent to Aegir.'

Fin stood frozen. 'Eric for God's sake what are you doing?' he called.

'Performing my duty. Don't you see...'

'Cover now!' yelled Fin and he ran with all his might across the courtyard. Rapid gun fire spat out from the cottage door at the same time. Shots from on high hit the ground beside him as he ran. He threw himself at the open door to the lighthouse tower. He was panting, his shoulders heaving up and down, and he tried to get his breath back. He pressed himself to the side of the entrance, pulling out the hand gun. A shot rang out from the top of the lighthouse smacking into the ground just outside the door to the cottage. Eric was at the very top.

Keeping his back to the wall Fin inched up the stairs of the lighthouse. He'd read that there were one hundred in total and he counted each one in turn, his concentration not wavering from the angled staircase above.

He could now hear singing coming quietly from above. The words from an unknown folk song drifted down to him. 'Eric' he called 'this is crazy. Why don't you throw down your gun and come down.'

'I am Thor, son of Odin. I need to save my people. Odin has commanded me.'

'And what about Becky. What was her sin.'

'Becky is no more. She is re-born as Sif. She will bring fertility again to this island.'

'That's your excuse for raping an innocent girl and drowning another'.

'Ophelia is not harmed. She will return as a selkie. One of us. Don't you understand Fin. All we are missing is your sacrifice. You have cheated us but now your time is come.'

He started singing again.

Fin was now just blow the highest level. 'I'm going to come up' he called and he took another couple of steps up. The entrance to the light room was now visible.

'Stay where you are!' shouted Eric and a shot rang out the bullet ricocheting off the stone steps.

'Help is on its way, Eric. Magni is dead and the island secured. The police will be here in a moment.'

'Liar!'

'Throw your gun down. It's over Eric.'

'I'm Thor' he roared.

Fin felt a breeze of fresh air rush against his face. He slowly climbed up. 'I'm coming up..' he said, but there was no reply.

In slow motion, he climbed the last few steps into the light room, holding the revolver in front of him. He drew in his breath as his head appeared over the entrance. The room stood empty. Wind came in from an open window. He went over and looked down. Eric's body lay spread-eagled by the base of the tower.

He waved down to Steve who came out from the cottage door. He walked over to Eric, lent down and then shook his head.

Fin turned to the seaward side. The trawler sat at anchor but a large Customs vessel was powering towards it. The men in the inflatable held their arms in the air.

***

Fin did not like the helicopter that evacuated them off the island. It was horribly noisy and shook like hell. He did not care. He was on his way off Dog Island. Looking down, he watched its patchwork of green fields pass, and then the bay by the bird observatory, turning out to the turquoise sea shimmering in the sunlight. He thought he saw a seal but was not sure.

Three months later - Edinburgh

He'd agreed to pick up Becky from outside the Baillie where he'd first met her. The VW had been cleaned up and he'd spruced himself up as well with a new jacket in place of his old army surplus. Sammy sat in the back chewing at a new toy.

She climbed in next to him, throwing a daypack into the back. 'Before we set off' he said 'I wanted to give you something.' He handed her a small paper bag. She opened it and took out her pendant. 'I found it in your room at the observatory' he explained. She lent over and kissed him on the cheek. 'Thanks'.

He'd said he wanted to take her out to lunch, somewhere out of town. 'A wee trip to the country' he'd said. She been uncertain but then had said yes.

As they reached Cramond she asked 'Where are we going, Fin?'

'Oh, it's a trip back to my boyhood' he said.

The Forth Road Bridge came into view. The work to the new bridge to its left had come on apace since he'd last crossed. It seemed a lifetime ago.

'I didn't know you came from Fife' she said.

'I don't' he said. He turned on the radio. She didn't press him further.

Turning off the motorway soon after, they took the tourist route along the coast passing picturesque Fife fishing villages until they arrived finally an Anstruthur. Dropping down into the old village Fin parked up by a small beach overlooking the harbour.

'Did you know the locals pronounce it *Anster*' he said. Getting out of the van, the day was sunny and warm and the harbour front was busy with families and children out for the day.

They sat down on a bench by a small beach where a few little children were playing in the sand.

Fin had not really spoken to Becky since they'd got back from West Hunday. He couldn't find the words. He knew she must be traumatized but while he hoped that time might heal a little, he didn't think it would.

He'd attended Ophelia's funeral, sitting at the back. It was been a small affair with only perhaps about twenty present. They'd been asked to wear something pink and he'd bought a new tie. The minister rattled on about it being a celebration of her life but all he could think was what a waste it had been.

Steve North had attended for the police. Fin had never discovered exactly which department he worked for, but he was happy to see him again. He'd told him the observatory had been converted into a welfare centre for the islanders with a group of drug therapists posted to try to detox them from their dependencies. In reality they doubted the island had a viable future. The three children at the school, all found to the fathered by Eric Branson, had been taken into care and Frigga and Fulla were in psychiatric care on the mainland.

Becky interrupted his thoughts. 'Where are we eating? I'm starving'.

'Right here' said Fin. He pointed across the road to the Anstruther Fish Bar. 'The best fish and chips you can buy.'

There was a queue out the door, but soon, they were sitting back on the bench overlooking the beach with cod and chips for Becky and a haddock supper and portion of mushy peas for Fin. They had two ice cream floats to wash it down. Two seagulls stomped around them and Fin threw one a chip.

'Oi' said Becky 'that's not good for birds.'

'How are you Becky?' asked Fin.

'Recovering slowly. It's going to be a long process but I'll be all right.'

'I'm sure you will'.

As he said it he was not convinced. Becky was a tough cookie but he knew it would take time for her emotional wounds to heal. He was determined to be here for her.

An old lady had joined them on the end of their bench.

'Becky' said Fin. 'There was another reason I asked you here today.'

She gave him a puzzled look.

He took her hand. 'I wanted to introduce you to your grandmother.' He opened his palm towards the old lady. 'Becky, this is your grandmother, Grace Harper.'

'Hello' said Grace and she took Becky's hands in her own.

Becky was shaking with tears in her eyes.

Fin looked at her. 'I shouldn't have done this'.

'Yes, you should' insisted Becky.

'Well I'm going to leave you two alone to get acquainted. Save me some cola for when I get back.' And with that he clipped on Sammy's lead and started to walk with him down towards the harbour. He didn't look back not wanting to intrude into their moment.

He must have been gone for a good hour. Wandering back, he was pleased to see them sitting together on the same bench eating two ice-creams. Becky jumped up, excited. 'I'll get you one Fin' and she ran along to the ice-cream van.

Fin sat down next to Grace.

'She's very like Georgie. I can see it in her eyes.'

'She's a good kid' said Fin.

***

They sat speaking until Grace's son arrived for her. As Grace got up to leave, she handed Becky a small envelope. 'It belonged to Georgie. She really loved you.' Becky opened up the envelope and took out a faded photograph. It showed Becky laughing as a toddler as her mum held her on her knee.

'Do you mind if we take a detour' asked Becky. They were driving back down to Edinburgh.

'Sure, where do you want to go.'

'Kinross.'

'Ok'. He turned north and took the B road up past Kelty and towards Kinross.

'Where are we going' he asked.

'The RSPB centre at Loch Leven.'

When they arrived it was after five and the car park by the loch was empty.

They got out and wandered down to the loch side. Becky picked up a pebble and skimmed it across the water.

'Did you know that Mary Queen of Scots' was imprisoned on the island out there by her sister Elizabeth?' she asked.

'Is this where you came camping with Offie?'

'Yes, she really loved it here.'

They wandered on a little.

'Offie and me were like sisters. We used to cycle up from Edinburgh on our bikes and spend the day bird watching.'

She opened up her back-pack and took out the urn. Tipping it up she scattered Offie's ashes in the water.

'We can go home now Fin.'

The end.

o205

Printed in Great Britain
by Amazon